About the author

Dr Anita Heiss has published poetry, non-fiction, historical fiction and social commentary. Her novel *Who Am I? The diary of Mary Talence, Sydney 1937* was shortlisted for the 2002 NSW Premier's Award for young fiction. She was awarded the ASA Medal (Under 35s) for her contribution to Australian literature and community life in 2004. Anita is a member of the Wiradjuri nation of central New South Wales, lives in Sydney, believes in love at first sight and enjoys being single!

Not Meeting Mr Right

Anita Heiss

BANTAM

NOT MEETING MR RIGHT
A BANTAM BOOK

First published in Australia and New Zealand in 2007 by Bantam

National Library of Australia
Cataloguing-in-Publication Entry

       Heiss, Anita, 1968–.
       Not meeting Mr Right.

       ISBN 978 1 86325 511 0 (pbk).

       1. Dating (Social customs) – Fiction. 2. Man–woman relationships
       – Fiction. I. Title.

       A823.3

Transworld Publishers,
a division of Random House Australia Pty Ltd
20 Alfred Street, Milsons Point, NSW 2061
www.randomhouse.com.au

Random House New Zealand Limited
18 Poland Road, Glenfield, Auckland

Transworld Publishers,
a division of The Random House Group Ltd
61–63 Uxbridge Road, Ealing, London W5 5SA

Random House Inc
1745 Broadway, New York, New York 10036

Cover illustration and design by saso content & design pty ltd
Internal design by VJ Battersby
Typeset in 11/16 Warnock Pro
Printed and bound by Griffin Press, South Australia
10 9 8 7 6 5 4 3 2 1

Australian Government

This project has been assisted by the Australian Government through the
Australia Council, its arts funding and advisory body.

Contents

one

I love being single

'I love being single!' I said, with such conviction I almost believed it myself. All of a sudden I was desperately trying to convince myself and the table of proud married mothers that I really, really loved my single life just the way it was, and had no desire to marry and/or breed, thank you very much. Until I'd arrived at the pub that night, it had pretty much been true.

It was two months after my twenty-eighth birthday and I was at my ten-year school reunion at the Hub in Bondi Junction, our stomping ground in our late teens. Back then it had been known as Jack's Bar. I'd dreaded the night since the invitation had arrived and had spent the previous three months mentally scripting and planning the event. It was sure to be an unpleasant reminder of what school had been like. I'd been a self-conscious teenager who never really fit in – me being a Blackfella from La Perouse and the rest of the girls whitefellas from Vaucluse and Rose Bay. A triangular peg in a round hole, I used to say. I'd never felt skinny enough or pretty enough compared with the other girls.

I wouldn't even have gone, if Dannie hadn't almost physically dragged me along. I'd much rather have stayed away – or boycotted, as Bianca had put it. Bianca had better things to do, like 'hanging out with her man', she'd said. The three of us had remained friends after school, but Dannie was married now, Bianca had just got engaged, and me, well I was *loving being single*. We seemed an unlikely trio, but somehow we were mates.

I was now the head of the history department at a private Catholic girls school, living in a funky two-bedroom flat, full of sunlight and right on Coogee Beach, and I'd aged well compared to my old school buddies. I'd thought that would be more than enough to see me through the reunion with head held high, but within minutes of ordering my first gin and tonic, it was clear that my old classmates weren't impressed. In their eyes, I was without the one key ingredient that determined success and true happiness: I did not have my Mr Right. I was the only one at the table who didn't, but they made me feel like I was the only one on the planet. This time I was prettier and thinner than most, but they had all moved on. They had all joined the 'club' – the 'I have a significant other and significant little others' club.

The reunion was set up like a speed-dating event. Everyone was allocated a specific amount of time speaking to the person opposite them; when the time was up, one side of the table moved left to face someone new. The idea was to keep on doing this until everyone had the chance to catch up with everyone else. The conversations so far, though, had all been about wedding planners, floral arrangements, dress fittings, honeymoon locations and gift registries. I'd never had a bridal register, or a wedding planner, and with no similar experiences of my own to share or compare, I felt left out.

Now I sat opposite Estelle and just listened, sucking on the ice from the bottom of my first drink.

'Excuse me, Alice,' she said as she rearranged her rather bulky bra, 'My nipples are killing me.'

'What!' I spat ice back into my glass. Was there a new dinner-table etiquette I was unaware of that meant it was okay to discuss sore nipples in public?

'Still breastfeeding and my son just *tugs* on them.' She put her whole hand in her bra.

'Really …' I didn't know what else to say, but it didn't matter. She continued right on.

'At least the pain isn't long term – not like stretch marks or the need to do pelvic floor exercises every day.' Estelle grimaced and I guessed she was tightening her fanny. It wasn't a good look. Right at that moment I seriously loved being single: sore nipples, loose fannies and stretch marks didn't appeal to me at all.

I was bored already, and food wasn't even in sight. I eavesdropped briefly on the conversation next to us.

'I registered at Peter's of Kensington – they do the best bridal baskets,' I heard Louise say.

'I was with DJs, but seeing as it was my second wedding I wanted to keep it low key,' Judi responded. I couldn't believe these women were actually for real.

I love being single! had been my daily mantra for the last couple of years. Serial dating and short-term relationships suited me fine. My single life was great compared with the lives of some married women I knew. God knows the teachers at school who had kids always looked tired and were on the run all the time.

No-one I'd spoken to so far had seemed convinced by my *I love being single!* mantra, though. They'd responded only with 'Of course you do!' and 'There's absolutely nothing wrong with being single.' But to me they sounded condescending and that got my back up. Within the first half-hour, all my insecurities about not being skinny or pretty enough compared to the other girls in the school grounds had come flooding back.

I should have taken note of my horoscope that morning: 'Expect the unexpected! Remember your own value.' Let's face it, while I hadn't expected to have a raging good time at the reunion, I sure as hell hadn't expected to be tripping over my self-esteem because of it either. Aria's Super Stars were nearly always right when it came to Leo predictions and I always, *always* relied on her words of wisdom to see me through the day, but somehow they weren't providing me with enough positive affirmation to deal with the reunion.

Someone gave me the shove to move left again. I didn't know whose idea the speed dating set-up was, but it was genius. I moved on, leaving Estelle's sore nipples for someone else to soothe.

'*I love being single!*' I said to Linda, before she had the chance to talk about any part of her anatomy or any special exercise regime she might be following. I looked down at my cleavage. 'And my nipples are fine.' I thought I'd get in first. 'No stretch marks, and I haven't been too stretched downstairs either!' I laughed.

Linda looked at me oddly, and asked, 'How many kids have you got, Alice?'

'None. I'm a bleeder, not a breeder,' I said, half trying to be funny, half serious. Linda just smiled politely and showed me a couple of photos of her children. Admittedly, they were cute, but when she put them back in her wallet, we looked at each other blankly. I hadn't really ever even thought about kids, not seriously. Not seriously enough to have a meaningful conversation with a mother about parenting, anyway.

Of course I'd dreamt about meeting Prince Charming and having a fairytale wedding. All girls do. I'd started planning my wedding when I was only twelve and we'd had a mock ceremony in the street where I grew up. Richard Barker played the groom. He wore a school tie with his shorts and t-shirt and I wore a pink dress and a shower curtain on my head as a veil. Since then I hadn't become Muriel by any means, but I had bought the odd wedding magazine over the years, just to look at the pictures, and I'd been to one or two bridal fairs.

All women did, didn't they? I called it research. I was a teacher; I liked to be organised. No-one wants to be running around at the last minute once the question has finally been asked. Yes, even single girls have bridal dreams occasionally. Women who say they've never thought about a fancy wedding are lying. Problem was I'd not given any thought to what would happen *after* the wedding. All I really wanted was a man. A wedding would be fun too. But married life? Not for me.

I was glad to get the nod from Jen, the class bossy-boots, to move on. 'I think our time's up, Linda. Pity …' We both half smiled. Even if I only had to spend a short time speaking to every woman there, it was still going to be a struggle. I was beginning to feel inadequate: I was an intelligent, educated, capable woman, unable to make conversation, even basic small talk, with girls I'd spent six years at school with. Why didn't we have anything to talk about?

Don't get me wrong. It wasn't as though I wanted to talk about current affairs all night – refugees, Indigenous health, peace in the Middle East – but *some* diversity would've been appreciated. Talking to Jen would be a welcome break. She'd been great to have in my Society and Culture class in senior years – she always brought something quirky to every discussion.

'So Alice, I've been looking forward to speaking to you. You were always so political at school. I've just joined this new party, and I thought you might be interested in it.' Thank god – Jen hadn't changed at all.

'Cool, which party? What's its platform?' I was already feeling more comfortable. Politics were a level playing field. Didn't need kids to be political.

'It's the Family Party – we advocate for protecting traditional family values, the family is the most important thing.' She rattled this off as though she was reciting the strict party line.

I nearly dropped my drink. Was I sitting with a mobster's wife, a John Howard fan, or just a lunatic?

'So, what does the party think of same-sex marriages?' I asked, baiting her.

'They don't endorse anything that's not in the Bible.'

'Female clergy, then – you always believed in equality for women in society.'

'No, there are definite roles for men and women, and the clergy isn't for both sexes.'

'Abortion?' I could tell I'd hit a nerve as Jen started to fidget. Her politics were bad politics, but she wasn't an idiot. I'd thought if I made her say the words out loud she might see how ridiculous her position was, but she didn't respond at all. She knew I knew the answer to this question already. It seemed even the political conversations tonight would be hijacked by notions of motherhood and womanhood and narrow definitions of family.

'The party does support a formal government apology for the stolen generations, Alice,' Jen said almost proudly. 'You'd appreciate that. Wasn't your grandmother stolen?'

So the party had *one* decent item on their agenda – their support for Blackfellas didn't discount the fact that they were homophobic and sexist. Who'd want an apology from that mob anyway? I knew my grandmother wouldn't.

'Why exactly did you join this party, Jen? You seemed so broadminded at school.' I was blunt.

'Because my husband did, and I support his views. That's what married life is about. Support and compromise.' My stomach turned. Not only had Jen taken on extreme right-wing political beliefs, but she hadn't even thought them through for herself. Or had she? Did she truly believe she had to adopt her husband's views? I'd marry a guy with political beliefs for sure, but if his beliefs didn't match mine – highly unlikely – *I* sure as hell wouldn't be crossing the floor in the name of wedlock. I had to do a reality check. Was it 1950? Was I actually at Jack's Bar listening to this? Had we all been taught the same things at school? If so, what had gone wrong? Was it me? Surely not!

I looked around the table for some answers and all I saw was a group of women who had lost their own sense of identity. They were all now known as Mrs Joe Bloggs or Mrs Sue Jones-Bloggs or Emily Bloggs's mother. But they all seemed happy. Why was I so angry? Was it possible I was feeling envy?

As luck would have it, I was opposite Dannie next, and our entrees arrived, so I had some respite from trying to fit in. It was an opportunity to bone up on some birthing detail, too, before I had to move left again.

'So, how many waters are there anyway?' I whispered. 'And what do you do if they break on a bus?' Dannie – my only married friend – thought I was joking, but in all honesty, I had no idea what my old classmates had been talking about. Why would I? There's an unrealistic expectation that every woman is maternal and is born to breed. Not me. I wasn't maternal at all.

'Seriously, Dannie, does meeting Mr Right and breeding with him mean that women can't think or talk of anything else from that moment on?'

Dannie wasn't offended, she just laughed and changed the subject. 'What did you think of *The Daily Terror*'s report on Black deaths in custody last Saturday, Alice? I've been waiting all week to hear your opinion.'

Dannie was the least wife-and-mother-like married woman I knew – partly because she hung with me so much. She was doing a media degree part time at uni, so we had common interests still. Dannie was writing a paper about the fuss there had been over whether or not 'God Save the Queen' would be sung at the opening ceremony of the Commonwealth Games in Melbourne early in 2006, and she had bit of a rant about it now:

'It's a song for Christ's sake! Forty-five wars going on around the world, and you've got news anchors on TV reading their scripts like the bloody Queen has been shot or something. I don't think stories like that should even make the news, let alone a headline.' Dannie was a staunch republican. I loved her even more for that.

She hadn't been sucked into any void of wifedom and motherdom; she was on top of the rest of life's responsibilities as well. The other women at the table could have learned a lot from Dannie.

After we'd finished our entrees, we moved on again. Vicky was across from me now. She was considered the tramp of the class back when we were at school, because she spent so much time up the Bronte gully with boys from the surf club. The gully was far behind her, though: she had gone on to become a highly paid lawyer with one perfect child and a second husband who was a well-known QC. She specialised in corporate law, and didn't do any pro bono work at all. (I asked.) She couldn't really afford to, she told me, with childcare fees and a huge mortgage on their Point Piper home.

'There's such a limited number of childcare places in this state that some of us have to pay double just to find someone to mind the kids.' Vicky made it sound as though raising her own child was an imposition. It was an attitude that always made me angry.

I'd been waiting weeks to have this conversation, after listening to whining mothers on talkback radio and I launched straight in. 'I don't understand women complaining about the government not providing enough day care centres.'

'Women have to work too.' Vicky sipped her wine.

'Have to or *want* to? You wouldn't *have* to work if you lived somewhere other than Point Piper, surely.' There was no way she was getting away with not admitting it was her lifestyle that meant she *had* to work.

'We're part of society – why shouldn't we be out there in it every day?'

In my mind, there was a difference between participating in society and dumping your kids with a stranger so you could make money.

'If *you* choose to bring a child into the world, *you* should be responsible for raising it. Feeding it, playing with it, looking after it until it has to go to school.'

'What's your real problem with working mothers, Alice?' Vicky asked. It sounded like a challenge, as if the issue was really about me, and not about working mothers.

'I don't have a problem with mothers working. I just don't understand how parents can admit publicly that they're pissed off they can't find a stranger to raise their children for $100 a day. Aren't kids supposed to be your most prized possessions? Or are some things more important than children? I wouldn't be off-loading my little one to some stranger to raise, just because I wanted a big house in an expensive suburb.'

'Ah, but you're single and childless, Alice, it's different for you.'

'That's right – it should be different for me! I am single and childless, so I can work long hours without it affecting anyone else. I can be – what would you call it? Selfish?' I was getting hot, my face felt flushed.

Vicky remained cool. She wasn't buying into the argument. Her kid was probably in some private centre that cost a fortune anyway. Vicky would've had a cleaner and probably a cook, dog-walker, social director and third husband on the way. She clearly had more than me – even though as a single woman I was socially permitted to be *selfish*.

We'd reached a stalemate – but our time was up. Neither of us bothered with a polite smile; I just stood up and moved one seat to the left again.

I persevered with the reunion chatter for quite some time, fighting hard to find new adjectives to describe each family portrait and baby photo I was forced to look at over the course of the next hour. I tried to expect the unexpected, as Aria had advised, hoping that among all these women, there might be a Toni-Morrison-reading, Koori-Radio-listening, Villawood-visiting mother who perhaps sent her kids to a Steiner school or something, and taught ESL to refugees once a week. Anything was possible, wasn't it? I mean, that's the mother I knew *I'd* be.

Eventually I found myself opposite Ronelle. She was the one person I'd actually been looking forward to speaking with. Obese at school, she was now the most glamorous and healthy-looking woman at the table. Softly spoken and relaxed, she told me she had three kids, but didn't mention stretch marks or lack of sleep or sore nipples or the need for more day care centres. Instead she talked about her life as a yoga instructor – she'd been to India, done a course, changed her name to something like 'Swami' (I'd forgotten it five minutes later). It was all going well until she asked if I'd like to attend one of her classes 'even though they were for new mums'.

'You might still get something out of it,' Ronelle said with one eyebrow raised. 'Your bust would look better if you sat straighter, and yoga is fabulous for posture. You'd learn to relax at the same time, too.' So she thought that I *needed* yoga – that I had a drooping bust line and that I was uptight? My bust was fine, and I wasn't uptight, just annoyed at the lack of interesting conversation so far that evening. I didn't need yoga – I just didn't need to be at the reunion.

'I have too short a concentration span to make yoga work for me, Ronelle, but thanks,' I said, and moved on, even though our time wasn't up, demonstrating that what I said was true.

After making a monumental effort to adhere to the rotational rule, having spoken to almost everyone, I took a break, leaning back in my chair. The metal was cold on my skin. I looked around the pub. Jack's had been gentrified, like all the pubs in the eastern suburbs had been in the past five years. Dark wood tables and comfy cushioned lounges had been replaced by streamlined chrome tables and chairs. The antique-looking carpet you still find in old people's houses had been replaced with ceramic tiles. The jukebox and dance floor had given way to a roomful of pokies. (I noticed they still had Coopers on tap, though.)

The space wasn't as warm as it had been when we were young, and while the pub's owners had changed its name, and spent millions on updating the interiors, they hadn't really managed to change their clientele. I scanned the room and saw the same private-school rugby players who'd been drinking there ten years before. They didn't seem as attractive now. Funny that, everyone's a spunk when you're young. That thought brought me back to our group. There had been more of us back then, when we were teenagers. I looked around and counted heads: we were a table of fifteen. Why had only fifteen showed up? Probably because the others were single and out having a raging time meeting gorgeous men, not worrying about their pelvic floors.

Then I noticed it: each and every woman in the group wore an engagement and/or wedding ring. That's why I was on the outer. That's why I didn't fit in. It was a clear case of 'Us' and 'Them'. I couldn't even pull the race card this time; it wasn't about being Black and white. It wasn't about being rich or poor, as it had been at school. Rather, at twenty-eight it was about the haves and the have-nots. I was definitely a have-not. No wedding ring – not even an engagement ring. No husband. No kids. Not even a date lined up any time in the near future. I had nothing to contribute to this Mothers' Club meeting. No-one was the slightest bit interested in what I did for a living, what I drove (unless it was the latest station-wagon or oversized four-wheel drive with airbags to protect the kids), or where I lived (unless it was near a good day care centre).

Debra, who had once crushed biscuits in my hair at the school bus stop, arrived late. She hadn't changed a bit. Thin frame, thick hair, bushy black eyebrows, and a sense of self that had always put me on edge. Where did she get that confidence? I knew straight away she'd be married with children. I really didn't care if I spoke to her or not, but she planted herself opposite me just as the main course was being served, everyone else quickly moving to ensure there wasn't a spare seat across from them. Debra was known as the class bitch at school, but no-one was ever brave enough to challenge her. Dannie had told me that no-one really wanted her to come. I'd had five gins and two glasses of wine by this time, though, so I was ready for whatever she dished out. Biscuits or otherwise.

'So, how many children do you have, Alice?' Debra had four.

'None. But here's a photo of my brothers.' Did it sound as weird as I thought it did? Probably. I quickly put the photo back in my wallet and left it there for the rest of the night. Some may have thought it was sad, but my brothers and my dad had always been the most important men in my life. At least I could rely on them to be there for me.

'But you're obviously involved with someone special, though,' Debra said, looking at my hands.

'No. I bought this ring as a present for myself.' I was proud of my ability to teach, and that I made a good enough living to take myself shopping at Tiffany's. If I were ever to get a wedding ring or even just an engagement ring, it would come in a pale blue box. Not some chain-store faux suede one.

'That's funny. I thought Aboriginal women had children young – married or not. We all thought at school you'd be the first to have children.' Bitch! Had they all really thought that?

Debra was wrong about me being the first pregnant, but she was right about Koori women and kids generally. Fact was, most of the Koori women I knew had squeezed their kids out in their early twenties, some even before that, and none of them had blokes around now. Some of them had never had a bloke around at all. Many of the young girls I knew now were still doing it. It was a hard thing for me to understand, coming from a two-parent family and a Catholic background. We'd always been taught no sex before marriage and no kids out of wedlock. Even as times changed, the morals of the Church were upheld, at least in the Aigner house. Christian values worked for me in a very general sense – do unto others and so on – but I'd had to work out my own beliefs when I left school and started to live the life I thought best for me and the world. I tried to live by the Aboriginal value systems of the past – community benefits over individual gain, cooperation over competition, responsibility over rights.

Debra was still staring at me.

'Some do have children young, Debra, because when there's nothing else to do – no employment opportunities for instance – and you have low self-worth, why not create a life – someone who will love you back unconditionally?' She looked at me, unbelieving. I was struggling; she'd dealt me a low blow and I didn't really know how to recover.

'As for me, I've got plenty of love around me. And plenty of work to do. I'm not looking to fill any gaps yet,' I said, getting to my feet, loud enough for some of the other women to look at me and then Debra, wondering what had sparked the clear disagreement. Debra looked at me with contempt. She was ticked off, but I didn't care.

I already had my mother nagging me about breeding and maintaining the race. ('Wouldn't it be lovely to have a little brown Koori kid around the house?') All the other women in her ceramics class had photos of their grandchildren. ('I just need one photo in my purse, Alice.') She said she was the only Koori woman without grandkids. ('It's our job as the matriarchs to have families, Alice.') Now whitefellas I didn't even like were on my case about it too.

Dessert was being served and I moved four seats away, so I could sit alone. Half the table, the 'responsible homemakers and mothers', were outside, irresponsibly sucking on cigarettes. Yeah, get lung cancer and who'll look after your man and kids then? Dannie was happily engrossed in conversation with two other women and looking like she was having a great time.

I repeated my mantra, *I love being single!*, over and over.

❤

By ten pm *I love being single!* had become *I hate school reunions*. The more I drank the more difficult it became.

'Here's one of Lulu as a princess and Davey as an elf – aren't they cute?' Another couple of photos were shoved in my face.

I looked around the table at all the women, now totally sloshed. It was their one big night out and they were going to make the most of being kid- and husband-free for a night. It was funny that I'd been at all worried about what to wear to the reunion. My 'competition' hadn't worried at all. They might have been happy with husbands and children and shared mortgages, family holidays and family rooms, but they also bore a few more laugh lines than I did, and some were in need of serious tszujing from the Fab Five. These minor details at least brought me momentary comfort. It always bothered me to see women in bicycle shorts, t-shirts and thongs out shopping, though I realised that mothers had more important things to worry about than coordinating outfits. It was okay to look sporty or beachy, I thought, but not both at the same time, and regardless of priorities and income, one should never leave the house without a bra and lipstick. It was like going to work without cleaning your teeth.

'You haven't changed at all, Alice.' At last some positive recognition! It was Leonie. We had been good friends in Year 8 but then drifted apart. I faked a modest smile.

'Thanks, it's the eye cream and citrus face peels,' I said, trying desperately to make my existence as a single woman with a disposable income sound a little less pathetic and perhaps even indulgent. If I could make my life sound like an attractive option to just one of these women I would be happy.

'You never got that chipped tooth fixed, did you?'

I gasped. My god, she wasn't complimenting me at all.

'Not that you needed to. It's like a signature look for you.' I rarely even thought about the tiny chip on my front tooth. It had happened in second class. I was laughing so hard I hit my mouth on a chair. I usually have to point it out to people, it's so *not* there. I was so pissed off that I felt like chipping *her* tooth, the married, mortgaged, motherly bitch!

Dannie could see I was distressed, having difficulty just being there, let alone having a good time. She handed me a glass of water.

'Why did you come?' she whispered sym-pathetically.

'You dragged me here, remember? You didn't want to come on your own.'

'Oh, come on, Alice. You've never done anything you didn't want to in your life. You can't blame me. Why did you *really* come?'

'Because if I didn't people would've talked about me.'

'Don't be ridiculous.' She was right. They wouldn't have talked about me. They hadn't been talking about anyone else. They were lovely women, and genuinely keen to catch up and share baby photos and birthing tales, because that's what *normal* women our age did.

'I'm not normal!' I said.

Suddenly I wanted my own special moments to share: the moment when I 'just knew'. When I'd met 'the one'. The wonderful roller-coaster ride from wedding planning to broken waters.

I felt a growing desire to fit in with this group, this new community I'd never been part of. I was part of the

Koori community, my local community in Coogee, and the school community (as a teacher, of course, not a parent) – but I'd never been a member of the 'married with children community'. Now I wanted in.

I wanted more than that, though. I wanted to prove it was possible to maintain your identity and keep up to date with current affairs even while changing nappies and doing tuckshop. I knew I could manage it. I wouldn't be like *they* were. I was up to the challenge.

A man, marriage, career, kids and happiness: I *could* have it all, I decided. I *would* have it all.

'I'm going to get married,' I blurted.

Dannie shook her head. 'Listen, you're just pissed, Alice. You love being single. You're always big-noting about how good you've got it. A husband and kids? That's not for you.'

She didn't understand my resolve: I was already excited about the new path my life was going to take – until I was momentarily side-tracked by another conversation about pregnancy.

'I just loved the feeling of Sky and Fern as babies inside me,' someone said, and another round of discussion began, not about the appalling choice of names (there's a conversation I could've participated in), but about what it felt like to have a rug rat *moving* inside you. Shouldn't those kinds of things be kept private? Did these women have no sense of decorum? Obviously not. I tried to imagine what they were describing, but the only thing moving in my gut was the baby octopus I'd had for dinner, and if I were to break my waters now they'd have a very high alcohol content.

I started to feel sick. It wasn't just the conversation: the G&Ts weren't mixing well with the huge slice of tiramisu I'd eaten for dessert. I got up to go to the loo. Dannie jumped up too and raced towards the door, pushing past me on the way.

'I'm busting. Haven't had a chance to escape all night,' she said. Did that mean she was over it as well?

As we both sat in adjacent cubicles, I reminisced a little about the nights we used to spend as teenagers with fake IDs, hiding in the toilets until the police raid was over outside. I recognised the old tiles and wooden doors and wondered why the ladies were the only part of the pub that hadn't been brought into the twenty-first century.

'There's no paper,' Dannie said, sticking her hand under the dividing wall.

'Want to leave?' I asked as I passed her some paper.

'Why? It's only early.' Of course, this was a big night out for Dannie too; her husband George was minding the kids for the first time in months.

'Because this is soooooo painful. I don't fit in. I'm not even a bloody peg, regardless of shape. I want to go home.' I actually wanted to do a thorough post-mortem of the evening and decide once and for all – by morning, if that were at all possible – whether I wanted a man and a kid or not.

'We need to speak to everyone at least briefly.' Dannie was happy to leave with me early, but she would never be impolite, not even for her mate. We both stood at the sink washing our hands.

'I haven't spoken to Karly yet,' I said. 'At least she might be good for a laugh.' I was trying to be positive, as Dannie hadn't bitched about anyone all night.

'I haven't spoken to her either – why don't we do it together? That way it will be only *half* as painful for you.' Dannie was trying to point out how unreasonable I was being, but I just said 'Ha! Ha!' and pushed her out the toilet door.

Dannie took a seat on Karly's left and I sat opposite them. Karly had been the class dimwit. Since then she'd been to East Timor, set up a communication network, met a missionary, and adopted three kids.

'So you're a full-time mother, then?' Dannie was more interested than I was in the motherhood side of things. I wanted to hear about the 'missionary work' and saving souls.

'Yes. These children need all the love they can get. Poor things, it's very hard raising them outside of their own culture and society.' Karly had that martyr sparkle in her eye. I saw it. Dannie saw me see it. I saw Dannie start to move.

'Well then why are you doing it?' I asked Karly aggressively. Dannie stood up and grabbed her things.

'I thought I might call Bianca and let her know what a great time we're having. Maybe I can persuade her to come down. Why don't you come with me and say hello, Alice?' It was an escape plan: we could finally leave. I didn't care about Crusading Karly if it meant I could get out of there.

'Great idea. I'm sure she's wishing she were here,' I said, holding up my hand and mouthing a lie at Karly: 'Five minutes!'

Dannie and I linked arms and giggled as we headed towards the door.

two

Strategic planning

Once outside, Dannie called home to check on her kids, and I called our friends Peta and Liza. 'I'm getting married!' I explained, and told them to meet us at my place immediately – I needed their help. They were a little worried, they both admitted later, so they agreed to meet me at mine in half an hour.

Dannie was sober enough to enjoy the opportunity to drive my sporty red VW to my place. She'd sold her Land Rover when she moved to Paddington; the street was simply too small for it.

Within the hour, the four of us were sitting around my lounge room. The globe had blown, and I hadn't replaced it, so I lit some candles. Dannie and Liza sat on the groovy red sofa they had all helped me choose, and Peta and I sat on cushions on the wooden floor. It was a balmy night, so we opened the windows and venetian blinds wide to allow as much breeze in as possible. Just being home, I felt more secure in myself; I was in my own space, with my friends; two of them were happily single, childless women. In their company, I was normal, one of the majority.

'So how was the reunion?' Liza asked.

'All married women can talk about is honeymoons, anniversaries, pregnancies, Lamaze classes, sore nipples, breast milk, stretch marks, school fees, nits, mortgage repayments—' I took a breath, '*Apparently*, all the *important* things in life. Important to whom, I ask you?'

'Important to those women, Alice. Don't be so bloody harsh – or are you jealous?' Dannie was defensive. I *was* being harsh and, truth be told, I was perhaps a little jealous, but even though I admitted quietly to myself that all the women at the reunion were happy, and none of them looked like they'd trade their lives for quids, I would never let my insecurities be known publicly. Not Alice Aigner.

'Jealous, hah! I love my life. I could *build* on it, of course. In fact, I'll get myself a man, and breed, and show that it's possible to maintain a marriage, motherhood, and a mind of my own. Yep, I'll have it all by the time I'm thirty. I'll marry the most gorgeous man on the planet, have a HUGE wedding, so big it'll end up not only in the social pages of the *Koori Mail* but in the daily papers, too. You girls will be there, of course: Liza, the wedding coordinator; Peta, the producer; and Dannie, the matron of honour.'

'Why can't *I* be matron of honour?' Peta jokingly whined to Dannie.

'You're not married, and if you were, you'd be matron of *dis*honour,' Dannie said adamantly. Peta and Dannie occasionally sniped at each other, because they were so different – Peta out partying every night, Dannie relishing reading to her kids before tucking them into bed – but their exchanges were nearly always in good humour.

'Can I finish?' I felt we were losing focus. 'The difference is *I* won't be limited to conversations about cradle crap, booster shits or nappy thrush.' The girls keeled over laughing, but I had no idea why.

'Cradle *cap*,' Dannie chuckled.

'Booster *shots*,' Liza added.

'And it's nappy *rash*, Alice. Even I know that.' Peta rolled her eyes.

'Whatever! So now there's a whole language I need to learn as well. I can do that. I'm a bloody history teacher. I could learn the whole history of birthing techniques and baby things if I really wanted to. But I don't.'

Liza and Peta smirked at my outburst, but I think Dannie was a little bothered about how I pictured her as a mother. She frowned out the window into the black night, elbow resting on the arm of the lounge, her chin cupped in her palm. I wasn't talking about her at all – she had to understand that.

'Dannie, you know I don't think of you as *really* married or *really* motherly at all, don't you?'

'I don't think of you as *really* an Aborigine, either.'

It was the first real laugh I'd had all night. Dannie wasn't just our voice of reason; she often provided the comedy for the group, too.

'So, you're going to be married by your thirtieth, are you love?' Liza was good at getting things back on track.

'That's right. I've got two years. I want what all those other women have, like Dannie. I can do it, I know I can.'

'Do what? Learn how to function without sleep?' Dannie was always pragmatic.

'No, I like my eight hours' sleep per night.'

'So, you want to be able to read only when you go to the toilet, and even then have someone banging on the door calling out *Muuuuum* – your only name?'

'No, I like to be left in peace on the loo, and to read at night in bed – and on the beach too.'

'Ah, the beach. Well, be prepared to spend hours packing bags with towels, buckets, spades, cordial, sandwiches, tiny packets of chips, spare clothes and sunscreen. And don't think for a minute you'll ever be able to lie down and read anything, because you'll have to be watching the kids the whole time.'

'Okay, so forget the kids and reading for now, what about Mr Right? You have him. Tell me about how wonderful that is – having a gorgeous man who has vowed to adore you forever – your own Mr Right!'

'I have Mr All-Right. When the kids come along, it all changes between you and your man, Alice. There's hardly any more romance. George and I don't even kiss properly anymore unless we're having sex.'

'But there you have it! You *have* sex! On tap! Right?'

'We fall into bed every night exhausted, look at each other and smile, then agree to wait until we have more energy – which of course we rarely have.'

Personally, I thought having sex with a bloke called George would be difficult at any time, but I pursued my line of questioning.

'What about the mansion? The freshly cut lawns? The young, built husband washing the car on Sunday morning, your kids riding bikes and getting good school reports, the dog you take for walks?'

'The so-called mansion takes hours to clean and keep tidy because the kids leave everything, including their bikes, everywhere. Jeremy looks like he'll have to repeat kindergarten – kindergarten! Sarah's one of the school bullies, so naturally I'm proud of her. We pay a fortune for a gardener who is so old I'd rather he *didn't* take his shirt off. George's sixpack has turned into a slab. The car is always dirty because George won't use a bucket to wash it and is too tight to pay to get it cleaned, and the fucken dog is a Siberian husky and should be in Siberia. It malts fur all over the place and eats more than me and the kids put together.' Dannie stopped and took a long sip on her drink. 'Sorry for swearing.' There was sweat on her forehead.

'Okay, okay, I get it. It's not *all* rosy, but I want *some* of it. I'll trade the kids off for a trip to Venice or Paris or anywhere each year. At least say you'll help me find a bloke. Based on what you've told me, without the kids we'll at least have the energy for sex.'

Liza jumped in. 'What you need is a strategy.' She pulled out a steno pad from her bag. Her preparedness comes from being a lawyer, always making case notes. Liza works for the Aboriginal Legal Service in the city. She's white like Dannie, but with Italian heritage. I call them my token white friends; I reckon everyone should have at least one or two. It's politically correct.

Liza and I met at a justice forum back in the 1990s and have been tight ever since. Liza's really smart, she always has her head in a book, and it's always non-fiction. She has a real thirst for learning. I like her because she's genuine. Her work at the ALS isn't some patronising attempt to help Blackfellas, and it's not about making herself feel warm and fuzzy about being in the cause either. Some might see it as her bit for reconciliation, but Liza has a holistic approach. Her philosophy is that helping anyone in anyway makes the world generally a better place to live. I love that about her. Also, I think she enjoys pissing her parents off. They're really well-known solicitors. They wanted her to join the family firm, and hate that she works at the ALS for next to nothing. She does heaps of pro bono work as well, which her parents simply don't understand. They didn't walk the Harbour Bridge with her in 2000, and she didn't speak to them for months afterwards. She is so passionate about social justice that she has culled almost everyone from her life who doesn't think like she does. She can be extreme, but that's what I like about her.

Once we were in a restaurant when another member of our group – a friend of a friend – kept putting on a racist Indian accent. Liza was furious; she threw money into the middle of the table and stormed out, shouting, 'I only want to surround myself with people who think like I do!' She was accused of being narrow-minded, but I agreed totally with her, and followed her out. That was when we became really close.

Peta, Dannie and I watched Liza tear off pages from her notepad and lay them on the table. Then she pulled pens from her bag. I imagine this is what she does as part of preparing for a case, but I can't be sure, because I've never really seen her in action. Unlike most of my girlfriends, Liza is all for confidentiality. If she learns something at work that she thinks I really should be on top of or might just be interested in knowing, she'll tell me, 'What I'm hearing out there is ...' or 'The word on the street is ...', but she never gives away anything she shouldn't. She's a good confidant, which is why I felt safe pouring out all my business in her presence. I knew she'd take it to the grave. She better.

'Okay, so let's be clear about your goal first.' Liza was methodical, too. 'What exactly is it?'

'Haven't you been listening? I want to meet Mr Right and get married *and* I want to have a HUGE, all-star-cast, social-event-of-the-year wedding!'

'Okay, Muriel, good. Is there a timeframe?'

'Hey, I'm no Muriel. I'm not constantly fantasising about getting married.' (I had of course fantasised, but not constantly, and I hadn't been trying on dresses — there was a difference.)

Peta coughed and laughed. 'Bullshit.'

'Can we focus, please? Is there a timeframe, Alice?' Liza asked again.

'By my thirtieth birthday!' Had she been hearing me at all? But Liza was just in lawyer mode, double-checking the facts.

'Right, that gives us just under two years. Now, how would you define Mr Right, Alice?' Liza was talking to me as though I was a client and she was questioning me on the stand. I didn't mind, though, because it was all helpful.

'You want a definition?'

'Well, in order to know who Mr Right is when you meet him, you should have some idea of what you're looking for.' Liza was so, so organised. 'You talk and I'll scribe. Let's start with the most obvious of your requirements. What *must* he be or have?'

'He must be single, straight and wanting to be in a relationship. Not like Gus, who was already in a relationship, or bi-Max, who was just discovering his sexuality at the age of twenty-five, or Richard, who preferred watching football to having sex.' At least my past lovers had taught me something.

'Did Richard really choose the game over you?' Peta was astonished. She'd known him from around the traps as well.

'Sure thing. I asked him straight out if he'd rather go to the football or spend the afternoon making love, and his response was ...'

The girls waited anxiously for the answer.

'Depends on which code!'

'What!' they all screamed. I was sure my neighbours could hear us.

'Okay, so what else? Let's keep it moving, Alice.' Liza sat with pen poised.

'He must be good to his mother and like children – because clearly they're all going to be around at some point.'

'And because there's a good chance that you won't like his mum *or* the kids.' Dannie was on a comedy roll.

I kept adding to the list. 'I want him to love his job. Scott used to complain all the time about his work, I couldn't stand it. He acted like he had no control over his own happiness there. He was such a bloody victim.'

Liza was writing furiously.

'I want a man who is only addicted to me.'

'Your problem, Alice, is that it's always just about you,' Dannie said. She turned and looked directly at me. 'No addictions? None at all? Who are you going to date, a bloody priest? Can he drink coffee?'

'Coffee, yes; beer for breakfast like JC, not on your life. One alcoholic in my life is one too many. Now fill me up!' I held out my glass for another drink. Peta did the honours and we all laughed.

'I want him to think I'm the most gorgeous woman on the planet.' The others nodded in agreement: it was a fair request for any girl to make.

'And I don't want him to adore me because I'm Black. I don't want to be someone's "exotic other". Do you know how David used to introduce me?'

'How?' they asked in chorus.

'This is Alice, she's Wiradjuri.'

'What?'

'I know, I know, and he'd say it to whitefellas, like I was some freak. He didn't understand it was different when *I* said it, to place myself. That he didn't need to do it at dinner parties.'

'So what did you do?'

'I'd say "This is David, he's my own personal anthropologist." ' We laughed some more.

'Anything else for the list, Alice?' Liza was the only one truly keeping on track.

'He *has* to be non-racist, non-fascist and non-homophobic, and believe in something, preferably himself. And, apropos of nothing, he must be punctual.'

'But you can be on Koori time whenever you want, right?' Dannie couldn't help herself.

'That's right,' Peta chipped in.

'He must be romantic and be comfortable with showing affection in public, and by that I don't mean grabbing me on the tit every time he kisses me.'

'Who did that?' Peta wanted to know.

'Jason, the young surfer I met down the coast last New Year's. Every time we kissed he grabbed my left breast, didn't matter where we were.'

'Why not your right one?' Peta asked.

'Left one's slightly bigger. He loved it more,' I said matter-of-factly. The discussion was getting off track again, so I brought it back. 'I want a man who is financially secure and hopefully debt-free.'

'What about a mortgage?' Liza asked.

'A mortgage is fine. I just don't want him working twenty-four/seven to pay off his gambling debts.'

'*Now* who are you outing?' Dannie said. 'You're a bloody serial dater, Alice.'

'Grant – remember him? We met at the Leukaemia Foundation ball. Turned out he backed the horses to the point where he was working seventy hours a week to cover his debts. That's not the kind of man I want to marry. Would anyone?'

'Depends, was he built?' Peta always managed to bring it back to basics.

'Okay, you've got a pretty strong list here, Alice. Anything else you want to add?' Liza was trying to wrap up her side of the work. She'd been a very objective scribe and facilitator.

'Yes, I want a loyal, faithful, sincere, chivalrous, witty, competent and responsible man.' I was completely serious, but Dannie burst into giggles.

'That's it, then?' Liza asked, almost impatiently.

'No. Can you add that he should be a good communicator as well?'

'You've got to be kidding, Alice. I've never met *any* man like the one you're looking for,' Dannie said, marvelling at the long list of criteria I'd come up with.

'What about George?'

Dannie squealed with laughter. 'George! That's it, I'm going to pee myself! You live in a fantasy world sometimes, Alice.' She got up off the sofa and ran along the hall to the bathroom.

'Well, Alice, no-one could accuse you of not aiming high.' Even Liza, whose standards were generally rather exacting, was surprised at what I expected in a potential partner.

'Based on previous experience, as you have just heard, sis, I've got to aim high. The more you ask for, the more you're likely to get, right?'

'Or the harder you might fall, Missy.' Peta wasn't convinced.

When Dannie came back from the loo, Liza read out my final list of essential selection criteria for the position of Mr Right, or, as she called it, 'Alice's ten-point plan'.

Essential selection criteria for Mr Right

1. *Must be single, straight and wanting to be in a relationship*
2. *Must be good to his mother and like children*
3. *Must love his job (don't want him whinging every night about his day)*
4. *Must only be addicted to me (not alcohol or narcotics, and he must not smoke)*
5. *Must think I am the most gorgeous woman on the planet*
6. *Must be a non-racist, non-fascist, non-homophobic believer in something, preferably himself*
7. *Must be punctual (although I am allowed to be on Koori time)*
8. *Must be romantic and be able to show affection in public*
9. *Must be financially secure and debt-free (mortgage will be acceptable)*
10. *He must be loyal, faithful, sincere, chivalrous, witty, competent, responsible and a good communicator (i.e. he must be a good listener)*

'Actually, I'd like to add some non-essential criteria as well. Just a couple of desirable characteristics that might help me identify the *real* potentials.'

'I'm going to need another drink, then,' said Peta, and took herself out to the kitchen.

'I'd like him to be in the property market – or at least thinking of getting into it. And I don't anyone with a criminal record, so don't be lining me up with any of your clients, Liza, okay?'

'What about teeth and hair?' Dannie asked cheekily.

'Well yes, he should have both, and they should be his own, of course.'

She wasn't giving up. 'Here's one for you, Al: what if he's got kids from a previous marriage?'

'Nup, don't want an instant family either, or stalker ex-girlfriends, been there with Terry – had to get an AVO out against them both eventually.'

'Okay, that's gotta be it now, Alice – you can't possibly have any more criteria, surely?' I was turning into one of Liza's more difficult clients.

'Actually…' – I admit I was a little embarrassed to add yet another criterion, but it was important to me – 'It would help if he were a compatible star sign.' Aria said that for a harmonious relationship, the perfect matches for Leos were Tauruses, other Leos, Scorpios and Capricorns. If I wanted passion – and what girl didn't? – I should try Aries, Gemini, Libra or Aquarius, and if I was looking for a challenge, then I should date Cancerians, Virgos or Pisceans. I wanted it all – harmony, passion *and* a challenge – so that just ruled out Sagittarians, really. I trusted Aria.

'I think you should stop there, Alice, and move onto your strategy for meeting this one-in-five-hundred-million guy. Your so-called Mr Right?' Liza made me feel like I was in one of those little rooms with the one-way mirrored windows where they grill baddies on TV. She was taking it all so seriously. But then, so was I.

'You mean Mr Unbelievably-Perfect-Needs-To-Be-Cloned,' Dannie said, shaking her head. She stood up and headed to the kitchen, where Peta was still busy making some late-night cocktails.

Peta was the real party girl of the group. I met her in the Bachelor of Education course at Sydney's University of Technology when we were in first year. I went on to teach and she decided to go into policy making. She was good at it. She'd never have made a schoolmarm anyway; she was too effortlessly glamorous for that, with her trendy clothes, flawless make-up, and about 300 pairs of shoes. Imelda Marcos had nothing on our Peta. She knew that a career in teaching would never have allowed her to maintain her elaborate wardrobe. I was happy with her decision, because I often borrowed her clothes. Yes, Peta's career in policy furthered Indigenous education and helped two Indigenous women to look good at the same time.

Peta was also the prettiest of the group. We knew it. She knew it. Her broad smile lit up any room she walked into. Her buttered body was toned and golden ("Cos I'm a Murri from Queensland,' she always said), and her long, luxurious, mahogany ponytail drove guys wild. It wasn't unusual to see Peta surrounded by a swarm of young admirers at our local, the Cushion Bar down at Coogee Beach, on a Friday night. She just seduced men with her presence. I could've learned a lot from Peta on that front. She was always positive, no matter what, and incredibly likeable as well. She could be sharp, sometimes, but only when dealing with ignorant whitefellas, and even then she made sure she had good cause. Between Peta, Liza and Dannie, I had the best mix of friends a single, childless woman of twenty-eight could hope for.

Soon Peta and Dannie brought out fresh drinks, and we settled down to work on the strategy. I had read in *Aria's Almanac* that feng shui-ing your home would not only bring peace and harmony, but could bring love as well. So I started my list with that: *Feng shui flat.*

'Secondly, you'll need to get your friends to set you up with their single friends. Blind dates. Don't get too blind yourself, of course,' Peta said. 'You should also suss out people at work – maybe there are some single dads floating around. And what about Mickey? He must have some mates.' I wasn't too keen on the single-dad idea, but Peta was right: Mickey *should* know someone I could date. Mickey was my only close friend at St Christina's. He taught science. Being gay, he was great at getting in a huddle for girl-talk, exchanging dating horror stories and fashion disasters. Most of the time, we met at the Cushion Bar to debrief. Mickey liked a few G&Ts too, and there were fewer suspicious Christian eyes upon us there than in the staff room.

'What about attending a few work-related events, like conferences and department functions? I'm sure the school will pay for some professional development. At least at those kind of gigs you can meet people who do similar work,' Liza said. It seemed a sensible, practical suggestion; the list was coming together nicely.

'You could place an ad in the classifieds. I knew someone who met her husband that way. She also got shagged a lot along the way.' While I wasn't just looking for a 'shag', Peta's idea might be a valid strategy.

'Can we just say I'll check out the classifieds, as opposed to placing an advert myself? That's just a little too desperate for me, I think.' They rolled their eyes collectively. Obviously I was desperate; otherwise, I wouldn't have dragged them all to my place in the middle of the night to workshop my problems.

'Same with internet dating. I heard one of the mothers at the school saying her sister's friend was doing it and met an engineer,' Dannie added. She was clearly impressed with 'engineer status', but that was okay – so was I! I was quite open to becoming Mrs Engineer.

Liza was next to offer a strategy: 'I recently read about this annual singles picnic at Bondi. It's called "Singles Uprising." You might want to check it out.'

Liza never ceased to amaze me with the amount of useful trivia she knew. 'How on earth did you come across that?' I asked.

'I googled "uprisings" for a paper I was writing for the *Indigenous Law Bulletin*, and that was one of the sites I found.' Thank god one of my friends was an internet nerd!

Looking for an excuse to take a trip, I added 'holiday romance' at the bottom of the page. 'That's it,' I said. 'We're done.'

Liza read the list out loud:

Strategies for meeting Mr Right

- *Feng shui flat*
- *Go on blind dates with suitable (single, heterosexual) friends of friends*
- *Suss out potential dates through work – single colleagues and their friends*
- *Attend professional gatherings – conferences, meetings*
- *Place an ad in the classifieds*
- *Try internet dating*
- *Attend 'Singles Uprising'*
- *Be open to holiday romances*

Liza paused. 'I guess we could sum these strategies up with one simple command,' she said. She took a fat purple texta and wrote across the top of the page:

'BE OPEN TO ALL OPPORTUNITIES!' Then she stood up and went straight to the kitchen, where she removed all the takeaway Thai and pizza menus stuck to my fridge and used the magnets to put the lists up in their place. 'Leave these here as a daily reminder of the process involved in achieving your goals before your thirtieth birthday cut-off date, Alice.' Ever-efficient, she recognised something else we needed to do: 'I think while we're at it we should make a short list of the strategies for *not* meeting Mr Right.' She was onto something. Whatever I'd been doing in the past obviously wasn't working.

'The first strategy should probably be *not* to stray from your list, Alice! Stick to the strategy!' Liza was right, of course and that would be a useful mantra during down times.

'Don't get too pissed and make a complete dick of yourself when you're out on dates, either.' Peta knew what she was talking about, having spent many weekends cursing herself for things she'd done on a Friday-night date under the influence of alcohol.

'Never talk about exes on your first date, Alice. Actually, don't talk about them at all. That's probably the best advice I can give you,' Dannie said. The last man she went out with before she'd met George was the local mayor, who had moaned about his ex-girlfriend dumping him for another woman. It had been so bad Dannie had walked out of a restaurant mid-meal.

'It drove me nuts, so I dumped him. So, if we don't like them talking about their exes, I'm sure they won't like it either.' She was right, of course.

'Don't forget the rule about no sex on the first date.' Peta stood, as if to give a public oration, took a long slug on her drink, then continued: 'Men might like you to be as wild as a tiger in bed, but they'd also like to believe that you are virtuous, at least for the first date.'

'When's acceptable these days?' Dannie had been out of the game for some time, and so had I, compared to Peta.

'The third date is usually acceptable. By then the juices are well and truly flowing and you can count the previous dates as foreplay.' Peta could be crude, but she sounded like she knew what she was talking about.

Liza added the no-sex-till-the-third-date rule to the list, then said, 'Alice, don't even think about dating any of your friends' exes. If she dumped him, you can rest assured there's a good reason for it.' Liza had gone out briefly with one of Peta's exes, who we had all called 'The Root-Rat'. The emphasis was always on *rat* – he just couldn't be faithful. Even for Peta, a notorious good-time girl, it had been too much, so she'd dumped him. The Root-Rat had always fancied Liza and we all knew it. Liza had believed he would be different with her, that she could tame him. She couldn't and didn't. Luckily the friendship between the girls hadn't soured; in fact, they still joked about it.

As the clock hit two am, Liza went to read back the key points, but I had two more of my own to add first.

First, dating Cancerians or Geminis was out, I explained, because I was superstitious. I didn't like the thought of dying from cancer and every Gemini I had ever met was constantly sick. I was probably being irrational, but I wasn't going to change my mind.

Second, under *no* circumstances was I to pick men up at the pub. I didn't want any one-night stands. I was smart enough to know I couldn't really build a solid relationship on a night spent with a near stranger. I'd tried it a couple of times and the result had only been long-term one-night stands. Anyway, part of me was terrified at the thought of taking a stranger home. What if the guy I picked up turned out to be an axe-murderer?

'Don't be so ridiculous, Alice, they don't want to kill you! They want to shag you, that's all.' Peta had had enough one-night stands to know. She'd spent some time as a serial dater as well.

Liza read out the new list:

Strategies for NOT meeting Mr Right

- *Straying from the list of strategies*
- *Getting pissed and making a complete dick of self*
- *Talking about ex-boyfriends on first date*
- *Putting out on the first date*

- *Dating friends' exes*
- *Dating Cancerians or Geminis*
- *Picking men up at the pub (i.e. No one-night stands under ANY circumstances)*

Peta and Liza nodded, accepting the drafted policy and its key points. Dannie, slightly pissed by this stage, was silent, but very busy at the same time.

'What *are* you doing?' Peta asked sarcastically. She'd had a few drinks by now, too. I could feel one of their meaningless spats on the way.

'I'm doing a SWOT analysis for Alice meeting Mr Right.'

'A what?'

'SWOT. Strengths, weaknesses, opportunities and threats.'

'Oh for god's sake, Dannie, I know what a bloody SWOT analysis is. I've finished *my* degree, Mummy.' Peta was getting messy and Dannie was clearly upset by her display of bitchiness. Liza moved straight into appeasing facilitator mode.

'Actually ladies, I think we can do something with this.' She tore off a few more sheets of paper, preparing to be scribe again. 'Peta, why don't you come up with the threats and weaknesses, and Dannie can do the strengths and opportunities.'

Peta didn't need prompting. 'Well isn't it obvious, Alice? The threats are to your independence, individuality, disposable income and ability to party. Dare I say it, a threat to the depth of your friendship with other singles.' She ran through this spiel like a well-rehearsed script. 'Haven't heard you mention Bianca for a while, come to think of it. Now why would that be? My bet is that it's because she's getting married and her whole social calendar has changed – no single friends in sight, eh?'

Dannie wasn't fazed at all. She was married, and managed to maintain her friendships, so she didn't think Peta's remarks warranted rebuttal.

'The opportunities far outweigh the threats,' she said. 'You'll have opportunities to love and grow and be enriched by a partnership with someone who shares your beliefs and opinions. That's something too great to deny yourself, Alice. And meeting Mr Right will also provide you with the opportunity to have children. Little images of yourself.'

'Yeah, needy, reliant little images of yourself,' Peta mumbled into her glass. She'd once told me she *never, ever, ever* wanted to have kids. 'The world's overpopulated,' was all she'd said.

'Look Alice, I know you've always wanted to have little brown kids, as you call them.' Dannie was right. Who didn't want to see themselves reborn in another little human being? That's why people bred, wasn't it? I also wanted someone to look after me when I was old and sick. I didn't mind going into a retirement village and playing bridge and bingo, but I sure as hell wanted to have visitors. Yes, meeting Mr Right would be the best way to ensure that I'd be taken care of in my old age. Perhaps that's what having children was really about.

'Now the weaknesses,' said Peta. 'You'll become reliant on someone else to do all the things you do for yourself now.' I wasn't convinced – quite the opposite. I had already started thinking about how nice it would be to have someone else put my garbage bins out for me – the one thing I really hated doing as a single girl. In fact, there were several things I had to do for myself that I'd be happy to have a man take care of.

Dannie's response was calm: 'And the strengths, Alice, are that you'll meet your soul mate, share your life, have unconditional love and support.'

Unconditional love and support. That was the deal breaker for me. Dannie had found the missing elements in my life. I wanted both of them bestowed upon me, even though I had always doubted my own ability to give unconditional love in return. Perhaps it would be easy to reciprocate once Mr Right showed me how it was done. Yes, meeting Mr Right could even help me grow as a person, and so it became even more important, and urgent, to make a firm commitment to the strategy.

In true peacemaking style, Liza called the exercise a tie at three am, even though we all knew that the strengths and opportunities we'd discussed far outweighed the weaknesses and threats. Dannie had to get home because the kids would be up at seven looking for breakfast and cartoons. Peta had a draft policy to read and a plane to catch the next day for a department meeting in Canberra, and Liza had to prepare for a hearing on Monday morning. I needed to process all that had happened that night and find time to mark essays as well.

Finally in bed, my head pounding, but only lightly, I considered what my Mr Right might be like. It was *my* dream, so I made him drop-dead gorgeous, and as he began to undress me, he grew even sexier. I went to sleep smiling: I would soon implement my strategy for meeting Mr Right.

three

Feng shui-ing Mr Right

I rose with a hangover and stumbled and groaned my way to the kitchen, but after an orange juice and some coffee, the seediness subsided. I contemplated the lists on my fridge and felt inspired. Today was the first day of my soon-to-be-Mrs-Right life, and I was keen to swing into action. The first strategy on my list was feng shui-ing my flat, and I decided to start straight away.

I'd recently cut an article on feng shui out of the local paper, and following its instructions, I completely rearranged my bedroom, rotating my bed to face my south-west 'love corner'. I also decided to replace two of the mirror doors on my wardrobe with frosted glass. In feng shui, pairs are auspicious, representing couples, but this wasn't really about feng shui – I just didn't want to roll over in bed anymore and see my naked reflection. I kept one mirrored-door for future use, though.

Calling my father in to help wasn't originally part of my plan for the morning, or his for that matter. As fathers do, though, he came to my assistance. He always did. He often replaced light globes for me, fixed leaking taps, hung pictures and screwed, nailed and hammered things when needed. He was the reason that I hadn't really noticed not having a man around. I was a feminist, but I was also quite comfortable with not having to swing a hammer or turn a screwdriver. I knew what I was good at, and it wasn't home maintenance.

He seemed puzzled today. 'Why fix something that isn't broken, Alice? There's nothing wrong with these doors.' How could I possibly explain to my father the self-nudity thing, and that the two new doors were supposed to symbolise a couple? He simply wouldn't get it. Nor would he have cared, I'm sure. My dad is from the old school. Man meets woman, man courts woman, man marries woman, man supports woman and they live happily ever after. Just like him and Mum. They were both outcasts when they met in the 1960s. Mum was a Koori from the country, not even a citizen in her own land, and Dad, a migrant from Austria, was simply a 'wog' to just about everyone he met, but to each other, they were immediately the world. Their love knew no racial or class barriers. They were married in their early twenties and were still happy after nearly thirty years together. Dad still brushed Mum's hair when they got up every morning, and she still had his meal on the table at the same time every night. They were complete opposites, and both Scorpios (Aria would not have approved!), but they were bound by shared notions of respect and family and hard work. Their relationship was my benchmark; was it any wonder I'd been avoiding commitment by dating losers and long shots? My marital bar was unbelievably high because of them.

My Dad believed there were certain ways to do things. The way *he* did things. The way he and Mum did things. They expected my brothers and me to meet someone, fall in love, get married, just as they had, and they would expect the same of their grandchildren and great-grandchildren. It was the natural course of events – in my Dad's world anyway.

I might subscribe to Dad's happily-ever-after approach if I actually met someone who loved me the way that Dad loved Mum. Until then, I was happy to have him do all the 'boy jobs' around my flat; I only wished he lived next door so he could put my bins out as well.

After Dad had gone home, I spent the rest of the day creating a feng shui love and romance shrine in the south-west corner of my lounge room. At first it posed a problem: my TV currently sat in the same corner that, by feng shui law, should bring me love and romance. Unfortunately, it was the only place in my flat where I got decent reception. I did a Liza, and tried to analyse the situation dispassionately. What was more important to me: watching another series of *The West Wing* alone, or finding love? Somewhat reluctantly, I relocated the TV and replaced it with red candles and paper lanterns, as prescribed by my newspaper clipping. The love corner was a must if I wanted lasting romance and love-related happiness. My TV-related happiness from now on would just have to take second place – and another corner.

In the late afternoon, I went to the florist on Coogee Bay Road and bought two matching bonsai plants in terracotta pots and brought them home. Then I dug out two ceramic painted tiles – red and black, with matching calligraphic designs – that I'd bought at a garage sale around the corner three months before. I hung them one on each wall in the love corner. Two of everything symbolised the coupledom I knew I would soon enjoy. Perhaps I should just buy another TV: I could put them both in my south-west love corner as well, and *all* my happiness would be realised.

four

I'm not a lesbian

Living in a large block of units, with snowdroppers stealing underwear regularly, I tended to do my washing at Mum and Dad's. Twice a week I'd stop by before school to do a quick wash and hang it out. Sometimes it didn't seem worth it, though; I often came away upset, and fumed all the way to work, if not the entire morning. Without fail, my mother would spend my whole visit following me around, asking me why I didn't have a man. Then she'd try to set me up with an unlikely suitor – like Cliff.

'Cliff just got back from Venice!' Anyone would've thought Cliff was her own son, she was so pleased he'd returned after three years abroad. Cliff was actually the son of Janet, one of Mum's friends from ceramics class.

'He's landed himself a great job as a hair colourist. Some salon in Darlinghurst.'

'That's nice.'

'You colour your hair, don't you?'

'I *have* a hairdresser, Mum.'

'He lives at Clovelly. Just round the corner from you. That's an omen, don't you think?'

'I'd say coincidence, Mum.'

'He's still single too, Alice, and Janet said he hardly dates. Now *that's* a coincidence. We both think you'd make a lovely couple.'

Both Mum and Janet were in denial. Cliff was actually gay, and he wasn't dating anyone special because he was a serial slut. I never said anything about it, though. I knew Janet would have been delighted to see us together. I reckon in her heart she knew of his sexual preferences but naively hoped he would grow out of it. Cliff was thirty-three and had never had a girlfriend, so there was little chance of *that* happening. I was sure Mum knew Cliff was gay, but she just wanted me to get married anyway.

I thought Cliff was a right-wing fuck-knuckle. He and I had had a number of arguments about our prime minister's concept of the black armband view of history, and his assertion that there was no such thing as generations of stolen children. Cliff was a huge fan of John Howard and his views, and Keith Windschuttle was his favourite historian. Come to think of it, perhaps I *should* tell Janet he's gay, just to get back at him for his appalling take on Australian history. Mental note to self: save telling Janet about Cliff until real payback is needed.

Mum had been going on about Cliff for ages, which was why my daily visits had of late trickled down to a couple a week, but I dropped in on my way to work on the Monday following the disastrous school reunion at the Hub.

'I don't know how much longer I've got, Alice. I'd like to be a grandmother one day, and you are my eldest.'

'Only by a couple of years, Mum.' My brothers were both younger than me, but not by much: Arnie was twenty-six and Dillon was twenty-four.

'Don't you worry about being alone?' She followed me around the kitchen as I unpacked some fruit I'd picked up from the fresh food market on Saturday morning.

I just couldn't bring myself to tell her about my new strategy; she'd want in on all the dates and processes. I simply couldn't have that.

'I'm not alone – I have you guys, and great friends.'

'You spend too much time with Liza and Peta. People are going to think you're a lesbian if you don't start spending time with men. Go on dates. What about one with Cliff?'

'Liza and Peta are the best dates I've ever had, Mum.'

'I knew it, you *are* a lesbian, aren't you?' She clasped her head dramatically.

'I'm not a lesbian, Mum. I actually like my single life and having no-one to worry about, being able to sleep and read when I want to.'

'Are you sure you're not a lesbian? It seems like everyone's a lesbian these days.' I think Mum just liked saying the word *lesbian*.

'Oh for god's sake, I'm not a lesbian, Mum, I'm just saying that it's much easier to hang out with the girls. They're far less work than men – I don't have to try to figure them out or organise them.' My mantra for the day seemed to be *I'm not a lesbian, I'm not a lesbian.* As much as my mother enjoyed saying the word, I didn't!

'Well, you'll have to settle down one day, and with a MAN. Look at your brother Dillon – it looks like he and Larissa'll be together forever. As for Arnie, well he's just sowing his wild oats. That's what boys do.'

I'd lost count of the number of times I'd head Arnie on the phone to women saying 'Trust me, babe!' He was always breaking innocent hearts, but my mother would never have anything bad said about her sons. It was pointless arguing with her.

'Yeah, that's what boys do. I wouldn't trust most of them as far as I could throw them. I've got to go to school now, Mum.' I headed for the door, but she called after me.

'Alice, you know, your father worries about you too. About who will look after you when he's gone, hang your pictures, nail things, fix things. He'd like to see you married too.'

'I can look after myself,' I shouted back to her, already on my way out.

'Then why don't you? Why do you get him to help you all the time? He's getting old too, Alice.' What? This was the first time I'd heard anything about Dad's age and me having to fend for myself on the home improvement front. He must have said something after the feng shui effort. There were no secrets between Mum and Dad. They were as tight as nun's knickers.

Mum was hanging out her bedroom window as I got into the car. 'I can call Cliff if you like.' I pushed my foot hard on the accelerator and drove off, wishing Dillon and Larissa would just get married and take some of the heat off me. Actually, as Dillon was the only source of straight male input into my personal life, I should probably run my new strategy by him at some stage.

For a young fella, Dillon was pretty wise when it came to matters of the heart. It was not unheard of for me to SMS him the middle of the night to ask for 'boy advice': What does it mean if he said this? How many days should I wait till I call him? Should I call him at all? Why hasn't he called me? Is he going to call me? If not, why not? What's wrong with me? What's wrong with him? And so it went. Dillon always answered my messages, but he didn't hold back if he thought I was being desperate or if I was way off base. If he needed to be blunt with me he would. He wouldn't sugar coat his frustration at my raving or my commitment to finding reasons for dragging out relationships that were obviously over. 'Build a bridge and get over it!' was his favourite response, but more than a few times he'd sent me a text saying: 'You've fucked it up, now it's time to move on.' Nine times out of ten Dillon was correct in the advice he gave me, but I didn't really listen to it, because it was generally the opposite to what I really wanted to do. Perhaps I needed to add 'Heed Dillon's advice when it comes to relating to the opposite sex,' to my list of strategies.

It wasn't that I didn't want advice or assistance in finding a husband – god knows I needed both. It was just that I hated everyone knowing my business and feeling sorry for me. It made me seem desperate, and I wasn't. I just hadn't been in such a rush before. Having a deadline made it all seem more of a priority than it had been in the past.

As I drove on, I started thinking about my wedding and considered the options. Mum had always said I could have Archie Roach sing at the reception. I love him singing 'Love in the Morning', probably because I've always preferred making love at dawn. (Then again, I don't mind a bit of afternoon delight either.) Archie rarely performs without Ruby, though, and I didn't know that Mum and Dad could afford to fly them both to Sydney.

Perhaps an island wedding? The Cooks. Or Fiji. That'd weed out the real friends, wouldn't it? Who'd pay to travel across the Pacific to see me finally get married?

Or what about a Sydney Harbour wedding down at the Park Hyatt? A celebrant rather than a priest, of course. Mum would really struggle with it, not being in a church and all, but it would be *my* wedding. I'd wear a tiara rather than veil. Designer dress, not one off the rack. The groom would wear whatever I told him to. A cocktail party would follow, as opposed to sit-down meal. Dillon would MC, but I would write his speech, or at least check it – I was a teacher, after all. I'd have a big heart-shaped chocolate cake, with fresh red roses around the base. We'd spend the night at the Hyatt and then fly out the next day to honeymoon in Venice or Paris or maybe both. We'd live happily ever after. Yes, it was all planned.

I was so excited about the plans for my wedding that I needed to share them with one of the girls. My first class that morning wasn't until second period, so I had time to make a quick call. Dannie would be at her kids' school, helping out with reading group, and Peta was in Canberra discussing the future of Indigenous education, but I knew Liza would still be at home with her face in a book or file, so I dialled her number.

'Liza, it's Alice. I'm sorting out my wedding plans, you busy?'

'Not really, Al, just working on keeping a young fella out of Long Bay. I'm sure his case notes can wait – your pretend love-life is a case with far more importance.' Was she was being sarcastic or just joking?

'So you're organising a wedding, are you? What about the groom?' she asked almost accusingly. As though I was breaking the law because I was trying to organise my wedding without having found a man first. Liza could be a real wet blanket sometimes.

'Don't bother me with details, darling!' I said, sounding like some social butterfly and waving my free hand nonchalantly, as though I knew the hired help would fix the problem. I was glad Liza couldn't see me. I wished I *could* hire someone to find a groom for me. Hell, these days you could hire someone to find and buy your dream home for you, so why not your dream man? Anyway, I now had all the other elements of the big day organised – the only thing I needed to worry about was finding someone to fit into the suit. How difficult could it be?

five

I am deadly and desirable

I was determined to prove to my family that I was not a lesbian, but there was no way I was going to succumb to the pressure and go on a date with Cliff to make two in-denial mothers happy. Instead I carried on with my project, my strategy for finding Mr Right. I had already feng shui-ed my flat; now it was time to get serious. I was ready for 'Phase I': blind dating. I thought hard about the mantra I would cite daily, playing with combinations of words. Finally, my new mantra for meeting Mr Right wrote itself: *I am daring and dynamic, deadly and desirable.*

I launched Phase I at school. I strolled confidently into the staff room with a sense of hope. Surely some of my colleagues would have eligible brothers, uncles, ex-husbands or sons who were open to a date with me, the newly crowned Ms Deadly and Desirable. Most of my own staff in the history department were middle-aged, married men with unattractive beards and bellies. There was nothing about them that suggested they would be at all helpful in my new quest, but as Peta had pointed out, teachers from other departments were bound to have single friends – connections to get me into 'The Club'. Conscious that some of the older staff members considered me a floozy simply because I was single, and that others probably thought I was a lesbian, because they'd never known me to have a relationship with a man, I was cautious about who I approached.

I decided to follow the younger, more upbeat, not-so-uptight teachers for a few days, and thought about how best I could befriend them. The head of the history department really *should* mingle more with the English and maths staff, I thought.

I made my mate Mickey my pilot project. He was gay, and the only friends of his I'd ever met were batting for *his* team, but it was still worth a try. I often wondered why, as a straight person, I had lots of gay friends, but few of my gay friends had straight ones. When Mickey had dinner parties, I was always the only straight person there. His friends probably all thought I was a lesbian too. Shit, I really did need to get some dating happening – not just to meet Mr Right.

Mickey was a well-dressed country boy who wore R.M.Williams gear with an Oxford Street sashay. He was gorgeous, single and looking for love, just like me, but was willing to take all the lust he could get along the way. Mickey knew a lot of other gorgeous guys seeking that ideal love, but none of them had proved right so far.

I briefed him on my new mission and all he responded with was, 'Love, unless you're having a sex change, I can't help you. And should you actually be calling it a *mission*?'

I'd been ranting about politics and history to Mickey over cocktails for years, so he knew quite a bit about the missions many Aboriginal people had lived on under the Protection Acts. He was right; for many Blackfellas it was a word that brought back a lot of bad memories. 'Goal' was definitely a better choice. It sounded more professional, too: 'I've set myself a life-goal of meeting Mr Right'.

Later that day, however, Mickey grabbed me in the corridor and melodramatically mimed hitting himself in the head. He'd forgotten to tell me about his 'spunky cousin Daniel' – captain of a touch football team. 'He's single and hot'. Mickey admitted that Daniel was 'a lad's lad', but we both agreed that one date couldn't hurt. Mickey added, 'I'm sure he'd be great in bed too'. How Mickey knew this I wasn't quite sure, and I didn't want to know. He often slipped into graphic detail about his own sex life that made me feel uneasy.

'What star sign is he?' I asked, more to change the direction of the conversation than anything else, but I was mentally going through my criteria for Mr Right at the same time.

'God, I don't know. Does it matter?'

'Yes.'

'Well, probably Taurus – the bull'. And he made some disgusting thrusting gestures, just as the bell rang.

I wasn't really worried at this stage about the star sign, and there was a spring in my step as I walked away. Mickey was already on the job. Perhaps finding Mr Right wasn't going to be that hard after all. I put on hold the prospect of harassing any of the other teachers for the time being.

❤

Having made minor progress towards my goal, I had some time to focus on my other job – my *real* job. That of teaching my Year 11 class about significant moments for women in Australian history.

The students had done research for homework and had come up with some suggestions. We spent the class narrowing these down and identifying what the girls believed to be the most important moments. After half an hour or so, I faced the blackboard and started to write up our final list:

- *1881 – Women are allowed to enrol in the same subjects as men at Sydney University for the first time. (Medicine is the only exception.)*
- *1901 – Women are granted the right to vote.*

'Miss Aigner, only white women got the vote in 1901. Aboriginal women didn't get it until the 1967 referendum.'

In a class with only one Koori girl, Kerry, it was actually a non-Koori student, Bernardine, who had picked up on this fact. It made me proud. I'd once heard feminist Dale Spender say that if a man ever made a sexist remark in public, it was up to another man to correct him, not a woman, and I totally agreed. It was the same with race issues. Aboriginal people were always expected to challenge the ignorant whitefella when racist comments were made, when in fact it should be another whitefella doing it. Just as a man correcting a man packed a punch, so did a whitefella correcting a whitefella.

'Good point, Bernardine.' I kept writing:

- *1907 – Australia's first female architect, Florence Parsons, wins wide acclaim for the design of her houses.*
- *1943 – Senator Dorothy Tangney (Western Australia) and MP Edith Lyons (Tasmania) are the first women elected to Federal Parliament.*
- *1967 – Aboriginal women (and men) get the right to vote.*
- *1976 – Pat O'Shane is sworn in as Australia's first Aboriginal barrister.*
- *1992 – Women are ordained as priests in the Anglican Church.*
- *1996 – Jennie George becomes the first female president of the ACTU.*
- *2000 – Cathy Freeman wins gold at the Sydney Olympic Games.*

Looking at the blackboard, I realised that the moments we had chosen were all 'firsts'. As the first female head of department at St Christina's, black or white, I was almost tempted to add myself to the list. Humility was one thing we prided ourselves on at the school, though, so I resisted the temptation.

The class had been a great success, and I'd enjoyed the girls' arguments. They had really gained a broad view of the contribution women had made to Australian history. Many had only ever mentioned male historians in previous classes, so today I was pleased to have heard the names of female historians for the first time – Beverley Kingston, Shirley Fitzgerald and Wendy Brady – women who had influenced my own understanding of Australian history and had even been my inspiration for teaching it.

I was also pleased that the girls' debate and final list had included Aboriginal achievements, given that Australian and Aboriginal history were often treated as two separate subjects.

No doubt about it: I'd taught them well. I was confident that my students were going to be valuable citizens once they got out into the big, wide world.

My daydream was broken by an unexpected question from the back of the room. 'With equal rights came the right for women to ask men out – didn't it, Ms Aigner?'

The discussion had apparently turned to questions of equity in relationships, etiquette and dating. I had no idea how it had happened; I'd been too busy indulging in thoughts of my own achievements.

I tried to make a joke of it.

'Did it? I thought women just got tired one day of waiting for men to work up their courage.'

'What do *you* think about women asking men out on dates generally, Miss?' Bernardine asked.

I was the last one to give advice. The last guy I'd asked out had almost taken out an AVO on me. I'd read in *Cleo* that men loved confident women who went after what they wanted; that men loved being asked out, because many of them were too shy to do it themselves as women grew more and more confident. And so I'd tried being that confident woman. I asked a man out. I sent him flowers. I sent emails and invitations to make it easier for him to ask out a daunting and desirable woman like me. None of it had worked. It turned him right off. I'd thought I was being assertive, but he saw it as harassment.

I'd felt embarrassed and shamed, and since then I hadn't asked anyone out again. I'd gone from one extreme to another, as my brother Dillon would say. How could I tell my students that I hadn't had a real date for months, that men didn't ask me out, and I didn't ask them, and now my friends stayed up late workshopping the problem and my family all thought I was a lesbian?

'Miss, have you ever asked a man out?'

'I think we're getting too far off the topic, girls,' I said, and turned my back to them, hoping they wouldn't notice my wobbly hand as I cleaned the blackboard.

'What about arranged marriages, Miss? What do you think of them?'

I wouldn't be in my current predicament if I'd had an arranged marriage. Then again, I might just be married to my mum's friend Janet's gay son, Cliff, a right-wing hairdresser who secretly desired Keith Windschuttle.

'Arranged marriages are often very successful, but they don't necessarily work for everyone.' The bell rang.

'Class dismissed, and don't forget to read Chapter 6 of *Butterfly Song* by Terri Janke to discuss next week. It will be on the exams at the end of the year.'

six

Holmesy

That night the phone rang as I finished the last of a bowl of two-minute noodles. I picked up, my mouth still full.

'Hello?'

'Hi, I'm Mickey's cousin, Daniel.'

Mickey must have got to work on organising my blind date already. I was caught completely unaware. No script in front of me, no points to follow to keep the conversation going. I didn't have my 'Strategies for not meeting Mr Right' in front of me as a reference either.

Daniel continued: 'Mickey told me you're interested in playing touch football?' I nearly choked. I couldn't run with a football even if there was a guarantee of a wedding ring and husband waiting at the end of the field. I'm simply not fit enough, and too top heavy, and I look ridiculous when I run. And ... And ... And ... what was Mickey *thinking*?

'Orrright,' was all I could muster in response, sounding like a complete yob.

'I thought you might like to come to a game on Thursday, meet the team and maybe have a drink afterwards.'

Okay, so that's what Mickey was thinking – I could pretend to be interested in sport and have a casual drink. Sure, I could do that.

'Sounds good.' I got the details from Daniel and hung up. I was so excited I jumped up and down like a teenager, running on the spot, singing a new mantra: *I've got a date! I've got a date!* The strategy was working, my plans were coming together, I would reach my goal! I walked down my hall and did a little side kick in the air like they do in the movies.

♥

Before the game I went shopping for some flattering sportswear and the sexiest sports bra I could find, then agonised over how to wear my hair: up or down or baseball cap? I called Dillon, because he was a sports fanatic. He just said, 'It doesn't really matter that much what you wear, Alice, just don't say anything stupid. You don't know anything about sport, so don't pretend you do. It won't help.' I'd planned on asking him to give me some pointers on the game itself, but it didn't seem the right time.

♥

I was looking very athletic when I met Daniel at the sideline before his game. We just said hello, as the starting buzzer was about to go. I did a quick check, and I looked just like every other sporty chick there.

The others were on the field, though, or getting ready to play. I couldn't have run the length of the field if I tried and I made up some lame excuse about a bad ankle.

I watched the game with as much interest as a non-footy-kinda-girl could muster. I had no idea who was winning, what the score was, or even what the rules were, but I honestly didn't care. There was so much eye candy I could feel myself putting on weight just looking at the sweet, sweaty men.

Then there was Daniel; stylish and agile, a pleasure to watch in action. I stood there wanting to sink my teeth into his thighs. People were screaming at him from the sideline, 'Go Holmesy, go Holmesy!' and I joined in. Everyone was rooting for him each time he got the ball. They knew – and he knew – that he was the best player on team; you could see why he was captain. He scored five tries which, apparently, is really good for touch football. Or any kind of football.

When the game finished, he was panting and covered in sweat. His team had won and everyone walked in a group to the pub across the road to celebrate.

As everyone sat around a table, I was the only one left standing. 'There doesn't appear to be anywhere left to sit,' I said awkwardly to no-one in particular.

'Here, let me make some room for you,' Daniel said, and he mimed cleaning his face.

It was the kind of comment I'd expect from a rugby league player, given all the bad press the code had had in recent years with players involved in assault claims and so on. He was disgusting, and clearly had no respect for women.

'Don't worry, he's tried that line on every girl on the team,' one of his female team-mates said.

'Yeah, he's nicknamed after John Holmes for a reason,' another added, rolling her eyes. 'The porn star, you know.'

Daniel ignored them and gave me a sleazy grin. 'Mickey didn't tell me you were so gorgeous.'

'Let's just say that Mickey doesn't really *appreciate* women the same way you do,' I said.

'Nor did he say you were so ...' He looked at my double D's. 'It'd be great to watch you running on the field.' Oh god, was this fella for real?

Even while he was trying to chat me up, he had one eye on another woman across the bar. He saw me see him checking her out.

'Don't mind me, I've got a lazy eye. It wanders sometimes.' He must've thought I was an idiot to give me such a lie.

'There doesn't seem to be anything lazy about your eyes at all, Daniel.'

I wanted a one-woman man – make that one-Alice man – so I finished my drink, took Daniel's number – at his insistence – and left with no aspirations at all of joining the team.

seven

Mr Moonwalker

Daniel didn't really count as a blind date, he was just a way to test the waters, to get out there and give it a go. The experience made it clear to me that Mickey wasn't the best person to ask for assistance in setting up blind dates with straight men. He just didn't know anyone suitable. Onto Phase I, Step II: blind dates with friends of friends.

On Saturday night, I sent an email to close friends, giving them my list of what I was looking for in a man.

> Dear so-and-so,
> Do you love me? Do you want to see me happy? I know
> you do, so help me find a good fella. My criteria for
> Mr Right are attached.
> With eternal thanks,
> Alice xo

I sent it to a small but trusted group — Peta, Liza and Dannie, of course, although they already knew what I was up to, along with a couple of old uni friends I saw occasionally at Cushion. I couldn't really cast the net too wide in case Mum got wind of it. I'd never hear the end of it. Mum still believed, like Dad, that women should be demure and ladylike and men would eventually ask them out. She was wrong.

Within days my friends were sending me details of all sorts of men, telling me that I could cull them to a short list. I didn't actually cull any, recognising that I wasn't really in that strong a position. I'd be able to line up a series of dates throughout the whole of November if I wanted to. Even if I didn't find Mr Right I'd at least be having a half-decent social life. It was summer and nice to be out and about.

The first 'real' blind date didn't come from the spam email I'd sent, though. Rather it was arranged by chance, as I trudged up the stairs with Gabrielle from across the hall, her with her washing, me with bags of groceries. She suggested I go out with her Filipino brother-in-law Renan. I immediately thought of great food every night; a honeymoon in the Philippines; giving painless birth to small children; and the stories I'd be able to tell at the next school reunion. It was all sorted by the time we reached the top step and she called him immediately from her mobile. This was the quickest date I'd ever landed.

Gabrielle was married with two children and spent her days cooking and cleaning. For her, organising my date with Renan was something to get excited about.

'I love the thought of playing cupid for you, Alice.' Gabrielle had never said anything, but I'm sure she'd heard the conversations Peta and I often had as we sat with my flat door open, doing post-mortems on our disastrous dates and ex-boyfriends. She'd probably heard the whole strategic planning meeting two Saturdays before. I wouldn't be surprised if the whole Arden Street block had heard. Next time, I thought, I might ask her in to help. She was obviously a fast worker, and time was of the essence now that I had a deadline for meeting Mr Right.

❤

Renan arrived promptly at eleven-thirty am the following Saturday. He was drop-dead-make-you-scream-inside-gorgeous with dark hair, mysterious eyes and a small, cheeky smile. He looked muscly even under his loose white shirt. He was slightly shorter than me, but I didn't care. 'Short men try harder!' were Peta's words of wisdom once when a George Costanza look-alike had asked me out and I'd declined.

'What a spunk!' I whispered across the hall to Gabrielle as Renan walked up the stairs. 'Yeah, I married the wrong brother,' she joked. 'Seems so – thanks!' I was grateful for Gabrielle's choice: it left me with this hunk for lunch. I suddenly appreciated that this was one of the joys of being single – the excitement of going out on first dates.

We went for yum cha in Chinatown and even though I generally refuse to queue for anything, I wasn't bothered at all by having to wait in line for twenty-five minutes. The queue moved up the stairs, Renan constantly one step above me, so the height issue wasn't even obvious. The date was off to the perfect start. I could see the wedding already. We could have a Filipino-inspired menu, and Renan could have some lifts inserted into his shiny black patent-leather wedding shoes. Perhaps my bouquet could be orchids or lilies. What was the native Filipino flower? I'd have to google it at work later in the week. My mind was ticking over and I was smiling inside and out. My dream wedding was planning itself.

We were eventually escorted to a table up the back of the bustling restaurant, leaving fifty people behind us still waiting to be seated. He had chosen the most popular yum cha restaurant in the city. Every single table was full, and crowded with food; the conversation chaotic.

The food tasted great but I hardly noticed as we yarned away easily, comfortably, like soul mates: just add water and we were an instant couple. I liked the way Renan took charge and ordered yummy things as the trolleys trundled back and forth. I had no idea what was what.

'I think you'll like this dish, Alice,' he'd say as he motioned to the waiter to put something on the table. His confidence on the culinary front turned me on a little. I liked the way he used my name, too.

'I make the best seafood egg rolls this side of Manila *or* Beijing, Alice. But these aren't bad.' I smiled at the thought – my kitchen repertoire was quite bland and very *Australian* in comparison. Yin and yang. Clearly the feng shui was working for Renan and I. We were getting on fantastically. Renan was an Aries, and according to Aria, a union of a Ms Leo and a Mr Aries had great marriage potential. He was also incredibly witty, always an aphrodisiac. I could've jumped him there and then, until I remembered Peta's rule: no sex on the first date – and I'm guessing especially not in the middle of the Dragon Castle restaurant. I had decided before the sweets trolley arrived that I could easily fall in love with Renan.

Then we started talking about our career aspirations. 'I want to be principal of St Christina's one day,' I said, even though I knew they'd never had a layperson in the job in the past, and I sometimes wondered if I'd only landed the job as department head at the age of twenty-eight because no-one else applied. The nuns were all getting old and there'd been some talk in the staff room that the principal's position might be opened up in the future. It was a personal goal that I'd told very few people, but I thought I should tell Renan; I was on my third glass of wine and it seemed to me there was a good chance we'd be getting married one day and sharing *everything*.

'I could see you as principal, easy. You're a strong, capable woman. A fantastic role model. If I had a daughter, I'd want to send her to your school.' He had a sparkle in his eye. 'Though if you were principal, it would mean you probably wouldn't be able to teach, and that would be such a loss to the students.' Clearly, Renan was impressed by my career goals. I dare say he may have had the future in mind as well. Why wouldn't he? I was a bloody good catch. Strong and capable, as he rightly pointed out.

'And what about you? What are your plans?' I was really keen to see how we could make our careers work together.

He dropped a bombshell: 'I've been working for years towards being one of the world's best moonwalkers and male hula dancers.'

I nearly choked on my dumpling. This was his career dream? His personal goal? No, no, no! 'I'm already in the *Guinness Book of Records* for the longest unbroken moonwalk.' Renan sprang out of his chair and moonwalked from one end of the restaurant to the other, giving a fine display of his skill. How long was it since I'd seen someone moonwalk? Twenty years? I had thoughts of him moonwalking down the aisle with me after we'd said our vows. I reached for the carafe of house wine in the middle of the table.

I refilled my glass as Renan moved from Michael Jackson to generic Polynesian. With a smile that spanned his entire face, he began to do the hula at the table. To my surprise, the predominantly Chinese audience started applauding, which only encouraged Renan to shake his thin hips even more. I thought he was never going to stop. He only ended up back in his seat when a trolley of chicken feet accidentally collided with his left hip. Shit! Would our wedding waltz be a bloody hula?

I wanted to slowly disappear under the table. While I wanted a man to be able to move in time with the music, or at least give it a go, I definitely couldn't date and simply would not marry a man who looked better in a grass skirt than me. Nor would my self-esteem ever allow me to be with a man who had thinner hips! I sadly scratched Renan's name of my list of potentials, even though at that stage it was the only name there. My wedding plans came crashing round my feet.

The date ended with the promise of a hula lesson or two whenever I had time, and I smiled to myself thinking that lessons with Renan might actually be fun.

Gabrielle was more disappointed than I was that we didn't have a second date, and she was quick to suggest her cousin Ernesto as a follow-up attempt. Ernesto couldn't dance, but had been on *Red Faces* once and played the spoons. Gabrielle was obviously part of a very talented family. I didn't even have to think about that one, just lied and told her I had a few other dates lined up and I'd call on her during the next dry spell. I'm sure she was aware that my whole life was a dry spell, though, and she looked hopeful that I would be enlisting her services as cupid again shortly.

eight

More blind dates from hell

I was surprised how well I bounced back from Daniel and Renan. I really was giving this blind dating gig a go. So far I'd hooked up with a womaniser and had a nice Chinese meal with an offer of free dance lessons. Going on dates was actually entertaining. I couldn't really complain about not having met Mr Right at this stage, because I wasn't at all bored, or lonely. I continued to chant my mantra on a daily basis: *I am deadly and desirable and desperate!* Whoops! *I am deadly and desirable and delicious!*

Not long after, I went on my third blind date in two weeks. Dannie was determined to prove Peta wrong and find me my life-partner, so she had arranged a date with her cousin Charlie, who liked to play pool. I'd been known to sink a few, and Dannie thought we might have some fun together. Charlie and I were to meet at the Marlborough Hotel in Newtown the following Saturday.

Just before leaving for my date, I sought Aria's advice, and was puzzled: 'Leos won't have to travel far from home to find love and romance today, so don't go looking outside your own perimeter.' Did Aria mean my physical or mental perimeter? Was inner-city Newtown too far from home?

I met Charlie at the pub, and the first thing I noticed was his daggy, tan, eighties-style sand-blasted leather bomber jacket. That would have to go for a start. The skin-tight, pale blue jeans, turned up at the cuff, with white Dunlop Volley shoes, would be following behind quickly. I didn't even know they still made those shoes. Or perhaps he'd bought them with the jacket two decades ago. Charlie also wore an akubra hat that pushed down his dark hair, and even though he did the gentlemanly thing and removed it when he greeted me, I wished he hadn't. The hat-hair look didn't sit well with the jacket and jeans.

Dannie had told me Charlie was 'cool'. She seriously needed to get out more and see what today's fashions were. She may have been okay with George's clothes, but I wasn't ready to settle for a man dressed in time-warp garb.

Bad dress sense wasn't the worst of Charlie's problems, though. He had dreadful skin, clearly the result of a bad bout of chicken pox as a teenager.

It's what's inside that counts, I told myself. *Our bodies are mere shells for our souls to walk around in* would be my mantra of the night. I'd read somewhere that scars just show that you've survived something horrible, that you're strong. Surviving chicken pox wasn't quite the same as surviving a fire or an appendectomy, but it must have been hard growing up with those pock marks.

I should just stop being such a lookist, I thought. I wouldn't focus on Charlie's skin. It was the scars I couldn't see that I really needed to worry about.

Charlie came back from the bar with two schooners. *Don't look at his skin*, I thought. 'So, did you have trouble finding a park?' I asked. 'King Street can be a nightmare.'

'I don't drive. I'm car-free, I like to say.'

Oh god, I was going to have play chauffeur to this fella if we dated. That was not an attractive option at all. I wanted to play passenger occasionally.

Charlie read my face. 'I can drive,' he said. 'I just don't want to pollute the environment. I believe it's worth suffering a little inconvenience to save the planet.'

He was right. I felt ashamed of my reaction. I noticed that Charlie had a beautiful smile and dreamy chocolate-brown eyes hidden under the rim of his hat.

Over the next few hours we played pool and put money in the jukebox, both choosing some old favourites from Blondie and ABBA. We had exactly the same taste in music – appalling taste, Peta would say. Neither of us knew who was at the top of the charts, and at one point Charlie asked, 'What's an ARIA?' Peta would have been mortified, but I really liked his unashamed pride in not being up-with-it. We were having fun, and the time passed easily.

I was warming to Charlie, no doubt about it. After a few more beers, I found myself making plans. My hairstylist could fix the hat-hair permanently, and we could burn the hat with the jeans and jacket. The shoes he could keep for sport if he wanted to. Dannie, Peta, Liza and I could do a Fab Four makeover. It might even be fun. The full transformation. Surely there'd be some way to take care of his scars? I couldn't stop thinking about or looking at Charlie's skin.

My stomach had started making noises: dinner was well overdue. We'd spent the entire afternoon talking and laughing, and I'd had too much to drink on an empty stomach. 'Let's eat!' I said, and we ordered at the bar.

Sitting across from Charlie as we ate, I imagined him post-makeover. His scars were bad, but a dermatologist could probably help. They can do amazing things with lasers these days.

Suddenly Charlie wasn't looking happy.

'You've been staring at my skin all night, Alice. Is it that much of a problem for you?'

'Have you thought about having your scars, umm, you know?

'So my skin *is* a problem for you.'

'Not as much as your jacket,' I joked, hoping to make light of the situation, and immediately wished I hadn't.

'I'm sorry you find my jacket and skin so problematic, Alice.' And with that he up and left me there; drunk, alone, disappointed in myself. I was shallow. I was a lookist. I had hurt Charlie's feelings. For sure I would've been hurt had someone said that to me.

I am cruel, I thought. I am not deserving of love from anyone, not even crater-face Charlie. I am not deadly and desirable and delicious. My new mantra became *I am dreadful! I am a lookist!*

I left the bar and blind date #3 behind.

The next day, when I'd sobered up, I realised I'd left my sunnies behind at the pub, so went back to get them in the early evening. As I waited for the barman to fetch them from the office I stood at the bar and watched a gorgeous guy saunter across the smoke-filled room. A handful of people were dancing to the sounds of a local grunge band. I'm a retro chick, so the music didn't do much for me.

'Wanna buy me a drink, babe?' Even the pathetic opening line didn't put me off, because this guy just made me weak, standing there in his jeans with no cuffs, and tight black t-shirt, sixpack obvious underneath. No hat. Doc Martens. He looked totally shaggable. I was back to being the lookist again. In no time at all we were slow dancing to the grunge music I hated and I was thinking that I owed Dannie a huge thank you. My blind date with Charlie hadn't been a dead loss after all.

For the next eight hours we danced and drank. We tried to talk over the live music occasionally, but it was too loud. I didn't care. I was having a great time. Then, as the clock was about to strike two, I sensed that something wasn't quite right. I looked around the room, briefly frisked myself to check I was still totally clothed, rummaged through my bag to check my phone and wallet and sunglasses were there, but all seemed to be as it should be. Then it hit me. My wallet was much, much thinner than it had been when I entered, and *he* hadn't bought one drink all night.

I wasn't impressed with either of us: him for being such a sponge, and me for being such an idiot. I was possibly daunting and desirable and delicious, but definitely a loser.

'I've gotta go,' I said. 'I have to get up early and mark essays tomorrow.' It wasn't a complete lie, I did have some school work to do.

'No worries.' He was cool about it. Let's face it, he'd had a good, cheap night out and managed to cop a feel as well. 'Don't s'pose you can give me cab fare home?' He winked and grabbed my arse as if that would seal the deal. I was gobsmacked. I said bluntly, 'I guess I can drop you off somewhere.'

I was shitty as hell, but I wasn't quite sure what I was doing, and needed to buy some time to think. 'I need to go to the loo first.' I grabbed my bag and pushed through the crowded room as he turned to the bar to finish his beer. The beer *I* had bought. What a tool. When I glanced back towards the bar again he wasn't looking in my direction, so I just walked out the front door and escaped without notice, leaving Mr Welfare and a good chunk of last week's wages behind.

I wrote it up in my journal when I got home: 'At least it was a night out with straight male company.' Yeah, but at what cost to my dignity and wallet?

Aria had been right. I shouldn't have travelled so far from home. Somewhere between Coogee and Newtown I'd gone from having some dignity to almost none.

❤

On Monday I got a curt email from Dannie:

> Alice, sometimes I think you really are sabotaging your own happiness. There are decent men around you, kind, caring, faithful and funny; politically and environmentally sound. The way you treated Charlie on Saturday makes you seem, well, a bitch. And no-one wants to date a bitch. I know you're not *really* a bitch. But you don't even give men a chance to get to know you properly. That, my friend, is why you're single. And I say this out of love, you know that. Dannie

I cringed with shame at the truth in her words. I didn't respond and Dannie and I never spoke about Charlie again. We actually didn't speak at all for a couple of weeks, which was odd for us. And I felt bad. Friendships like ours shouldn't be lost over bad skin – even if potential husbands could be.

nine

Looking via the mobile network

Mickey, Gabrielle and Dannie had failed me, but Liza hung in there, trying desperately to palm me off on one of her relatives. Uncles, cousins, second cousins, third cousins, the suggestions never seemed to end. She came from a big Italian family and often joked about how it would be great if I married into it. They had huge weddings, if nothing else. On top of that, she reminded me, most of the men in her family were great cooks.

Liza was adamant that I should meet her cousin Marco, who'd just returned from Italy and was working in an exporting business. (I wondered if he'd met Cliff at all.)

'He's gorgeous, and I know he would love you. Just have a coffee with him. He fits most of the criteria you've got scribbled all over those bits of paper on your fridge. I just know you'll hit it off.'

'I'm trying to give up coffee and I'm not interested in meeting Marco. I already have a strategy in place that I'm supposed to be following, remember?'

'I don't recall not dating Liza's family being on that list.'

'It is now!' After dating Dannie's cousin and the stress it had caused between us, I didn't want to risk it with Liza as well. I'd come across as abrupt, though, and hated myself for it. The last thing I wanted to do was hurt Liza's feelings when she was trying to help me meet my Mr Right, but she'd had years of dealing with me being gruff, and bounced back quickly.

It was dusk. We were sitting at a table on the footpath outside Barzura, a restaurant overlooking Coogee Beach. Liza's phone beeped, interrupting our conversation. It was a text message from someone in her basketball team. She was the manager of a men's amateur team in the western suburbs, but didn't talk about it much. It was something she did out of obligation really, having started years ago when she'd had more time. She was too nice to just quit now. Didn't want to let anyone down, because that's the kind of girl Liza was. Several years ago she'd admitted to me that she first got involved so she could meet men, after being advised that the best way to a man's heart was through 'sport, stomach and sex', in that order. Liza claimed her experience proved that theory wrong: she said the more she got into sport, the hungrier she was, the more she ate and the more weight she put on, making her feel less attractive; she ended up having less sex rather than more.

'That was Shaun.' Liza had a wicked look in her eye. 'And you know what? He might be a good date for you. Who knows, Mr Right even.'

'Tell me more.' I could feel a wicked smile starting on my own face.

'He's your age and single. A bit of a lad, but not like Mickey's cousin Daniel. He's actually very respectful and kind. He's the only one on the team who asks if I'd like a drink after the game. You should just send him a message for fun and see where it goes.'

'What? You mean set up a date? You know I can't ask a bloke out, not straight up like that. I'm not that desperate.' Of course we both knew I was, but Liza let me pretend I was still the sought after, not the seeker.

'So, it's okay for you not to seem desperate, but have your friends act desperate on your behalf? I just want to be clear about it!' Liza laughed and sipped her wine.

'Well, yes.' It was completely ridiculous and, some might say, irrational. She knew it and so did I, but the whole blind date thing was bad enough without me actually having to ask out men I didn't even know.

I suddenly wondered why Liza hadn't set me up with someone from the team before. There must've been at least a dozen men to choose from. Take the married ones and young ones out, and there'd still have to be at least a couple to choose from. Fit men. Tall men. Sydney men. Most likely straight men. Hot, sweaty, sexy men!

'Come to think of it, Liza, why haven't you set me up with one of them before?' And why was she doing it now?

'It would be unethical to use my position to suss out people's relationship information. I'd also have needed your consent to pass on your details to them as well.'

'You have my consent now.'

'I'll give him your number, then.' Liza looked around, trying to catch the waiter's eye.

'Do it now,' I said.

'What? Can't we order first?'

'Do it now and do it often. That's the approach I'd like you to take when you're helping me with the strategy, okay?'

'Except when it comes to my family, right?' Liza knew how to make her point strong and clear, but she did it without any drama. She didn't even look up at me when she spoke. She punched a few keys on her phone and sent a message.

'That oughta do it. If I know him, he'll be back to you in no time. Can we order now?'

The young Italian waiter took our orders, refreshed our glasses of verdelho and left a basket of bread on the table. We both lunged for a piece, starving.

'Liza, why haven't you dated anyone on the team?' I was concerned that she'd set me up with a guy she wouldn't go out with herself.

'Alice,' she explained patiently, 'I'm the manager, and it's just not kosher to date the team members. Anyway, this mightn't even end up in a date, you know, it's just to take your mind off all the womanisers and hula dancers you've dealt with so far, and to give you some fun. The whole thing seems to have become an obsession, and you need to lighten up.' She was right. It had become an obsession. Setting a deadline, developing a strategy, risking my friendships – and all in the name of finding myself a husband by my thirtieth birthday. Was it too much? I wasn't sure. But my thirtieth birthday was now only nineteen months and six days away.

Another young waiter arrived – English this time, a backpacker, I assumed – and put our meals on the table: mine salmon and spinach, Liza's a massive bowl of pasta, which she dived into as though she hadn't eaten for a week. I'd always admired Liza's metabolism. She only had a small frame but she could pack it away, eating masses of carbs but never putting on weight, despite what she said.

I noticed a good-looking guy at a table inside the restaurant. He looked familiar, but I couldn't place him. I must have seen him at the Cushion Bar. It was like seeing a Blackfella walking down the street, giving that nod or raised eyebrow in recognition of belonging to an exclusive club, even though you'd never met. Same for the regulars at Cushion. I smiled at him across the restaurant, hoping I didn't have any baby spinach in my teeth, assuming that he was also wondering why I looked familiar. He was wearing a funky navy and white

Mambo shirt, and when he stood to greet someone, it accentuated his slim waist and broad shoulders. He was actually very, very sexy. Mental note to self: keep an eye out for Shirt Guy at the Cushion. Then my phone beeped. Checking, I saw an unfamiliar number: it was probably Shaun. Shirt Guy disappeared from my thoughts.

> Hello. Liza said I should contact you. Why?

Shaun's first text message almost stumped me and then I remembered my mantra.

> Because I'm daunting and desirable.

And clearly confident while under the influence of alcohol.

The SMS dialogue between Shaun and I went back and forth for the next three hours. Liza and I ordered more food, more wine, dessert, coffees. I didn't even think about how much we were spending, or what my phone bill would look like either. Thank goodness I'd signed on for one of those capped plans and could spend up to $500 – I'd need it if my dating habits were going to be like this. I regarded the exchange as an investment in my future wedded happiness. As the night wore on, though, what started as innocent flirtation became somewhat sleazy. I asked Shaun what he was reading, a safe question, I thought, and the answer would give me some insight into his character. His response?

The Karma Sutra!

What was I supposed to do with that? 'Do you think he's serious?' I asked Liza, a little unnerved. I motioned for her to fill my glass again.

'You're a puritan, Alice. It's a great answer.'

Texting was a dangerous form of communication. Dillon had once told me that no matter what you said in a text message, a man would read it as meaning sex. 'Even if I just said "Do you want to see a movie?"' 'Even if you sent the word *fish*,' was his answer. I thought I should be sensible and choose my words carefully.

Good book?

Was that the best I could come up with?

Shaun didn't respond for some time, and I was grateful, as things were moving into territory I wasn't overly comfortable with. A couple of cocktails at Cushion Bar later that night helped me relax, though. I looked for Shirt Guy, but didn't see him. Maybe he wasn't a Cushion regular after all. But where did I know him from then? He had looked so familiar – and hot.

I was home by eleven-thirty. At quarter to twelve I had one final SMS from Shaun, asking what my favourite sexual position was. Prudish Alice appeared immediately. I went to bed without texting him back, but actually thinking of my favourite position and, for some reason, Shirt Guy. God, had I kissed him drunk one night? Perhaps that's why he looked familiar. If so, where? When? I drifted into slumber with a smile on my face.

The next day I hit Bondi Junction. My wardrobe was in need of a summer clothing injection. I bought a black dress with a slightly Spanish hemline, some black strappy heels, a black silk skirt and a red top. By five o'clock I was exhausted and so was my credit limit, so I decided to spend the evening in with a movie and some chocolate. No sooner had I settled in than my phone beeped with a message. It was him, the SMS guy, the basketballer, the Karma Sutra man, the STALKER!

How are you, Al?

He was being familiar, calling me Al. I panicked, not sure why he had sent me a message. It was over. Surely he knew that. I hadn't responded to his last text. That meant, at least in my books, hasta la vista, baby! We'd had a few hours of flirting and that was it. Why was he still contacting me? Weirdo. It was my fault. I'd started it. It was meant to just be a little bit of fun during dinner – *maybe* something that would help me find a husband, or maybe just a date. Now this guy thought I was a skanky ho who picked up blokes over SMS and just wanted a shag.

What if he wanted to meet me? What if he was an axe-murderer? All of a sudden I was scared of a bloke who'd already been given a character reference by my dearest friend! Where was my commitment to my future happiness now? What about that wedding before my thirtieth birthday? Why was I panicking over a bloody text message from someone who'd never seen me and didn't know where I lived? He'd just asked how I was.

I rang Liza and she laughed at me.

'Shaun's harmless. What are you afraid of? Text him back or don't, but stop being so weird.' She was right. I was being weird. I wanted to date, she pointed out. I wanted to get laid. I wanted to get married. I'd asked her for her help. I'd made her contact this guy as part of my strategy. '*Do it now.* Those were your exact words, Alice. *Do it now and do it often.* Do you remember?'

Liza was in lawyer mode; it was her way of telling me that she was only just tolerating my pain-in-the-arse behaviour. It gave me the shits, but I knew she was a good friend.

After I'd spoken to Liza, I walked into the kitchen and looked at the lists on the fridge. Just as I thought, there it was, written in purple texta: 'BE OPEN TO

ALL OPPORTUNITIES.' That included SMS-Shaun. But how could I tell my grandchildren I met their grandfather via a text message? It just didn't feel right; in fact, it felt really, really wrong, but I sent a reply anyway.

> Had a great day, staying in tonight, very tired.

I was sure that would put him off; he'd think I was a loser, staying in on Saturday night.

> Where's in?

He wanted to know where I lived. He *was* a stalker! Shit!

> Eastern suburbs.

That should be enough.

> I'm in Villawood.

Did he mean *in* Villawood? Surely not. Liza hadn't mentioned anything about a refugee basketball team, but she had been doing pro bono work for some asylum seekers. Now I was being stupid – of course he didn't live in an immigration detention centre. I didn't respond. I was glad there was distance between Coogee and Villawood. Could westie meet waxhead ever work anyway? It seemed to be working out for Bianca and Ben. They were engaged, soon to be married, and seemed likely to live happily ever after, but I couldn't see it working for me. I turned my phone off for the night, and thought briefly about having the number changed.

ten

Possibly the worst date ever!

Sunday morning was overcast and I was glad. It meant I could stay in bed and read, drink tea and enjoy the mellow sounds of Vika and Linda's *Love is Mighty Close* down low on my stereo. I couldn't help thinking that it wasn't close enough, because I was lying in bed alone. Still, I was happy. Life was pretty good. I stared out the window and looked at the choppy ocean and a few boardriders trying their luck. I smiled briefly as I imagined a couple of backpackers drowning in the whitewash, then slapped myself for enjoying such nasty thoughts.

My mobile beeped and my heart skipped a beat, but it was just Peta wanting to know if I was laying around like a slug or if I might be up for a coastal walk. I got dressed straight away, and headed off to meet her.

❤

Peta was waiting for me near the Bali bombing memorial on the headland. I could feel the southerly coming up, already bringing summer heatwave relief. It didn't usually arrive until late afternoon. Peta's hair was flying all about the place. We paused at the memorial for a moment and looked out to sea.

'I've got a surprise for you.' Peta was excited, and it was infectious. I like surprises.

'What is it?'

'I got some free tickets to that play you've been going on and on about.'

'What? The one with Marcus Graham about inter-racial relationships?

'That's the one,' said Peta.

'The one where he gets completely in the nick? How? When? How much do I owe you?' The thought of seeing Marcus in the flesh was so exciting I nearly peed myself. 'I've always thought I'd make a great reconciliation project for Marcus,' I said.

Peta laughed at me. 'You'd be doing it for the cause, right? Facilitating harmony between Black and white? That's what we need, a good Black woman like you with someone gorgeous like Marcus Graham.'

I could breed with a Black man, but we needed to unite with the whiteman as well. It would help water down the white race.

'It only takes one Black parent to make a few Black kids,' I said. 'I'd do it for my people. Anyway, how much do I owe you?'

'You don't owe me anything. It's a gift from me to you. It's this Friday, are you free?'

'Of course. Should we have dinner and a few bevvies first?'

'Sorry darl, I can't go, but I've lined up someone to take you. Bit of help with the strategy.'

'What? I can't go with a bloke and perv on Marcus at the same time. That's just not right. I do have some ethics, you know.'

'You asked for my help, didn't you?' Of course she was right, but there seemed to be something very sad about my friends now going out of their way to help me find a bloke. Did they actually feel sorry for me?

'Okay then, so who is it?' I didn't even think about asking what he looked like.

'A guy I worked with last year on the new state government policy for education and the arts. His name's Jim Akee. He's from the Torres Strait. He'll meet you at the theatre bar at six pm.'

❤

Friday arrived. I checked with Aria to see if she had any advice re my date with Jim from the Torres Strait. She said: 'Don't get carried away with expectations today Leo. Remember, no expectations, no disappointments, no regrets.' *No expectations, no disappointments, no regrets* became my mantra for my date with Jim.

I wore a black jersey dress and looked pretty hot. I had no expectations but I reckoned that if Mr Torres Strait Islands didn't work out, I might just hang round to see what else was in the offing. I arrived at the bar, looking casually around for 'a person of Islander appearance', (a description that could have come straight out of *The Daily Terror*). I spotted him immediately he walked through the door. Hair in a bun, theatrically camp, sauntering towards me with a self-assured air. I knew he was an actor straight away. Peta hadn't told me: she knew I'd never go out with an actor (except Marcus Graham), because they are so damned precious.

'Hi, I'm Jim. You must be Alice.'

'That's right, nice to meet you.' I put out my hand to shake but he didn't respond, not even with an air kiss to the cheek.

'Yeah, hey, I've just spotted someone I know on the other side of the bar, I must go speak to them. I'll be back in a second.' And he just walked off. I waited, downing a couple of glasses of the house bubbly to fill in the time until it was curtain call. Jim only came back to see me because I had the tickets – I knew it and he knew I knew it. I was already pissed off and the date hadn't even really started.

As we climbed the stairs to the theatre, Jim told me about himself, his acting, his career. We took our seats and he kept right on till the curtain went up. He didn't bother to ask me *anything* about *anything* – work, leisure, how I knew Peta. Nothing.

The play itself was brilliant. Marcus Graham was gorgeous and, although the script needed serious editing, no woman would ever complain at seeing him forced to be on stage longer than necessary. It was a bonus for the audience.

However, while the actors were taking their bows, my date just up and left. I was furious. I decided to go to the after party without him.

❤

'It was possibly the worst date I have ever been on, Peta, what were you thinking? Was it payback for something I've done to you I don't know about?' I had to ask. Surely she knew Jim could never love anyone but himself.

'Don't be ridiculous, Alice. I'd tell you if I were upset with you about anything. What happened? I know he's good-looking, so it couldn't have been that.' Peta tried to look shocked for me, but she was busy shovelling pancakes into her mouth. We'd planned to meet at Barzura for breakfast and a debriefing. I was nursing a hangover from the glasses of cheap bubbles I'd lost count of the night before.

'To cut a long and hideous night short, he pissed off five seconds after he met me, came back only because I had the tickets, talked about nothing but himself right up until the show started, didn't ask me one thing about what I did, and walked out before the audience had even finished applauding at the end.'

'What? Did you speak to him at the after party? You did go, didn't you?' She wiped some maple syrup from the side of her mouth.

'Oh I went all right, and as soon as I was surrounded by other blokes *your mate*' – I felt the need to give her ownership of the jerk – 'butted in, trying to make small talk, acting like he was my fucken date. He was only cramping my style by then, so I told him in front of everyone that he was the worst date I had ever had.' Both Peta and I knew that was a blatant lie, but we were both prone to dramatics at times, so she nodded, agreeing with me like sistas of similar temperaments do. 'By the time I finished with him he was ready to get back in his canoe and paddle home!' We both laughed and ordered more coffee.

eleven

Mr Dick Fiddler

Having forgiven me for the Charlie episode, and still determined to prove Peta wrong on the whole SWOT analysis, Dannie made a second attempt to set me up. She invited me to a dinner party at her place with George, another couple and a blind date for me named Philip.

I liked Philip at first glance, although I was trying hard not to be a lookist. His clothes were from the twenty-first century; he had a decent hairdo; no hat; and dress shoes on. And his skin was flawless. He was also polite, extending his right hand to shake mine. 'Great to meet you, Alice. Dannie's told me a lot about you.' He had a pleasant smile and obviously didn't smoke: his teeth were bright white. He drove a car. I felt quite confident he wouldn't ask me for milk money or start moonwalking in the middle of dinner. I was glad I'd made an effort to look good, and not only to show Dannie that I appreciated her latest attempt to help me find Mr Right.

I was seated next to him at dinner. We had a starter of orange and port soup. Philip complimented Dannie, impressing me again with his manners, but then he began rummaging furtively in his lap. I tried to look away, but I was curious: what *was* he doing? My god! Was he trying to hide a hard-on?

I'd never had a penis myself, so I wasn't completely sure that what he was doing was anything out of the ordinary. I cut him a little slack, assuming that he was possibly horny as hell sitting next to me. I was, after all, deadly and desirable.

We started chatting again, and soon I forgot all about it. Dinner was lovely. Dannie had prepared a delicious roast, something a single girl always appreciates – no point doing a roast for one person. It was a treat to be able to enjoy a grown-up meal.

'Let's have coffee and dessert in the lounge room,' Dannie said, clearing the table and ushering us out at the same time. It was all going smoothly, I thought, until I noticed that Philip was standing by the door firmly grasping his penis in his left hand. No-one else seemed perturbed by it; they all walked ahead, but I couldn't take my eyes off his left hand. Grasp, pinch, pull, fiddle ... he was very busy as he made his way into the next room. He accepted a port that George offered him, and then stood there with a drink in one hand and his dick in the other. Was I the only one who noticed?

I checked out the other men to see where their hands were. Was touching one's genitals in public now acceptable, given that research had shown that ninety-five per cent of men masturbated and the other five per cent lied about it anyway? Was sex with oneself not only the safest form of sex in the twenty-first century, but something that was now considered an after-dinner activity? Was it the male equivalent of a woman telling me she had sore nipples? He's probably just adjusting himself, I thought. Yes, that was it. Then he switched hands: drink in the left, penis in the right. Something was definitely wrong.

He made eye contact. 'I've really enjoyed talking to you tonight, Alice,' he said. 'If you're free sometime soon, I'd love to meet up again – would you mind giving me your card?' Not having one, it was easy to ask him for his instead, even though I had no intention of calling him. God knows what sex would have been like. How the hell was I going to get anything when he was all over *himself* all the time?

I walked into the kitchen to help Dannie with clearing up and organising dessert and handed her Philip's card.

'I'm not calling him,' I whispered as I put some plates in the dishwasher.

'Why not? What's wrong with *this* one? He hasn't stopped talking to you all night. He's obviously interested.' She was scrubbing at the baking dish in the kitchen sink.

'There was one little thing that bothered me.'

'Only one?' She was being sarcastic, but it was a fair question, I suppose – she knew about my long list of expectations.

'What do you think it means when a guy touches himself a lot?'

'Touches himself where?' she asked as she rinsed the good crystal glasses that couldn't go into the dishwasher.

'You know, down there.' I pointed to my groin.

'What do you mean? He exposed himself? When? I'll kill him!' She turned off the taps and grabbed a tea towel, violently drying her hands.

'No, calm down, he didn't do anything that dramatic. I just noticed he touched himself … *a lot.* It's weird.'

'It's boys, Alice, they do it all the time. Have to adjust themselves, you know. Get short'n'curlies caught under their bags.' Dannie was sounding like Peta and it really didn't suit her at all.

'You're disgusting sometimes, Dannie. A simple "It's normal" would have sufficed.' Just then, George came in for the coffees.

'Philip suggested we all do a bridge climb sometime, what do you reckon?'

'No way. I'm frightened of heights, but you fellas go.' It would be difficult for Philip to grip the rail and his dick at the same time, I thought. Nup, Mr Dick Fiddler was not in the running at all.

twelve

Mr Committaphobe

Liza didn't know much about Tufu, she said, except that he was gentle and shy and was interested in meeting some people locally. He'd only just moved to Coogee to play football and didn't have many friends. She'd met him at a fundraiser organised by the ALS. He was a friend of one of her clients: the only reason she wasn't going out with him on a date herself. 'Conflict of interest, Alice. But I'm happy for you to go out with him.'

He sounded perfect, too good to be true. Tufu lived in Coogee like me; he was thirty, single, employed, gorgeous and brown. Samoan brown. It was a little odd that he was single; there are nine single women to every straight bloke in Sydney, so he'd either not been looking or not trying at all. Or perhaps he was just waiting for Ms Right. I chose to believe the latter.

Liza had given him my number instantly, telling him I was a Blackfella who lived round the corner and could introduce him to some of the local Indigenous community. He called within the week and invited me to his 'tiny and not always tidy little flat on Beach Street'.

He had the sexiest voice I'd ever heard and I couldn't wait to meet him. I felt like I was on a hat-trick; he was single, he was brown, he lived almost next door. Mr Right might also have been Mr Right-Under-My-Nose.

I rocked up at Tufu's flat at dusk, hoping he was cooking me a Samoan feast. There was a pile of rubbish stashed in the hallway outside his door. Empty chip packets, pizza boxes and a pile of newspapers and comics in the corner next to a box of empty wine bottles. All the signs of singledom. It wasn't a very good look. He hadn't gone to much effort to impress his potential Ms Right. Did he need a man to take out the garbage, just like me? Maybe he'd been too busy. I knocked on the door.

'Hi Alice, come in.' Our eyes locked momentarily at the threshold, then I followed him into his crowded flat. The walls were covered in family photos and actions shots of him playing rugby.

'Coogee Wombats,' he said, assuming I was going to ask him the name of the team. I didn't let on that I'd spent many of my younger days hanging out at the local Rugby Club and knew the green and white uniform well, even if I didn't necessarily appreciate the game.

Tufu stood there in a lava-lava, his huge, muscly thighs hidden underneath. I looked from him standing in front of me to the photo of him in full flight in the green and white jersey, trying to make the link between the two. Pacific reggae played on the small radio as I did a very discreet scan of the room and saw his Randwick Council shirt hanging on his bedroom doorknob. I turned to hand him the bottle of wine I'd brought with me and caught him checking out my cleavage. We both instantly stepped back, trying to find a place to stand without touching each other in the tiny space of his flat, and he cracked a nervous smile. His shyness was attractive.

'I haven't actually prepared anything, Alice. I thought we could get takeaway and that way we could just relax and talk. I hope that's okay? We can sit on the balcony, there's a great view of the beach.' Even though I had a good view of the beach from my own flat, it would be different looking at it with this hunk of a man.

'That'd be lovely.'

We sat on plastic chairs and talked, with a glass of wine each to keep our hands busy. His shyness soon disappeared and we laughed about the backpackers we could see skylarking on the beach. He'd had his share of them, too, down at the Coogee Bay beer garden. They generally stayed out of his way, though, because of his size, no doubt.

Sitting there watching him, imagining his thighs under the loose cotton, I couldn't believe Tufu was single. He must have had women just sliding off him all the time, everywhere he went. Surely the Rugby Club would have provided a bevy of women for him to choose from. He was just too gorgeous. But he told me he'd never actually had a girlfriend. Was he really waiting for Ms Right? Had someone broken his heart? Was he perhaps really not interested in girls? Was he a closet gay? Did he know Cliff, who only lived one beach north? I hoped he wasn't gay; it would be a terrible loss to the heterosexual single women's community of Coogee. Surely he wouldn't last long in a rugby team if he were? Ian Roberts hadn't really paved the way for many others to come out – not yet, anyway.

By the time our delivery Indian arrived, we were completely relaxed and swapping stories about the Festival of Pacific Arts held in Samoa in 1996. We'd both been there. We discovered a whole range of coincidences and common links. He knew some of the people I'd met there and we were sure we'd been at the same events. Destiny was screaming at me, 'Tufu's the one'. He seemed too good to be true. The conversation too easy. The mood too right. Had Tufu been the one I was looking for all along? Thoughts of an island wedding flooded my love-struck mind. I had considered Fiji or the Cooks a little earlier, but perhaps it was always going to be Samoa. I was already thinking about having a family. Genetically, the Samoans were large people. I'd be squeezing out a bruiser of a baby. That'd hurt. But there'd be a great story in it for sure to tell everyone at the next reunion.

'I'm really glad you're here, Alice, I've been looking forward to meeting you since we spoke.'

'Me too!' He slid his hand on mine, sealing my future. Sealing *our* future. I was sure of it. I looked out into the distance as the last light of day fell on Wedding Cake Island, the rocky outcrop just off Coogee's shoreline. The view of it was much better when the sun came up over the bay, but sunset on Tufu's balcony wasn't bad either.

'I bet it's beautiful here in the morning with the sun rising over Wedding Cake Island.' I hadn't meant to say it out loud.

'You can find out for yourself if you like.' He leaned in and kissed me. It was a swift move, and it was all happening fast, but it honestly felt perfect. Suddenly Peta appeared in my head: 'Don't do the deed on the first date.' Tufu's hand made its way along the side of my breast. *Don't do the deed on the first date. Don't do the deed on the first date.* Against all my instincts, I leaned back and took a deep breath, but I couldn't stifle a moan of pleasure.

'Tell me what you're thinking,' Tufu whispered in my ear, and I could hear the smile in his voice. He knew what I was thinking. Could I admit to him that I was contemplating ripping that lava-lava off him and crawling over him in a frenzy of sexual need? I couldn't say it. A woman had to have a little more mystery about her than that.

'I was just thinking about Wedding Cake Island and hoping I'd have a wedding cake one day.'

Hell, had I said that out loud too? Clearly I had, and he backed right off, taking his arm from around my shoulders. All of a sudden the shy lava-lava lad became Jack-the-lad, all calm and collected and looking like a real player, with a sly grin on his face.

'Really, Alice? You don't strike me as the kind of girl to get tied up with just one bloke.' What the hell did that mean? Was he calling me a slut? Did he mean I wasn't marriage material? Or was this really about him? Either way, I didn't feel at all comfortable now sitting on his crappy plastic chairs on his tiny little balcony anymore. All I could do was throw the same back at him.

'You don't strike me as the kind of guy who would commit himself either.'

'I'm not. I like my life the way it is. My independence. Not having to be responsible to one person.'

'You mean accountable.'

'I like to have variety in my life.'

'So you like to play the field. No pun intended.'

'I like to meet lots of different people.'

'You mean you're a slut?'

'That's a bit rough, isn't it?'

I knew how irrational I was being. Just because I wanted to meet my one and only, it didn't mean everyone else wanted to. I left before I made any more of a fool of myself.

thirteen

Mr I'm-Just-Not-That-Into-You

'Alice, it's Mum, how are you?'

'What's up, Mum?' Mum never called me just to say hello. There was suspicion in my voice.

'Nothing. I just wanted to see if you had any time this weekend? The son of an old friend of mine from the Aboriginal Medical Service is moving to Sydney and needs someone to show him round. He's single.'

'Muuuuummm ...' I whined. I didn't want her in on my strategy. She'd only ever offered Cliff in the past, and I wasn't interested in another gay man to dodge.

'Don't be like that, Alice, he's a nice boy. Good-looking, too. His name is Malcolm, and he's a project manager with a youth service. He doesn't know anyone here. Can't you just meet him and introduce him to some of the young mob? He doesn't want to hang out with an old duck like me.'

She was right, he wouldn't. Anyway, I needed to be open to each and every opportunity. Malcolm from

Melbourne might just prove a positive experience, so I agreed to show him around, and before long I'd started to regard our first meeting as another blind date. It was always possible that he was doing the same thing. Actually, it was highly likely that he was. Men didn't think that differently, did they?

We agreed to meet at Redfern Park during a family day, with Koori bands providing the entertainment. I SMS'd him when I arrived and told him to meet me at the Koori crafts stall. Not expecting him to be there for a few minutes, I looked at all the wares and reached out to pick up a beaded necklace. An incredibly handsome young guy put his hand on the same set of beads, accidentally brushing my fingers. A shot of electricity went up my arm and somehow hit me right in my loins.

'I'm sorry, you have them.' I looked up into his black eyes and suddenly knew what love at first sight was. Or lust at first sight, anyway.

'No please, you have them – they'd look good on you,' he said. I thought I would orgasm there and then, with the soulful sounds of Emma Donovan singing in the background, kids with painted faces milling around, johnnycakes being fried nearby and Caro from Koori Radio calling it all live to air.

'I'm Alice.' I extended my hand. I couldn't believe I was being so forward. It wasn't my style at all, but I couldn't let him get away.

He took my hand and shook it. 'You're not Alice Aigner, by chance?' He'd heard of me, but how? 'What a coincidence meeting like this. I'm Malcolm.'

'That's not coincidence, that's destiny. Fate I'd say.'

He looked at me as if to say, 'What are you on?' and then laughed. Didn't he know that there was no such thing as coincidence?

We hung around the stall for a while, pretending not to check each other out. I kept my dark glasses on so I could perv without being caught. He looked young.

'So, how old are you, Malcolm?'

'Just had my twenty-fourth birthday.'

'Blinder, I bet.' Young guys usually get trashed when they go out, birthdays or not. Dillon was always doing it and driving Mum to the point of despair.

'I don't drink actually.'

'Really?'

'Just trying to be healthy. Don't smoke, eat hot chips or have carbonated drinks, either.' He was a health nut, but I liked that. At least I'd be healthier if we got together. 'Sounds boring to you, I suppose, but I spent a few years running a kids' dance group in Melbourne and I had to be fit. Cycled and kickboxed every day just to be able to keep up with them.'

He was the most attractive man I'd ever met. Healthy, fit, working with kids. Young. Black. In Sydney and knowing only me!

'Your body is a temple,' he said as we sat on the grass, half listening to Sean Choolburra crack some jokes. Yeah, I'd be happy for my body to be your temple, no worries, I thought to myself.

'What about you, Alice? You into the fitness kick too?' His piercing black eyes unnerved me, his smile made me melt.

I'd have to lie. How could I tell him I drank a litre of gin a week? Only ate healthy meals accidentally, loved hot chips and hadn't ridden a bike since I was eleven?

'I do my best. I'm big on the coastal walk from Coogee to Bondi and back.' At least that wasn't a lie. I did try my best and I did do that walk occasionally.

Malcolm was the strong but quiet type – *my* type. I knew straight away that he was the closest thing to my Mr Right I'd seen so far. He was four years younger than me, but there wasn't anything about age on my list of criteria. Anyway, his confidence and worldliness hid any age discrepancy others may have questioned. He'd be a great young father, have lots of energy to do sports with the kids, and keep up with me as I reached my sexual peak in my mid-to-late thirties. Yes, a younger husband would be a good option.

I felt a huge relief: I had almost accomplished my goal – and my thirtieth birthday was still more than a year away. Of course, it might take some time for Malcolm to recognise how right we were for each other – women process things much faster than men. He *would* realise it, though, eventually. A clever guy like Malcolm would manage to figure things out himself for sure. Or maybe he already had. I was deadly and desirable. I could give up soft drink and chips. I'd even been to a kickboxing class once. And he could use my body as a temple any time.

We enjoyed the day and went to the after party that night at the Strawberry Hills Hotel. I introduced Malcolm to everyone I knew, and encouraged him to exchange numbers, cards and email addresses with them all. I wanted him to feel at home in Sydney, have a good network of friends and acquaintances. He'd need them for sure if he were going to stay on here after his project was finished.

We had a great night. He got on with everyone. It was like we'd been friends for years.

Around midnight I was ready to leave. I had a long day of school starting early in the morning, and teacher-parent night at the end of the day. It was time to go home, hopefully with Malcolm on my arm. We walked outside into the crisp midnight air, his hand in the small of my back, gently guiding me through the crowd. It felt good. It felt right. It felt like the next step would be a good-night kiss. Then ... *nothing*. He hailed a cab, opened the back door and put me in it, closed the door and waved me off.

What had gone wrong? I tried to reassure myself: Malcolm was a gentleman, that was all. He was well raised and too polite to try anything sleazy when we'd only just met, even though there'd been enough electricity between us to light up the city. He was just showing me respect; after all, I *was* the daughter of 'Aunty Ivy', whom his mother had always spoken so fondly of.

♥

I woke the next day expecting to hear from him. But he didn't call that day, or the next, or the next. I reminded myself that he was busy settling into a new city, getting to know the ropes in his new job, and probably analysing his new feelings for the wonderful woman he'd been lucky enough to meet in his first week here. He was probably a little overwhelmed by it all.

When I hadn't heard from him by the end of the week, though, my patience and understanding started to turn to anxiety. We both knew I was his Ms Right. I was the love of his life. The woman who gave him his connections in Gadigal country. The one who'd encouraged him to swap numbers with a whole bunch of other single Black women. Gorgeous, strong, single, capable, single, sexy, smart, single Koori women. What had I been thinking? He was probably calling *them*.

Just as I was about to start doing some research on the Koori grapevine to see what he'd been up to, he texted me, saying, 'Hello, how are you?' I'd expected an invitation to dinner or a movie or *something* – anything. Still, I saw his communication as an invitation to make contact, so I texted back suggesting he call me if he had some time and wanted to catch up.

A week later the phone finally rang and we went out for dinner, at my suggestion. We strolled along Crown Street before deciding on a small but atmospheric Nepalese restaurant. We ate, we laughed, and he said I looked gorgeous and that it was lovely to see me. We drank copious amounts of wine – or I did, anyway – and then, as the night drew to a close, I panicked. What next?

'Would you like me to drop you home, Alice?'

'That'd be great, thanks.'

Naturally I assumed he expected to come in. I was getting that loving feeling as we drove to Coogee and all I could think about was his young, rock-hard body. He pulled up right outside the building in a spot invisibly marked 'Al and Mal'.

'Would you like to come up for a herbal tea? I've got sencha, green, fruit?' I'd stocked up because I knew Malcolm was a health freak. He turned the motor off and we walked upstairs.

He took himself on a tour of the flat at my insistence, then came and stood near me as I prepared the tea. I realised, too late, that all my lists were still on the fridge. *Shit.* I panicked. I'd have to kiss him. His eyes would at least be shut then, and I could probably manoeuvre him back out into the lounge room.

I had no choice but to glide in slowly, hoping that it would look like it was partly his idea. However it looked, it happened: his arms moved around my waist and our mouths connected.

The kiss was nice, easy, warm. Malcolm definitely responded – but after we'd pulled away from each other, he looked at his watch.

'I've got an early start, Alice, better be going.'

I was confused. He was, after all, a bloke. He was young and fit. Surely he was horny. *I* was, whether he'd been instructed to call Mum 'Aunty' or not.

Fair enough, though. I didn't want him to have to eat and run, so to speak. At least we were on our way to greater things, and I assumed we'd catch up where we left off soon enough. The anxiety was gone. We were now a couple – though we'd take things slowly, of course. We could discuss Malcolm's permanent move to Sydney in the near future. My thirtieth birthday was eighteen months off, so we had plenty of time.

I thought he'd call the next morning – but he didn't. I sent him a couple of text messages – nothing. I left a message on his voicemail – nothing. What could possibly have gone wrong? I needed to confer with Dillon. He was the same age as Malcolm, so perhaps he could tell me.

Dillon sat on my lounge, a pizza box in his lap and a juice on the coffee table in front of him. Like Malcolm, Dillon didn't drink fizzy drinks. It was good thing to see young men being health conscious. I handed him a serviette.

'There's some ice-cream in the freezer too, if you like.' I was sweetening him up for the big discussion. This was an old, familiar pattern.

'So, what's up this time? Who is he? Or should I say who *isn't* he?' Dillon knew what was going on.

'His name's Malcolm, he's Mum's friend's son. He's lovely and we get on really well, and I think he's perfect and he doesn't drink soft drink either, like you, and he's gorgeous, and he's Black and we'd be perfect together if he gave it a chance, and, well … he's a bit younger than me.' I knew Dillon would have an issue with the age thing. He'd think I was a cradle-snatcher.

He put his pizza down. 'How much younger?' he said sternly, wiped his mouth and took a swig of juice.

'Four years. And I think it bothers him. He hasn't called me for two weeks. Maybe he's worried about the age difference?'

'Al, I can't believe I'm saying this, but it's a bloke's fantasy to be with – learn from – an older woman. Personally, I'd rather that the older woman they were fantasising about wasn't you, but it's your life.'

'So you don't think it's the age thing, then?'

'Has he mentioned anything about age since you've been seeing him?'

'Well, no.'

'Okay, I'm sure it's not an age thing. Let's back up a bit. When's the last time you heard from this guy?'

'He sent a text—'

Dillon cut me right off.

'Stop right there. Text messages don't count. When's the last time he *called* you?'

'Oh, he didn't really call much – generally SMS'd.'

'So, he didn't want to actually *speak* to you, or hear your voice, then?'

'Do you have to put it like that?' I was a little hurt by Dillon's immediate and adamant response.

'How long have you been dating this dude anyway?'

'A couple of months,' I said, 'but we're not really dating as such.' I had to lie about how long I'd known Malcolm because I knew Dillon would think I was an idiot putting so much emotional energy and time – his and mine – into a brief fantasy. 'Why?'

'I'm just trying to work out why he disappeared so fast if you were so right for each other. How often did he *text* you?'

'Well, he always responded to my messages almost immediately.'

'So *you* initiated every communication?'

'Well, as the older of the two, I kind of took charge,' I explained, knowing I sounded pathetic. I kept going before Dillon could say anything. 'Doesn't it count that he replied immediately? Surely that counts for something?'

'No, Alice. *You* were telling him he was on *your* mind, but he never demonstrated the same about you, did he? He just responded politely to your communication. Seriously, if a man is really into a woman, he'll call her regularly to hear her voice, not just send the odd text every fortnight.' He was making sense but I didn't want to hear it.

'Malcolm is a very busy guy. He works long hours, home late, up early. He couldn't even stay at my place because he had to be at the office before seven am.' Dillon looked incredibly suspicious by this time.

'Alice, now please know I don't really want to ask you this question, and as your younger brother I feel uncomfortable doing so, and I'm only asking because I have to, to get to the end of this conversation, but did he *ever* stay over? Did you *ever* have sex?'

'No, like I told you … he was very busy.' Even I knew how pathetic this sounded.

Dillon shook his head. 'Al, no man is *ever* too busy for sex! It doesn't matter how early we have to get up. We won't sleep at all if there's sex on offer.'

'But his priority is his job! He's responsible for some very important community initiatives.'

'I'm sure he is, but Al, don't you want to be a priority? His *first* priority?'

'Yes, of course, but maybe he's just not ready for a relationship.'

'Maybe he's not Al, but it sounds as though *you* are. You need to think about what *you* want.' Dillon got up and walked to the kitchen.

His advice was painful, but it all made sense. It didn't sound like Dillon, though. It was far more measured and considered than his usual 'just get over it' or 'move on'.

'But he kissed me. Why did he do that, then?' I sung out after him. I wasn't ready to give up just yet.

'Maybe he liked kissing you, Al.'

'Not maybe – he did, I know that for sure.'

'Okay. So perhaps he gave you mixed messages.'

'Maybe I gave him some too. Maybe he's confused,' I said sadly, as Dillon returned with the tub of ice-cream and a single spoon.

'Al, stop it. You're being pathetic. Stop making excuses. Cut him loose, cut yourself loose. Enjoy the freedom of letting go.' Dillon was making me uncomfortable now, with his new-age insights and psychological analysis.

'Al, if you're making excuses for his behaviour, it can only mean one thing.'

'Do tell, Dr Dillon.'

'He's just not that into you. I'm sorry, but all the signs lead to this conclusion. Actually, just one of the signs would be enough. No phone calls, no sex, no time for you. They all mean the same thing.'

He was right. But how had my twenty-four-year-old brother become so articulate on the subject? It was as though he'd been workshopping it or something.

'I've got to run Al, but Larissa asked me to give this to you.' He handed me a book. I looked at the title: *He's Just Not That Into You*.

'What's this for?'

'Larissa saw the author talking about it on *Oprah* and she hasn't stopped going on about it since. She thought you might like it.'

Not only was my brother giving me counselling sessions, but his girlfriend seemed to be in on it too. I started to get upset.

'Is the whole fucken family sitting around having conferences about my pathetic love-life? Are you all feeling sorry for me? Don't you know I love being single? I can read and pee in peace, and I'm never too tired for sex – singledom is something to be relished! My married friends all *envy* my lifestyle. And Mum's wrong, by the way – I'm *not* a lesbian!' I was on the edge of hysteria, and Dillon sensed as much.

'Al, no-one's sitting around conferencing your love-life. And I'm not sure why you mentioned your toilet and reading habits, but you asked me for my advice and I gave it to you. Larissa just sent the book because she read it and thought you might be interested in it. I thought it was probably a chick thing, but don't bother reading it if you don't want to. But that's it for me, I'm not having this conversation with you anymore.'

Dillon wasn't angry, but he left soon after. He had one last look in my pantry first. He always did that, but

I didn't mind – it was the first thing I always did when I visited Mum and Dad's place too.

Once he'd gone, I sat down to think. I wept a little, because Dillon was right. Malcolm just wasn't that into me. Maybe I should read Larissa's book. Or maybe not. After all, *he's just not that into you* was not the kind of positive affirmation I needed. I decided to make Malcolm the bad guy. *He's just not smart enough, he's just not good enough, and he can get fucked!* That was better. 'They can all get fucked!' I shouted. Swearing off men altogether, I headed to the freezer to find some solace in what was left of the cookies and cream ice-cream. Being single meant you could eat the whole tub yourself without an audience judging you.

And that was that. I was done with Phase I of my strategy. It had been a complete and utter failure. No more blind dates for me.

fourteen

Stick to the strategy

I drove and parked in Abercrombie Street, where Boomalli Aboriginal Artists Co-operative used to be. Harry Wedge's paintings still added colour to the street. I'd always found his work eerie, and could never imagine one hanging in my little flat, but Harry was a Wiradjuri man, and I was proud of all his success in recent years, and glad that the new tenants hadn't sacrificed his political statements with the mission brown paint that covered the rest of the building.

I met Peta around the corner at the Sutherland Hotel at seven pm. We played two games of pool, then headed over to our old campus at about eight for the Koori graduation dinner

Country students came to Sydney to study for two-week blocks, four times a year. We called them 'block releasers', and we always had a good time when they were in town. Seems like all the partying Kooris in Sydney had to get together and run amuck too, in support of their cousins and friends' attempts to be educated in a flash white uni. Peta and I went along whenever we could, especially for the grad dinners.

They were always fun, and made us remember what it was like to be students. Luckily graduation was only once a year!

It started off as such a good night, catching up with old friends, dancing to local band the Koori Krooners. We all danced for what must have been two hours, then I sat down while all the aunties danced in a circle to the country and western tunes that reminded them of their youth and bush dances at local town halls. All I could see were skinny Koori ankles and flat Koori arses. It was worth a photo, and sure enough, Peta pulled out her fancy new digital camera and took a few.

'They won't even be shame when they see themselves in the *Koori Mail*, eh?' I gave Peta a big grin.

'No way. Blackfellas love being in *Mail*.' She took a photo, flicked her glossy ponytail and said cheekily, 'I know I do.' She walked off, flash-happy, and I didn't see her again until it was time to leave.

At about eleven, I walked outside and spent some time with my old mate Tim on the balcony, then flirted with a couple of the first-year boys. They were so young I felt I was pretty safe – until I remembered what Dillon said about young guy's fantasies about older women. Then in one great swoop, we were all on the escalators, heading downstairs and off towards Chinatown. (I'd always thought the escalators looked out of place in the middle of a university building; it was like being in a shopping mall.) I remember seeing the big clock at

Central striking midnight as we turned out of the tower and onto Broadway. Peta pretended she was Cinderella and said she'd turn into a pumpkin if she didn't get home soon.

'Well, come here, 'cos I'm Peter Peter Pumpkin Eater,' said Tim. She just slapped him on the back, like a mate does. Tim had fancied Peta for years, but she wasn't interested. Truth be known, Tim was too nice for Peta. She liked the bad boys, and she knew with someone as lovely as Tim she'd chew him up and spit him out in no time flat. Tim's look of disappointment had become almost permanent when he was around Peta.

We headed to the Covent Gardens Hotel for some Koori-oke. The Covent was packed with every lonely heart, wannabe singer and block releaser in Sydney. Lots of alcohol-induced energy and an almost unhealthy competition for the mike prevailed. I didn't want to sing, although, as usual, everyone was urging each other on. After my fifth Sambuca, I couldn't help myself when Helen Reddy's 'I Am Woman' was announced and no-one owned up to it. The MC called for someone else to volunteer, so why not me? 'Hear me roar' all right – right down to Darling Harbour and beyond, I'm sure. Scary stuff, singing, when you're not really any good at it. The best part, though, even if most of the audience thought I was tone-deaf, was when I replaced the words 'Till my brothers understand' with 'Till them gubbas understand' and the place went up with a roar. The Blacks outnumbered the whites, which was normal during block release weeks, and one thing I'd learned over the years was know your audience.

'Nice one, sis. Can I get you a drink?' Some guy I hadn't seen before was suddenly at our table, being friendly, calling everyone sis and bro and buying rounds. He was white, and a bit drunk, but he seemed harmless enough.

'Sure, gin and tonic.'

♥

I will never drink again! My head was pounding. Where was I? And why did it smell so bad? I held my breath and moved my eyes from side to side, trying to figure out where the hell I was. It mightn't be the side effects of twelve Sambucas that caused the nausea, I decided. I appeared to be lying on a foam mattress on the floor of an indoor garbage tip, with the resident caretaker. What the hell?!

My first reaction was to check I was fully clothed. Thank god, shoes and all. No penetration of any kind likely to have occurred. I noted that the caretaker was shirtless and had one hand strategically squashed down the front of his jeans, but at least they were still on. I was grateful for that small mercy. His upper body was blinding white; I doubted it had ever seen the daylight, let alone the sun. He was so white he was almost fluorescent. I decided to call him Casper because I couldn't remember his real name. There were faded green tattoos on his arms, cheap and dated looking, but I couldn't read them.

What had I been thinking? No one-night stands under ANY circumstances – it was on my list. Peta, Dannie and Liza would be appalled. I needed to get out of there fast.

I eased myself off the no doubt bug-ridden mattress and onto the floor, then looked around for a bathroom. I needed to empty the champers, gin and Sambuca from my full bladder *immediately*, and I would've killed to be able to whack some toothpaste in my mouth. I had to walk through a bedroom to get to the bathroom. There was a bed with no-one in it, piles of clothes scattered throughout the room and trackie daks hanging by one leg from the pelmet above the window. I was confused. Why hadn't we slept in the bed? Had I woken up in a squat? Was this building condemned?

There was an Anthony Mundine poster above the bed. Was 'The Man' meant to inspire Casper during sex? I didn't want to think of Casper naked, so I let go of the thought quick smart.

From the next room, I heard him moan, and stopped dead in my tracks, hoping he wouldn't wake. When I was sure he was still sleeping, I stepped into the bathroom. It had no door and it smelled worse than a public toilet. Straining my thigh muscles, I squatted to pee without touching the porcelain.

Searching in the cabinet for some toothpaste, I found a toothbrush wrapped in toilet paper, a one-kilogram tub of Sorbolene and three half-empty jars of Metamucil. No wonder the bathroom had a lingering odour. I squirted what was left in an old tube of Colgate onto my finger and pushed it across the front of my teeth, enjoying instant morning-breath relief. I swished some water around in my mouth and spat into what must have been the filthiest sink in Sydney. Assuming I was still in Sydney.

Peering around the doorway, I noticed Casper was still protecting the family jewels, but had changed hands. I just hoped he didn't start having a party-for-one while I was still here.

I was hanging for a Coke, so I tiptoed over to the kitchen, passing a table holding a computer, a statue of the Virgin Mary and some plastic yellow flowers in a cracked glass vase. When I opened the fridge an odour worse than sour milk gushed out, and I nearly puked on the spot. Taking a step back I saw what looked like spag bol in a huge stainless steel bowl. The mould across the top and the smell seemed to indicate it had been cooked some time ago. There wasn't any Coke or juice, just some dark green liquid in a saucepan. Frustrated, I gave up on the drink and moved on: I had to get out of there before Casper woke up, then find out where I was and get back to Coogee before the morning heat set in. There's nothing worse than a hangover on a hot day.

I found my bag and ran a comb through my hair, then took one last look at Casper before I made my getaway. He was sleeping in the foetal position, now, with a smile on his face. I hoped to god he wasn't dreaming about me – or if he was, that I was at least fully clothed.

I legged it out the door and into a stairwell that stank of cat's piss. I gagged. Where the hell was I? I held my breath, then sprinted down the stairs and charged out into the street, where I almost collapsed from lack of air. I shut my eyes and listened for anything that might give me a hint of where I was and which direction I should head in. I heard a train and was thankful: if I followed the tracks, I could at least get to Central.

I turned left out of the building and looked back. It was grouped with five or six more exactly like it alongside, all seventies designs, and depressing. I gathered they were housing commission. Shopping trolleys littered the front entrances, and laundry was draped from one balcony to the next, with the odd body passed out on the front doorsteps. No-one can tell me there's no correlation between money and happiness. The high rates of suicide and depression among people living in public housing are a perfect illustration of how socio-economic status affects self-esteem, the way we live and interact and essentially, how happy we are. No-one could be happy having to sleep on steps. Mind you, Casper wasn't doing much better, I reminded myself, yet he had seemed pretty happy lying there.

The sun was already hot. It was early December and the summer promised to be a scorcher. My legs were sweaty in jeans, but I was grateful I hadn't worn a skirt. At least I didn't look like a sex worker on my way home after a long night.

Everything was so bright, but I couldn't understand why. I realised I didn't have any sunnies on and there weren't any in my bag. Why would there be? I'd gone out drinking and dancing on Friday night, no need for them. The glare and the hangover and the heat and the nausea grew worse and worse.

'Thank god!' I said out loud as I saw a train station up ahead. At least I was on the right track, so to speak, but then I saw the sign: 'Blacktown'. I was almost an hour's train ride from the city.

I immediately harassed the drink machine near the ticket window for two cans of Coke. It kept my change but I didn't even care, I was so desperate for the effects of caffeine.

To my sheer joy, there was a newsagent-cum-dry-cleaner-cum-key-cutter who also sold eight-dollar sunnies. I spent five minutes deciding which looked best and donned a big black pair that made me look like a blowfly. They hid me perfectly from the sun and the outside world at the same time.

I bought a ticket to Central, sat down, and began dreading the trip home. I felt sick, and wary of the train journey itself – I'd been influenced by all the stories on the news about gang violence in the western suburbs and assaults on trains. My motto had always been 'If I can't drive there, I don't go.'

There was an announcement that my train was approaching, so I skolled the last of the second can of Coke. I boarded, found a seat facing forward (I hate travelling backwards), and eyed all the others in the carriage as we slowly pulled out of the station. I was relieved no-one sat next to me – I knew I reeked of stale grog and second-hand cigarette smoke. A good blast of deodorant probably wouldn't have gone astray either.

I pondered the name 'Blacktown' and where it had come from. I remembered a woman I studied with at uni who was from Blacktown, the Dharug mob. She reckoned it used to be called 'Blackstown' or 'the Black Town' because that's where Blackfellas settled after Governor Macquarie made the first land grants to Aboriginal people in New South Wales, around 1820. As a history teacher I really should have known precise dates, but I was just too tired. I wondered how many Kooris actually lived in Blacktown now, and where they all came from. Western Sydney has the highest population of urban Aboriginal people in the country. God knows they're not all living in Coogee, though if they were, that'd be cool. I wouldn't have to deal with all those pain-in-the-arse backpackers by myself then.

As we travelled station by station, suburb by suburb towards the city, two suspicious-looking guys entered the carriage. Were they suspicious or was it just that they were wearing baggy jeans, the ones I always wanted to pull up, the ones that show off expensive undies? Was it because they had shaved heads and little goatees? Was I buying into a stereotype created by the media? Who the hell was I to be casting judgements? I was no doubt fulfilling some stereotypical notions of Aboriginality myself right then, sitting on a train from Blacktown, in the same clothes I'd been wearing the night before, reeking of alcohol and body odour. I hate that, always having to be aware of fulfilling other people's fantasies of who I am or am not. I soon forgot the two guys and was drifting off into self-analysis when my mobile rang. At least I hadn't lost my phone as part of the misadventure. I'd already lost three in as many years.

It was Liza.

'Hey, Alice, where are you? If I didn't know better I'd think you were on a train. What's that noise?' I couldn't begin to tell her I'd strayed so far from the strategy that I'd ended up in Blacktown with a bloke called Casper. She'd flip her lid for sure. I was embarrassed, ashamed and disappointed in myself. I'd gone from swearing off men altogether to ending up on the floor with one in one mad rush.

'Are you organised for Bianca's kitchen tea this arvo?' I'd forgotten all about the kitchen tea. I couldn't go, there was no way. I had a severe hangover, and no idea when I'd get home. I increasingly hated the married and soon-to-be-married, as it was becoming overwhelmingly obvious to me that I'd never be either – by thirty or forty or fifty years of age.

'I'm not going.' I was adamant. No correspondence would be entered into. Or so I thought.

'There's no way out, not for you, Alice. You have to go. She's *your* school mate. I don't even know why she invited me. I'm actually *your* friend if we want to be particular about it, not hers. I could probably get out of it, but you can't. Bianca doesn't strike me as the kind of woman who would ever forgive you if you didn't show. And Dannie will be there too – she'll be furious if you don't turn up.'

I looked at my watch. It had just hit nine am. 'Fine. I'll pick you up at two – but I'm not staying long, okay?' I sounded like a bitch, but I was just so tired. I needed to lie down. 'What about a present?' I asked. Thankfully, Liza had it all under control.

I turned the phone off then, just in case Casper called. I wasn't sure whether I'd given him my number or not.

'Next stop Central,' came the much-appreciated announcement. As the train pulled in, I added up how many drinks I'd had the night before. I was okay to drive – just. I counted again to be sure. I couldn't afford to lose my licence, and I was always giving Mickey a hard time for even suggesting he drive after a couple of drinks.

I had no idea where to go once I got off the train, so I followed everyone else. I found myself in Eddy Avenue, near the country buses and coach terminal. I knew where I was, but felt despair as I contemplated the long walk to my car. I hoped it was still there.

I briefly considered getting a cab back to Abercrombie Street, but that would've been sheer laziness, and I'm not a lazy woman. I was just hungover, tired, hot and pathetic. These were the times when I needed Mr Right. He'd just pick me up in his flashy car and drive me home, stopping for a Coke or two on the way, lavishing me with sympathy. I started my trek towards Broadway half expecting that flashy car to pull up next to me. Maybe I *was* still drunk; there was no other excuse for such craziness.

Behind the wheel of my red Golf, I drove ever so carefully back to my little piece of paradise in Coogee, past Moore Park and the Randwick Race Course. Even though the air conditioning provided relief from the heat of the day, my belly didn't enjoy the hills of Alison Road and there were a few moments where I thought I might need to pull over. I didn't though, and I finally felt a sense of peace and belonging as I caught view of the ocean and a glimpse of Wedding Cake Island in the distance.

Heading downhill towards home in the weekend traffic, I reflected grimly that the hard work in finding a husband could only be matched by the hard work in finding a car space in Coogee on a Saturday morning in summer. I prayed, as I did regularly, to the creator: *Please Biami, not only bring me spiritual guidance and long life, but also let me find a parking space without effort and a long walk today.* Surprisingly, I managed to get a park right out the front of my unit on Arden Street. Biami was often good to me, even if I was still single. Biami not delivering me Mr Right just yet might well have been a good thing.

I didn't care that the security door of my building was wide open; in fact I was grateful for one less task to complete in order to get into my bed. I hiked the two flights of stairs, shakily put the key in the lock and almost fell through the door, so relieved to be home that I cried a little. I threw all my clothes off, gulped some orange juice from the bottle (a bit of an effort, as it was a three-litre jumbo bottle), then staggered down the hallway, bumping from wall to wall, finally collapsing on my bed. It was ten-thirty. I figured I could have three hours' sleep before I had to get ready for the kitchen tea. My eyes weren't even closed before I was asleep. The sound of my phone ringing in the kitchen couldn't raise me from my pillow. I'd let the machine get it.

❤

I woke in a dribbly haze to the sound of my phone ringing again. The machine picked it up before I got to it, and it was a few seconds before I recognised Liza's voice, wanting to know where I was. It was two-thirty. I'd overslept. I raced to the phone and grabbed the mouthpiece, breathless. 'I'm sorry, I'm sorry, I'm on my way out the door,' I lied, then hung up and checked the message waiting for me.

'Hi Alice, it's Simon. You didn't say goodbye. Guess you didn't want to wake me, eh? I got your number from the phone book. Lucky you're the only Aigner in Coogee. Just wanted to know what you were doing this arvo. I'll call you later on the mobile.'

Simon – that was his name. I didn't want to see him again, couldn't even remember really seeing him the first time, and he now had my mobile number as well. I'd have to change that message as soon as I got home from the kitchen tea, and maybe get myself a silent number.

I jumped into a steamy shower and relaxed, enjoying the jets of hot water massaging my shoulders and back, washing away the night before. Running some conditioner through my hair (I didn't have time to shampoo), I thought about what I would wear, how I'd crawl to Liza for being late, and what excuse we'd use for leaving the kitchen tea early. It was all too much – I was still so tired my eyes were barely open.

fifteen

The kitchen tea

The hostess greeted us with a cheery 'Welcome to my home and Bianca's kitchen tea. Please put your gifts in the room on the left and make your way through to the kitchen. The toilet is upstairs, but if you have to go, can you take your shoes off please? The carpet is new.' Why would anyone have a party where guests had to take their shoes off to use the toilet? I rolled my eyes at Liza, who just started laughing.

'Lucky we peed at Maccas on the way,' Liza whispered, looking at my shoes, knowing fully well how badly my feet reek. (We'd stopped for some fries – 'best thing for a hangover', Liza had said.)

'Yeah, wonder what would happen if I went upstairs with these clodhoppers on, eh?' I wasn't game to find out. Bianca would already be shitty that we were an hour late. Dannie was there, scowling at us for our tardiness.

In the kitchen, both Liza and I received our mandatory name tags so that everyone knew who the two slackers were. I joked that I was on Koori time, of course. Liza and Dannie chuckled, but no-one else seemed to get it. Bit of an in-joke perhaps. Liza and I took our seats in the chairs designated especially to us. We just sat for a while and watched, saying nothing to each other, or to anyone else. More to the point, no-one said anything to us. Most of the twelve or so women were engaged in conversation of some sort, eating mini-quiches and corn chips, party pies and sausage rolls. We weren't left in peace for long, though. The games soon started.

First we were given pegs to wear. In order to keep them, we couldn't cross our legs. 'For every leg crossed, is a peg lost – simple!' The woman wearing the name tag 'Mother of the Bride' was very good at explaining the rules. 'The one with the most pegs at the end of the game wins a prize.' Liza and I had already missed out on the lucky door prize – a set of tea towels and matching oven mitts. I felt like I was in some parallel universe.

I deliberately crossed my legs on and off enough times in the next ten minutes to ensure I'd lost all my pegs, and therefore didn't have to play anymore. I was over the game before it had even begun. The groom's grandmother, who was the most competitive of the otherwise conservative group, pinched most of my pegs. By the end of the game, which took about twenty-five minutes, I thought to myself that if marrying Mr Right involved brawling over clothes pegs with eighty-year-old women, I'd be happy to remain single. Mr

Right could stay where he was until his grandmother and great-aunties were well and truly dead and buried.

As the women all laughed and pinched pegs from each other, I pondered the absurdity of the ritual. Who came up with the concept of the 'kitchen tea' anyway? The whole event was simply about getting as many presents as possible leading up to the wedding. As if an engagement present and a wedding present weren't enough, without having to buy something for the kitchen too. How sexist anyway. Why doesn't the man have a kitchen tea to receive appliances *he* can use in the kitchen? It was such a fifties concept. The whole reunion came flooding back. Why do we maintain friendships with school friends anyway? Life is a series of cycles, but for some reason we feel compelled to make the school-friend-cycle go on past its expiry date. No-one wants to admit that we change, that who we are as teenagers may or may not determine who we are as adults, and that there is no guarantee that we'll get on with our old friends ten years down the track. Bianca really had broken the cycle now, though, I thought, because she was getting married, and her new life cycle was beginning. I hardly ever saw her these days. Yet here I was, pretending I was excited to be there.

'Where's the booze?' I asked Liza. I needed a drink to cope with it all. I looked around to see who was drinking what, and to my horror and disappointment

I couldn't see a drop of alcohol anywhere. 'Maybe we have to take our shoes off before we can have a wine or a beer. Should I ask Mrs New-Carpet or not?'

Liza put her finger up to her mouth, as if to say, 'Shhhh.'

'I need a drink,' I persisted. I got up and strolled casually through the kitchen, grabbed myself a party frank, and winked at Granny. 'Love the little boys, eh?' She didn't laugh, so I just shrugged my shoulders and made my way to the drinks area. Juice, mineral water, cordial and every soft drink mentionable, but not so much as a light beer in sight. I was getting agitated. While I mightn't be the best cook in the world, I'm a damned good hostess. Never let it be said that someone couldn't get a decent drink at Alice's place. Why hadn't the bride-to-be and Mrs New-Carpet organised any alcohol? How did they expect people to enjoy themselves during an afternoon of kitchen-teaing and all that entails *and* stay sober?

It was painfully clear that peg stealing wasn't entertaining enough for me and Liza, even though all the other girls seemed amused. Dannie *seemed* to be enjoying herself, but she had an excuse to leave early, and soon did. Had to pick up the school bully from netball.

She stopped to say goodbye to us on the way out. 'There's a reason to breed,' I whispered to her. 'Kids get you out of doing lots of things you don't want to.'

'But you end up doing a whole lot of other things you don't want to do,' she said. Perhaps motherhood was not a win-win situation.

The afternoon dragged on like a game of chess between two people who don't know the rules. Liza and I reluctantly participated in game after game that showed us just how pathetic the socialisation process into suburban wifedom is.

'I've been nothing but critical from the moment I walked in, so remind me why I'm so desperate to get married myself, Liza?' Seriously, sitting there I was truly happy to be single.

'You want to get married for the wedding party, the honeymoon and a guaranteed lifetime of don't-have-to-go-looking-for-it sex,' she said, as we lined up to play pin-the-penis-on-the-spunk. I was blindfolded and spun around and I did my best to cheat. I wasn't quite sure I'd be able to find it, but Granny assured me it was like riding a bike. I wondered how poor old Grandpa would cope when she got home that night.

Time ticked by slowly, and although Dannie had made her escape, Liza and I knew we couldn't leave before the presents were opened – that being the whole purpose of the event. Gift getting, and making your friends and relatives compete with each other over who spent the most on what. Or maybe the idea was to make others feel completely inadequate because they couldn't afford the top-of-the-range whatever it was you were expecting. Yes, gifts for the kitchen, that's what the kitchen tea was all about.

The next game was pass-the-parcel, with terrible folk music. I won a pair of rubber gloves and a scourer.

Liza and I both groaned with relief when we were finally summoned into the living room for the next part of the kitchen-tea program. Mrs New-Carpet was assisted by Mrs Sister-in-Law-to-Be in ushering us to our chairs, but by then Liza and I knew which were 'our seats'. The choruses of 'Ooooohhhh, aahhhh, isn't it lovely? ... Wish I had one of those ... That will come in handy ... I have one just like it ... I nearly bought one for myself ... I *did* buy one for myself!' almost made me want to puke.

I thought about kitchen teas I'd been to in the past, and realised none of them had been for Koori women. All my Koori girlfriends were relishing singledom, working on their careers, hanging out in the city, and, more often than not, terrifying men with their confidence and expectations, so that even a first date left a bloke in shock and in need of counselling. Many of the women in my circle did aspire to meeting Mr Right at some point, but I couldn't imagine any one of them going through this charade as part of *their* initiation into wifehood.

I wondered whether or not I'd do the kitchen tea gig, given that I rarely cooked anyway. If I did, the event would definitely involve lots of booze, good music and maybe even a stripper or two. Yes, that's the way a kitchen tea should run. Instead of Bianca's cookbook library, I'd get every marital aid on the market. I smiled at the thought – the first real smile after an afternoon of fake grins.

The kitchen clock Bianca received read six-thirty pm. (The gift-giver pointed out she had already put batteries in it!) The younger women talked excitedly about heading to a pub in Parramatta – a sign that it was time for Liza and I to leave. There was no way I was heading anywhere other than home. When I explained I needed to rest, Bianca didn't seem sorry to see us go.

'Yes, you do look dreadful, Alice.' Apparently I hadn't done as good a job on the make-up as I thought. We departed without fuss or fanfare.

On the way home, we discussed the urgency of the upcoming hens' night and wedding. How were we ever going to cope? Apart from the fact that we hadn't really connected with anyone else at the party, neither of us fancied doing the night-animal-bus-pub-crawl planned for the western suburbs the following Saturday, but we both agreed we should support Bianca in her hour of need: she'd be walking the streets of Parramatta with a shower curtain tied to her head and sixteen single, desperate girls and Mrs New-Carpet trailing behind.

I couldn't bring myself to tell Liza about my one-night stand with Casper just yet. I needed to be feeling healthy to do that.

sixteen

A date with Casper

'Alice, can you answer that? You *are* rostered on this week.' The sports mistress, who hated my guts because I was young and gorgeous, suddenly felt the need to remind me of my duties. But the phone ringing in the staff room made me nervous – I was frightened to pick it up in case it was Simon. If he'd managed to find my home number, he'd have no problem tracking me down at school. Just then my mobile rang.

'Sorry, I have to get this,' I said, waving it in the air. The other teachers were pissed off with me: I hadn't answered the phone in the staff room for three days. I pretended to answer my mobile, but sent the call straight to voicemail. Simon had already left three messages that week and I was sure it was him again. Mickey looked at me strangely.

'What's wrong?' he whispered. Even though Mickey was a mate, I didn't want to explain to him that I'd woken up next to a guy I had called Casper because I didn't know his real name. Mickey never judged me, though, so in the end I told him the full story and he laughed till he cried.

'Why don't you just speak to him? It's obvious he's into you. God, when's the last time you had a bloke pay you so much attention? And you didn't even sleep with him! Imagine if you had.' So he's into me is he? I thought. Great, never the ones you want.

Of course, Mickey was right. It'd been an eternity since anyone had paid me so much attention. But the thought of Simon and his apartment made me feel sick. Apart from the way he lived, I couldn't imagine what he and I might have to talk about. I couldn't even remember what we'd spoken about when we met – just that I'd been teasing him and calling him 'Simple Simon'. Whatever his line, it must have been good.

No sooner had I decided Simple Simon was *not* Mr Right than I received a letter from him in the post. He didn't know my flat number – thank god that's not listed in the phone book – but my postie must have just put the letter in my box. Simple Simon was definitely stalker material. I opened it cautiously, thinking that I'd have to photocopy it at school the next day and send a copy to Liza to use as evidence in case I mysteriously went missing. Then I read it and was surprised:

> *You have a beautiful spirit, Alice, the kind of presence other people want to be around. I feel good about the world just because you're in it. I can see how your friends draw strength from you, because you are so sure of who you are,*

*and that's something most of us struggle with
every day.*

The letter made me soft. I knew he was trying to flatter me — but it worked. His words had a sincerity and a charm that hadn't come through in the phone messages he'd left. Maybe he'd been nervous when he called. I knew I was like that sometimes, when I was ringing someone daunting, deadly and desirable. The man was only human; lily-white, but human.

In the letter, he said he wanted to prove that we had a chance at 'something special'. But how the hell could he claim all that from one drunken night at the pub — and from what I could remember, not even a kiss? Of course, there probably had been a kiss, but I'd been so horrified at the state of his apartment that I'd sent that memory to the darkest pit of my mind, never to resurface.

A few days went by and I kept thinking of the letter, reading and re-reading it between classes, at lunch, at home. Then I weakened. I would give Simple Simon a chance. He just *might* be Mr Right. He might be the love of my life. He might even be a dynamo in bed, I thought, if I could actually get him off the floor and into it. He mightn't really live in that flat anyway; maybe he was in transition. It certainly looked like a temporary kind of set-up. There had to be an explanation for anyone living like that out of choice.

I wanted a man to worship me and fill my life with romance. Simon had only seen me at my worst and still he was impressed. What more could a girl want? Was I mad? What was I waiting for? I dialled his number.

My gut feeling was that the phone call was probably a step in the wrong direction, but I had to be open to all possibilities.

He answered, 'Simon speakin'.'

I stumbled, 'It's Alice.'

'Oh, hiiiiii!' He sounded as happy as a puppy whose master has just come home from work and is going to stroke his stomach. His enthusiasm at hearing my voice was flattering.

I kept the conversation as short as possible. We arranged to meet for dinner and a drink in Chinatown, because it was on a train line and he didn't have a car. He asked if we could go on Thursday night because it was payday. I deduced that it meant he lived from week to week, and would never have any extra cash for romantic spur-of-the-moment weekends away. Already I was nervous, shaking my head at the thought of having to play chauffeur and banker for a guy who couldn't drive or manage money. Before we'd hung up I'd already decided that Thursday night's dinner was going to be a failure and Simple Simon wasn't Mr Right, but more than likely Mr All-Wrong.

♥

The next few days flew by. End of year exams were keeping me busy. Thursday arrived and I wanted to cancel, but that wasn't my style. *Always stick to commitments or don't make them in the first place* was a mantra my father had instilled in us as children. He was really strict on meeting obligations, whatever they were. Even so, there wasn't one minute fibre of my being that was excited about the prospect of dinner with Simple Simon, even if I could classify it as a date to the girls. *My* Mr Right had certain criteria to fulfill beyond simply worshipping me, and Simple Simon hadn't fit any of them yet.

I re-read his letter, which I had taken to carrying with me for regular self-esteem boosting. I did have a presence people wanted to be around, and either way we would have a nice meal together. I should at least give him a chance.

❤

At seven pm I sauntered into the Sutherland Hotel in a black and white striped skirt and black tee. I was wearing heels to add definition to my already toned calves. Walking up and down Arden Street had definitely helped get me into shape for summer – one of the reasons I chose to live in the hilly suburb by the beach.

I put on a smile and strolled over to the table where Simple Simon sat in a black and white Treaty t-shirt, rolling a cigarette. He was a bloody smoker as well. As if the way he mumbled wasn't unattractive enough without a fag stuck to his bottom lip.

'I need a drink, you want one?' I said bluntly. I knew I sounded rude and unpleasant. I probably deserved to be single.

'Hey Alice, great to see ya. Yeah, I'll have a schooner of black beer. Ta.'

How could someone who'd written such a beautiful letter be so inarticulate? I'd always thought the written and spoken word were very different in the white world. It's so obvious in their literature. Aboriginal writing is closely aligned to the spoken word. We write like we speak, and reality is, that's how our people read too.

And what was with the black beer? I thought only old men drank that crap. At the bar, I ran through what I knew about Simple Simon as I waited for our drinks. Simple Simon: hangs out at Koori-oke, has a poster of a Black boxer hanging over his bed, fancies me, wears a Treaty t-shirt, and drinks black beer. If he thought he was doing his bit for reconciliation by doing all this 'Black' stuff, he was sadly mistaken. Either way, I was going to find out what his go really was. I ordered myself a nip of Drambuie, checked to see he wasn't watching, and threw it back, hoping it might help.

The barman shot me a sleazy but sympathetic wink and smile that perked me up a little. I carried my G&T and Simon's schooner of old-man's-beer back to the table, where he was rolling another cigarette. Two drinks later (plus the nips I'd skolled at the bar when it was my shout), and Simple Simon wasn't looking so simple anymore. He almost looked attractive, and I realised I should probably stop drinking immediately. Then he rolled yet another cigarette. I'd lost count how many he'd sucked on since I arrived. The smell made me ill. Before I knew it I leaned towards him. 'Do you plan on kissing me tonight?'

'With an open mouth!' he laughed confidently.

'Well you can forget about having another cigarette, then.'

He tossed the half-rolled cigarette into the ashtray and grinned. We both knew I had the power at that moment, and I grinned too. All of a sudden he *could* possibly be Mr Right and I was really looking forward to that open-mouthed kiss. My short-term mantra for the evening became: *No more alcohol for me tonight.*

We staggered out of the pub, both very conscious any time we accidentally touched, and headed into the balmy night air towards Chinatown for dinner. I sobered up a little over dinner, downing three Cokes and some salt and pepper squid while he chewed away on beef and black bean.

While the pub had given us time to exchange basic information like preferred bands, football teams (he loved Nokturnal and went for the Panthers) and the like, we hadn't really talked about anything of substance, and I still had a list of questions I needed to ask him. I started with the most obvious.

'Why do you sleep on the floor in your living room when there's a bedroom with a bed in it?' Did that sound as logical a question to him as it did to me?

'Well, I like watching telly in bed of a night. Ya know, I can lie on the mattress with a bottle of Coke and packet of chips in front of SBS and have a party for one.' He was a bundle of contradictions – the least likely SBS watcher in the world. Then again, they did screen a lot of European soft-porn films. I hoped his definition of 'party for one' was different to mine.

'Right, well, I hope you don't mind, but I wanted a cold drink and went to your fridge. There was a pot with green liquid in it. What was it?' I couldn't wait to hear this explanation.

'Oh that, that's just the juice from the spinach I boil. It's really good for you.' Yeah, that'd wash down the month-old spag bol in the fridge, too, I thought, but I continued with my interrogation. I wanted to get to the bottom of what really made Simple Simon tick and what made him think we'd have a future together.

'What were you doing at the Covent Garden Hotel the night we first met?'

'I like hangin' out there with my people,' he said, without looking me in the eye.

'What, the wannabe singers and lonely hearts?'

'No, the Kooris. I'm Koori, can't ya tell?' He seemed a little surprised I hadn't understood him.

'Sorry, you're what? Koori? How?' It's not like he was sporting a deadly tan or anything. In fact, he looked almost albino. Identity's not about skin colour, of course, but there are definitely identifying characteristics that most Blackfellas can pick up with their Koori antennae. Language, an understanding of shared concepts and experiences, family connections, *something* – anything that lets you know the other person is one of your kind. Simple Simon didn't have any of it. He wasn't Koori, he couldn't be. I wasn't finished with him, though, and carried on playing the detective.

'So who's your mob? Where are you from?'

'Yeah well, not sure yet.'

Here we go, I thought.

'I only found out six months ago that my great-great-grandmother was Aboriginal. I'm still trying to trace the family tree, so I'm not real positive right now who my people are. I know I'm a Williams. So, I'm Koori too, like you eh?'

How dare he! 'Mate, you ain't nothing like me.' (My own language began to deteriorate as well.) 'Your great-great-grandmother being Aboriginal a century ago doesn't translate into you being Koori. And a Williams? From where? You want to be sure which Williamses you reckon you belong to before you start spouting off, or you'll end up on that bony white arse of yours.'

Simple Simon, Mr All-Wrong, was the latest in the Johnny-Come-Lately-family-tree spreading through the country. If he were smart, he'd just shut up. But on he went about 'feeling out of place all his life', 'always feeling different', and 'family secrets'. It was a common story, of course, but others had more dignity, didn't assume their identity until they were actually sure who they were. I was dying to tell him he'd felt out of place all his life because he was a deadset weirdo and a loser. It had nothing to do with Aboriginal heritage. Why should we all cop the blame for him being a dickhead? He started rolling another cigarette but I didn't care now. That disgusting wannabe-Koori tongue of his wasn't getting anywhere near mine.

'I'm doing the course in Aboriginal Studies at TAFE, too', he blurted out, and I did everything possible not to sing out 'Whoopee'. I was always fascinated how many wannabe Blacks and do-gooding whites went to college to learn what it means to be Aboriginal. Most of them never had and never would actually live it – just read about it, write about it and get glassy-eyed about it.

'So what's with the Anthony Mundine poster?'

'Yeah, well I'm real proud of my brother boy. He stands up for what he believes.'

Brother boy? *BROTHER BOY?* If he started on about 'gubs' I'd have to do something drastic.

'And what do *you* believe Simon? What would *you* stand up for? What racism and discrimination have *you* experienced as a six-month-old lily-white Koori that could give *you* the passion that Anthony has? Did *you* have to deal with taunts and stereotypes based on *your* race growing up? Did *you* ever get called names because of *your* skin colour?'

I stopped then, because he may well have been called names – he was so fucken white it was offensive.

'Okay, so maybe you got called whitey or Casper, but that's because you should really get some sun on your body.'

He just sat there stunned, mouth agape, and obviously offended.

'And what do you know about being part of an Aboriginal community, Simon? You think singing some songs at the pub with Blackfellas when you're pissed *makes* you Black? You think finding out your great-great-great grandmother was Aboriginal makes *you* Aboriginal? You reckon living in Blacktown makes *you* Black? Pulleeaaase ...'

'Aboriginality is spiritual, and it's a lived experience – not something you *find* by accident and then attach its name to yourself. I'm sick of white people deciding they're Black so they have some sense of belonging, or worse still, so they can exploit our culture.'

I was raving. I could tell he had no idea about what I was talking about. He rolled one cigarette, then another, then another. His hands were shaking, and he kept dropping filters on the floor. I was just waiting for him to get up from the table to go smoke any one of those cigarettes, because he'd end up shitting filters for weeks I'd shove so many of them down his throat.

I took a deep breath and looked around to see if anyone else in the restaurant could hear me. 'Well?' I prompted.

'I'm getting the Koori flag tattooed on my arm on Saturday,' he said nervously, hoping it was the right answer. It wasn't.

'You're an idiot!' I proclaimed in frustration. Like the beads and the t-shirts people wore like a second skin to show they were Aboriginal, I knew he believed the tattoo would somehow instill in him his new-found Aboriginality. I'd slap him then and there if he went on to tell me he was going to give himself an Aboriginal name as well. If I hadn't detested him so much at that point, I'm sure I'd have felt a little sympathy. He was suffering a complete identity crisis. I'd seen a lot of white Blackfellas go through it.

Simple Simon really wasn't that simple. He knew exactly what he was doing and saying with that letter he sent me. Trying to align himself with a strong Koori woman to help him infiltrate the community and be accepted by the local mob. He'd probably be asking me to organise a confirmation of Aboriginality for him from the housing co-op in no time, so that he'd have the paperwork at least to say he was a Blackfella. Not if he was the only bloke with the only tongue left in Sydney.

I shook my head. Simon wasn't just the antithesis of Mr Right, he wasn't even Mr Wrong, he was simply Mr Fucked-Up. I asked for the bill. To further cement my views on him, he divided the bill in two right down to the last cent. I left a generous tip to compensate the staff for having to listen to us argue, then we left the restaurant and headed off in opposite directions: he with a fag stuck to his bottom lip, on his way to the train station, and me to the parking station near UTS.

As I walked briskly away he sung out what a lovely evening he'd had and that he'd like to do it again sometime. I responded, 'Thanks, but no thanks', mumbling 'psycho' under my breath.

seventeen

Peta's brainwave: Perfect Paul

Saturday morning arrived soon enough and I was greeted with the news that another rich, skinny famous woman was getting married for the third greedy time. I was so uninterested I didn't even read the name. Who really cared? Wasn't there any *real* news that could go on the front page of the paper?

I turned the page of the trashy *Daily Terror* in disgust, only to learn that Brad Pitt and Angelina Jolie were arguing again. *Who cares!* looked to become the mantra for the day.

I wasn't at all surprised to find an article about a march and hunger strike protesting the government's treatment of refugees rated only two paragraphs on page eight. I was immediately ashamed of myself for even buying a paper and giving money to the fascist media empire that produced it. It was hard to believe that for some this paper was their only form of social education. Real news and issues of importance never even ranked in these tabloids. God knows Blackfellas only made the pages if they were throwing rocks at cops or fulfilling negative stereotypes that soothed the consciences of ignorant racist whites. I declared out loud that I would never buy another paper.

As I took the paper and other recyclables downstairs, I began to psyche myself for Bianca's hens' night, due to start in ten hours. It would take me that long to convince myself that I should participate in such an appalling event, the second-last step in the process of becoming Mrs Wife.

I dropped the paper and empty bottles in the appropriate sides of the bin.

'Morning, Gabrielle!' I hadn't seen her for a while, not since the last time I'd put the garbage out, actually.

'Hi Alice, what've you got planned for tonight? A hot date?' Gabrielle had hope in her eyes.

'No, a bloody hens' night. I can't think of anything worse, except for a kitchen tea. I don't even think I like the guy my friend's marrying.'

'Now Alice, didn't your mum ever tell you that if you can't say anything nice, don't say anything at all?' Gabrielle smiled at me like a wise mother as she walked off. I felt like a bitch. She was right. In an attempt to seek the Buddha within everyone and the positive in every situation, I would adopt a new mantra: *I will only say things that assist, contribute to, or are pleasant about any individual, place or event.* Before I reached my door, though, I was laying bets with myself on how long this mantra would last.

The phone was ringing as I entered the flat, but I didn't answer it in case it was Simple Simon. I let the machine get it and heard Peta's voice: 'Alice, it's me. I know you're there. You want to go to the Ladies' Baths?'

I picked up. 'Great idea.'

It was terrific having Peta living so close, both of us only walking distance from the secluded, women-only rock pool. It was always more peaceful there than the main beach, even if at times it was hard to find somewhere to sit. I was surprised a sundeck hadn't been built there for more women to sit on, but it was still just a natural space. We sometimes pretended to do laps in the pool but mostly we just floated and talked. Peta and I agreed to meet there in half an hour.

I ran the dry mop over the polished floorboards, sprayed some lemon citrus cleaner in the bathroom so that it at least smelled clean, and pulled the shower curtain right around the bath to hide the underwear hanging in there, then donned my expensive new bikini that made me feel like I'd had breast implants. Next I checked for unwanted pubic hairs hanging around the bikini line and plucked a few strays. I had planned on getting a Brazilian wax for summer but chickened out at the last minute. I had a really low pain threshold.

It only took me ten minutes to get to the Ladies' Baths, stake my claim on one of the few rocks left to sit on, and get settled with the latest *Who* magazine. I'd vowed to stop buying papers, not trashy mags. Like AA, it's a twelve-step program.

Peta arrived shortly afterwards. We didn't speak much for the first half-hour: we were old friends, and simply enjoyed spending time together. Eventually, though, Peta sat up and looked at me over the top of her sunglasses.

'So, I bumped into Mickey last night. He tells me you had a date last week. How was it?' Only because she'd asked, I gave a brief post-mortem on what I had chosen to call the 'Simple Simon Scenario'.

Peta laughed but I could tell she felt sympathetic. She did remind me, though: 'No one-night stands, Al – remember to stick to the strategy. See what happens when you don't?' She rolled herself a cigarette and lit up. It didn't worry me when Peta smoked, though I hated it when anyone else did.

I put some sun lotion on my chest, as my boobs hadn't seen the sun for some months, and lay back to absorb the rays. I thought about how many times Peta and I had sat there and analysed our disastrous dates. If the rocks could talk, they'd spill a million beans about our sad attempts at finding love, and even more disappointing attempts at finding decent lovers.

Vitamin D rays from the sun stung my shoulders but I didn't care. I love how it feels to have a good colour up. I started to doze, thinking about what I should wear to

Bianca's hens' night, when Peta's mobile rang. I listened to her making plans to meet people at the Coogee Bay Hotel later.

Snapping her phone shut, she turned to me. 'I've got Mr Right for you! That was him on the phone. He's an old mate of mine. Gorgeous. Slightly damaged goods, but aren't we all?'

I nodded, somewhat unsure, but encouraged her to go on.

'His name's Paul and he's Koori. Thirty-eight, single, straight, has a good job as an engineer. Plenty of walang, and doesn't mind spending it either. He's got perfect skin and he's not precious at all. Yes, he'd be perfect for you.' He did sound perfect, but if he was, why hadn't Peta scooped him for herself? What did she mean about 'slightly damaged goods'? And why hadn't she mentioned him earlier on in my search? After all, Phase I of the strategy was over. I wasn't supposed to be going on any more blind dates.

'Why aren't you going out with him yourself, then? Seems like an obvious thing to me.'

'No, he's not really my type. Doesn't do anything for me, you know, down there,' she said, gesturing to her loins.

'So he must be dingo ugly.'

'No, he's not. He's just not my type,' she assured me. I was no longer a lookist anyway, right? But what did she mean by 'slightly damaged goods'?

'You know we all have some baggage we carry. Don't try and tell me you don't. You practically need a porter for yours, Alice.'

Peta knew me well enough to know what she was talking about, so I trusted her if she thought Paul was okay for me. She promised to arrange something for the next week. Suddenly, the sun shone brighter. Wedding Cake Island was out in the distance and I peered at it hopefully. The prospect of having someone to wake up with on Christmas Day, only three weeks away, seemed almost possible again, maybe even likely. I pushed my straw hat over my face and lay back, imagining Mr Engineer telling our wedding guests that he was the luckiest man in the world.

eighteen

The hens' night

At five pm the alarm on my mobile rang loudly and I woke from my nanna-nap with a renewed interest in the evening's hens' night. Perhaps it wouldn't be that bad after all. Maybe sixteen women having a good time would attract a few guys having a good time, and amidst those few guys might be Mr Right. Yes, perhaps it would be a great evening after all. I had to keep all my options open, even though Paul-the-Engineer was looking promising. I didn't want to put all my unfertilised eggs in one basket.

I showered, shaved my legs, tidied up the eyebrows, and plucked one or two annoying hairs from my chin. Mental note to self: get oestrogen levels checked. I put on my lucky bra and knickers I saved for special occasions, donned my sexy black dress, styled my hair, put on blood-red lipstick, and dabbed a little glitter on the arch of my brow. I was happy with the elegant but fun look I'd achieved in just under an hour.

At six I cruised over to Liza's place, where she had a jug of sangria waiting on the balcony. I commented approvingly that Mrs New-Carpet could take some lessons from Liza on how to entertain properly, but couldn't help noting that she was drinking a lot for someone who'd been off the booze for so long. It really was all or nothing with Liza. Still, I was grateful to have my drinking partner back.

'So what's the deal with hens' nights anyway?' I asked, knowing Liza would have an answer.

'Funny you should ask that. Someone at work told me that the hens' night is meant to *replace* the old tradition of the kitchen tea. So you either do one or the other, I reckon. Get presents for your kitchen *or* go out with your girlfriends. Not both.'

'Don't tell me we were meant to get Bianca a present for this as well?' I asked. It was going to be a 7-Eleven job if we did.

'No way. We just pay for her dinner.'

'That's cool. This whole wedding gig's costing me a fortune. You know, engagement present, kitchen tea, wedding present, outfit, hair, nails, and of course, with the wedding happening out west, we're going to have to stay overnight.'

'It's the western suburbs, Alice. Stop making it sound like it's Broken Hill!' Liza joked.

'All I'm saying is that my own bloody wedding won't cost this much, I'm sure.'

'Which reminds me,' Liza said as she topped up my glass, 'we should book our motel too.'

'See, moooore money.' I rolled my eyes.

'Are you taking a partner?' Liza asked, sucking the alcohol-soaked fruit out of her already empty glass, then refilling it quickly.

'Yeah, well, I'm hoping there's still time before Christmas to meet someone, maybe even New Year's Eve. Else, it might have to be you!'

'Same, same. Mum said a woman she works with has a son who's just come back from studying in the States and—' She jumped up and down, spilling her third glass of sangria over herself and waving her hands about in the air.

'I forgot, I forgot! My cousin Marco, the one you didn't want to meet months ago, he's just arrived home again from Sorrento. He's here for a couple of years this time, working with my uncle's importing business. He's gorgeous, Al, I know you'd love him. The most beautiful green eyes you've ever seen, and tall. He's got the most beautiful head of hair and olive skin, and if he weren't my cousin I'd be taking him myself. I'm sure he'd love to go with you to the wedding. Do you want me to ask him?' She was so excited, and he sounded lovely, which made it harder to say no, but I did.

'I went out with Dannie's cousin Charlie and it caused tension between us for weeks. I don't even want to risk it with you.' I watched her body language to see what she was thinking.

'That wouldn't happen to us. Marco's better looking than Charlie, and I know that's why you didn't like him,'

Liza paced around as if she was addressing a jury, 'And he's perfect for you, Alice. Even though he looks like a true Italian Stallion, he's really a good Catholic boy, at the ripe old age of twenty-nine.' Liza was persistent, and she was making sense, but I wasn't convinced.

'I really think we should leave your family out of my search for Mr Right. I'll just try and get a pub-pash in before the wedding and meet someone too. If not, I'm sure we can coordinate our clothes and take each other – you know I make the perfect date, eh!'

We toasted each other and looked out over her balcony to the block of flats behind. Liza didn't have an ocean view, but it was enough just knowing we were close to the beach.

We had time to slurp down another glass of Liza's 'special sangria' before we left: the hens' night venue had been moved closer to home. Bianca had sent a broadcast SMS out after a few hensters from the east and the north-east had complained about doing the M4, M5 or M2 trip. We were going to Capitan Torres on Liverpool Street in the city's Spanish district (hence Liza's choice of pre-dinner drinks), and then onto the Bristol Arms for some serious seventies and eighties sounds. The night was already looking better than we'd anticipated. The warm glow in my cheeks was a bonus, especially given that I'd raced out without putting any blush on.

❤

A short time later we were eating garlic prawns and potatoes, squid in ink and the best paella I've ever tasted. Liza and I had a slight disagreement on how it was pronounced. She said *pay-ella* and I said *pay-eeya*. Dannie remained neutral and just ate it. As at the kitchen tea, we'd all been given name tags to wear. 'The Bride', 'Chief Bridesmaid', 'The Bridesmaid', 'The Mother of the Bride' and so on. I was grateful that 'Granny of the Groom' wasn't there, and that Liza's, Dannie's and my tags simply had our names. At least if we got lost or speechless, other people would know who we were. We were tempted to write our addresses on them as well for worst-case scenarios, but decided against it.

There was giggling and chatter, and some pretty crappy jokes were being told to the left and right of me. All noise stopped, though, when the Bridesmaid-To-Be mentioned that her hens' night would be in eighteen months' time and she was planning on taking her party abseiling in the mountains. Liza and I couldn't believe it. How had we managed to end up here amongst these people? Our snobbery must have shown on our faces, because Dannie threw us a mother glare – *behave yourselves* – across the table. Dannie's hens' night had been a gorgeous dinner down at the Rocks followed by very late-night cocktails at Level 31. Dannie was the classiest of us, even when she'd been a relatively new mother. She'd sometimes come out with baby food on her clothes, but she'd duck into the loos and minutes later emerge looking almost pristine again. She'd always had natural style.

'Even Bianca can't possibly fit in here.' Liza whispered in my ear.

'Ab-fucken-seiling?' I slurred back in hers. 'How does pre-wedding, freedom-ending socialising with your girlfriends translate into ab-fucken-seiling?'

Liza admitted to my complete surprise that she wanted to do the male strip show Bad Boys Afloat for her hens' night. 'You're supposed to do something daring on your hens' night, but I was thinking going a little crazy at a strip show rather than going crazy rock climbing.' Dannie's eyes even lit up momentarily, but I didn't know if George would give her a leave pass for that. Personally, I thought it was good for women, whatever age, to be reminded of that animal urge to jump a complete stranger in a leopard-print g-string. Not that I'd actually do it myself, of course.

'Pity most of the dancers are gay.' I thought I should tell Liza that up front.

After a few unflattering comments about male strippers, Liza asked me what I'd do for my hens' night. I liked to think I was a little more mature than Liza, who'd only just moved out of home at the age of twenty-eight. Besides, I'd done the Bad Boys Afloat gig more than once, in a number of venues, and with me playing a number of roles. I wasn't the least bit interested in abseiling or going to some old pub in Parramatta as part of my wedding preparations either. I confessed that I'd probably just have a girls' night in with pizza and good friends, but admitted that if someone *happened* to order a stripper, I wouldn't be the least bit offended. Liza looked at Dannie and they both winked, hint taken.

Just as I was trying to get the attention of a very sexy waiter to order another jug of sangria, an ugly pink cake arrived at the table.

'That is the aarrrrglllliieesst looking attempt at a cake I've ever seen,' Liza observed loudly. Unfortunately, the cook was 'The Bride's Cousin' (her name tag said so), sitting immediately to Liza's left. Silence almost strangled the table, and The Bride's Cousin threw a deathly look at my friend. I tried to break the tension: 'Looks better than any cake that I've ever made.' The cousin gave me a grateful smile, but Liza, who was really pissed by then, burst into laughter and fell off her chair onto the floor.

'Leave her there,' Dannie suggested. I wasn't sure if she was serious or not. I *was* tempted to leave Liza there, but helped her up anyway.

'You've never cooked a fucken cake in your life,' she said. 'So my arse looks better than any of your cakes ...' She was swearing, which wasn't like her at all. I couldn't help laughing, though, and Dannie was in hysterics. It was good to be with the girls like this, even though none of us really fit in with the rest of the party. It'd also been a long time since Liza had let all her inhibitions go. I was pleased to see her relaxed for once. She was always so uptight with work.

We all got a piece of the ugly pink cake and a big cheer went up for the cook, who'd bitten into the piece with a ring in it. Apparently tradition says that the hen who gets the piece with the ring in it is the next to be married.

'Riiiiiigggged, rriiiigggged,' Liza yelled across the table. 'She planted it in there, and she knew which piece had it. That doesn't count. Redraw! I want a redraw.'

'This isn't a chook-raffle at the RSL,' Dannie tried to explain, 'We can't redraw, look around the table, love – most people have eaten their cake.'

'Alice should've got that ring. You want to get married don't you, Alice? Why aren't you upset?' Liza was working herself into an unnecessary state.

'Calm down, Liza. It's just a cake.' She had the attention not only of the other women at the table, who were all clearly offended, especially the cook, but also other patrons in the restaurant.

'But if Mrs New-Carpet can get married, then why the hell can't you or I? This sucks.' Mrs New-Carpet got up and left the table. Liza did have a point. If Mrs New-Carpet could scoop a husband, then why couldn't we? I tried not to think about it, and focused on eating the leftover fruit in the bottom of the sangria jug, but I was increasingly aware of how drunk I was, and then suddenly the bill had landed on the table.

Liza, Dannie and I threw in a few extra dollars before anyone could comment that we'd drunk more than the rest of them. Surely they understood that they were all complete losers and the only thing that made them bearable was the three litres of grog we'd each had. Dannie was well and truly pickled, so we put her in a cab and rang George to say she was on her way, before following the crowd from Liverpool Street into Sussex Street, Bianca leading the way. I noticed the women at the front of the group wrestling with a huge bag, then passing things around. The penny finally dropped as I saw the women struggle to put them on – they were tiny little pseudo wedding veils. One by one they were being fitted to each henner's head. Bianca had a metre-long white one and everyone else had smaller pink ones. The big bag made its way to the back of the group, towards Liza and me. Liza said it for me: 'No way am I putting on some fucken pink tulle mini-veil because someone else is getting married.'

As luck would have it, the bag reached us empty. For some unexplained but much-appreciated reason, we were two mini-veils short. The others felt bad for us, but we both said with sincere gratitude, 'We'll manage.'

Before we knew it, we'd paid our $20 entry fee to the Bristol Arms and elbowed our way to the bar.

'More wine?' Liza shouted over Katrina and the Waves, but it was more a statement than a question. She grabbed the bottle by the neck, left the ice bucket on the bar and headed towards the first of the three dance floors. Lots of bodies were walking on sunshine, bopping along to some of the coolest music from the seventies. I loved it.

The evening became more of a haze the later it got, and Liza and I staggered between floors, minus the other henners. Before long I had some young gun gyrating against me to the sounds of the Hues Corporation singing 'Rock the Boat', and I started to feel seasick.

I love that my bedroom faces east and gets the morning sun — except when I've had a big night out. The temperature was already twenty-eight degrees and it was only seven-thirty. My room was like a sauna; the day was going to be a scorcher. I rolled over to see myself naked in the lone full-length mirror that hadn't been thrown out when I feng shui-ed my flat. I decided that the final mirror might have to go as well.

I hadn't made it under the covers when I got home, and I was lying on top of the bed, my clothes scattered across the room. My lucky bra hung on the doorknob like the warning sign used in a share house I lived in during uni. It meant 'Do Not Disturb', which translated to 'Sex In Progress'. I dozed on and off for an hour before my door buzzer went. I pulled on my knickers and cupped my breasts in my hands as I ran to the intercom.

'Yes?' My voice was croaky.

'Someone's hungover, then.' It was Peta. I threw on a top while she came up the stairs, then ran out to open the door and found her there holding two carrot and ginger juices.

'Moornniinnng, Missy ... oops, didn't interrupt anything did I? I see you've got your lucky undies on. Should I come back?' she asked, knowing full well that I was there by myself — I wouldn't have answered the door otherwise.

'Very funny Peta. What the hell are you doing up so early on Sunday morning? Piss the bed or what? And how did you know these were my lucky undies?'

'Just went for a run and thought I'd bring a juice and some good news to my friend. I was with you when you did that big shop for sexy underwear when you thought that surfer-dude was 'the one', remember? What was his name? Julian?'

'Jason.'

'Yeah, Jason, the left boob guy.'

'So what's your good news?'

'Saw Pauly yesterday at the pub. Gave a rave 'bout you, told him how smart, sexy and staunch you are. Didn't even need to suggest you guys go on a date. He asked me for your number straight away. I gave him your mobile number. Is that okay?'

'Absolutely! And here's cheers to someone *else* seeing this underwear in future.' My hangover seemed a little easier to manage all of a sudden.

We sat there for an hour while I milked as much information out of her as possible about my soon-to-be blind date. We both giggled like teenagers and she said, 'I have a good feeling about this, Missy. If he's not Mr Right, he's gotta be Mr Almost-Right. We just have to face the fact that sometimes that's the best you're gonna get.'

I was so excited about the prospect of the date with Mr Almost-Right that I smiled, inside and out, and sighed a big Sunday morning sigh.

I'd just started thinking about what to wear and where to go as the phone rang. I motioned for Peta to answer it, but she ignored me, and went out to the sunroom to read the paper.

It was Liza, naturally.

'You piss the bed too, Liza? Thought you'd be in bed at least till lunchtime.'

'No way, I've got loads to do around the house, and some case notes to write up. Working for the ALS is a twenty-four/seven job, you know. Just thought I'd see how you were feeling.'

In a sudden flashback, I had a vision of me kissing someone on the dance floor, and blurted out, 'I think I kissed that boy last night, Liza.'

'Yeah, you rocked his boat all right – and his mate's.'

'What?' I was horrified. 'Tell me you're joking, please.'

'What's the drama? You looked really sexy and you were having a great time dancing. Everyone wanted to be near you. Hell, half the girls wanted to kiss you too at one stage.'

'I'm not a lesbian, Liza. You know that don't you?' She thought I was a lesbian too!

'You're such a drama queen sometimes, Alice. No-one thinks you're a lesbian. And no-one cares you pashed two boys. You're allowed to let your hair down occasionally. But I don't know that your behaviour falls within the strategy, does it?'

I went into self-punishment mode straight away. Two decades of Catholic upbringing and sexual suppression made it easy for me to torture myself about my uncouth behaviour. Sure it was all right to kiss a boy or two or five when you were a teen, and even if you're a bit older, you can get away with it on New Year's Eve. Surely when you reached your late twenties, though, and you were a teacher at a Catholic school, and were supposed to act as a role model, you shouldn't behave like that anymore. By twenty-eight, you should be more refined and dignified – or at least a little more discreet.

'But Liza, that boy was about twelve.' I felt sick. 'You might have to defend me in court!'

'He was twenty-one, and he thought he was king of the castle smooching with you. Don't know about his mate, but just think of it as your community service to youth.'

My mantra for the day would have to be: *Don't worry about what you might have done yesterday, focus on what you can do tomorrow.*

nineteen

Waiting for Paul to call

It was a long week waiting for Peta's mate Paul to call. He didn't. I didn't turn my mobile off at all, but left it on silent when in class and in bed. I spent every recess and lunchbreak in the staff room, and even arrived early and left late just in case he'd lost my number and tried calling the school. My attendance was commented on more than once, and while I mightn't have been a good role model for my students, the principal seemed to think I was setting a great example for the teachers. If only they knew the truth.

All week, though, the phone was strangely silent, and I was fearful that it wasn't working, or that perhaps I was somehow out of range. Or, maybe, just maybe, Mr Almost-Right wasn't that right after all. I didn't want to seem anxious, so I didn't contact Peta, thinking I'd only mention it if she asked.

With only a couple of weeks until Christmas it was time to put the tree up and attempt to put some fairy lights in the windows. I dragged my pathetic three-foot green plastic tree from my linen press and stood it atop my coffee table in the living room window, overlooking the foot of Arden Street. I really wanted a new tree, but with the costs of Bianca's wedding sapping my funds, I'd have to make do with the no-frills number for another year.

I'd bought decorations at the clearance sales last year, so at least I had new shiny purple and silver balls. Enough balls and a bit of tinsel strategically positioned and I wouldn't even see the tree underneath.

It took me all of ten minutes to dress the tree, but almost an hour to hang the lights in the window. I'd failed year after year to get it right. I refused to ask Dad to help me after Mum's comments about looking after myself and not relying on him. I was determined that this year I'd be blinking along with the rest of the neighbourhood without his help. It was moments like these that I made a mental list of all the things a husband would be useful for: hanging fairy lights, changing the oil in the car, killing spiders and all those kinds of boy jobs.

I always emphasise that I don't *need* a man, but there are definite reasons for wanting one around anyway.

I wrapped a few presents and put them under the tree to add some more Christmas cheer, but I knew I was really just trying to keep busy as I waited for Paul-the-Engineer to call. 'You're an idiot,' I mumbled to myself. He didn't even have my home number, so why or even *how* would he ring me here? Why was it that Simple Simon was smart enough to look in the phone book but Paul-the-Engineer couldn't manage it?

I concluded that all men were basically emotional cripples or completely illogical or both. Even though they didn't think like we did, they could at least be considerate enough to think like each other, so that there was some consistency to their irrational behaviour. Santa would be coming in less than four weeks and it was unlikely that I'd get anything like a man in my stockings. Strange thing was, until I'd set myself the thirtieth birthday deadline to get married, I was fairly happy with my single life. Now I seemed to be disappointed a lot and either waiting by the phone for it to ring, or in Simple Simon's case, not ring.

I put on my bikini but it didn't make me feel at all sexy. How could I? I had my period and had been bleeding heavily for twelve hours straight. I felt completely bloated, and needed some sun to perk up my mood. Grabbing Linda Jaivin's *Dead Sexy* from my bookcase, I headed for the Ladies' Baths, where I'd have a good chance of bumping into Peta and a slight chance of seeing Liza, if she wasn't swimming at her usual Bondi spot.

Two hours later, I'd started going a golden brown and had read almost all of my book. At least I now knew the sex life I *could* be having. Sex with firemen, sex involving scarves, handcuffs, stilettos and so on. I planned on dragging out my stilettos and scarves when I got home, keeping them on hand for my next night of passion. Assuming I'd have one eventually. Mental note to self: be sure and put them somewhere not likely to gather dust too easily. Then I took a dip, needing to cool off in more ways than one. The water was chilly, and I didn't even go under, just wet myself and lay back down for a while.

As time passed I grew tired, and decided to ease myself off the steps into the rock pool for one last paddle before heading home for a nap and a night in front of the telly. Wading in, I saw arms waving and flapping about in the water in front of me. It was Peta.

'Well hello there, Missy … how's ya been?' Peta was so positive and energetic at times it could be almost depressing.

'I'm great!' I lied, with as much enthusiasm as I could muster. 'What about you? Haven't seen you all week.'

'Yeah sis, been out bush working on a community education model for the department. Just got back this morning.' Peta was always travelling, meeting interesting people and seeing a lot of countryside, but she made a point of saying 'It's all work,' trying to convince us that she never had time to shop or sightsee.

'Right. So what are you up to tonight? Thought I might see if Dannie can escape the kids and Liza will stop working long enough to watch a movie and share some food. Might throw some roo in the wok.' My body was screaming out for red meat.

'You doing that "fusion" thing again, Alice?' Peta did the inverted commas hand gesture. 'What is it this time? Roo curry? Sweet and sour roo? No, no, no, let me guess – Mongolian roo?' She fell back in the water, laughing at her own joke.

'Very funny. On second thoughts I might make Chilli Con Kanga. Yeah, and we can have margaritas to start.'

'Sounds good. I'll bring some tequila and corn chips and see you round eight.' She splashed off without even a mention of Paul-the-Engineer and I felt like bursting into tears. I decided I'd ask her later that night, and headed for home, where I'd have to take some vitamin B6. Maybe there was a message waiting for me on the machine, I thought, and upped my pace. There wasn't.

At seven pm I started to cook. I laughed out loud as I got the roo mince out of the fridge, recalling a conversation I'd had with Gabrielle a few weeks before.

'Oh, I don't think I could eat Skippy.' She'd frowned at me when I invited her over for some roo and bok choy.

'But don't you eat pork, Gab?' I was surprised at her immediate and definite refusal to eat my cooking.

'Yes, of course, I love it!'

'Well pigs roll around in mud and eat their own shit, don't they? How could you possibly have a problem with kangaroo?' I said matter-of-factly.

Gabrielle chuckled, and said I was disgusting. Eating different things really was just a state of mind wasn't it? I loved roo, hunted it three times a week at the supermarket: it was low in fat, high in protein and really cheap. I often wondered what the checkout chicks thought as I went through the register with roo kebabs, mince and steaks alongside Lindt chocolate, cottage cheese, strawberries, ice-cream, tampons and Pantene. Did they see that women of all colours are united by the need for beauty products, good chocolate and high-protein foods?

Eight o'clock on the dot and Peta was on the buzzer, tequila, corn chips and bag of lemons in hand – a hangover waiting to happen just standing in my doorway. Dannie and Liza were trudging up the stairs right behind her.

'Hi there Missy, picked up a movie too. *The Way We Were* with Redford,' Peta said.

'And Streisand,' Dannie panted. 'Know it?' She handed me the DVD.

'Know it? It's my all-time fave movie,' I said.

'Perfect choice,' Liza added enthusiastically. It had been months since all four of us had been together. Meeting at my place seemed to be the only time we ever managed it. We were all so busy.

We finished the chilli and corn chips and had a couple of potent margaritas as we went, then sat back and soothed our chilli mouths with bowls of French vanilla ice-cream while we watched our movie.

On screen, Barbara tried to make her passion for politics mesh with Robert's passion for himself. I cried at the end: Barbara was still fighting for her political causes and Robert was happily off with a nice young wife. Sometimes true love was simply not enough.

Dannie reckoned she could see me in Streisand's character, Katie, which didn't help. With all Katie's passion, she still ended up without her man.

'Do you reckon you could sweep aside politics for the love of a good man, Al?' Liza asked. It was a fair question. Had I reached the point at which I could give up my passion for politics to keep the man I loved? I wasn't quite sure.

'I'd only really know if I met someone as gorgeous as Robert Redford, I guess.'

'Closest thing you'd get to that round here is Robert Redfern!' Dannie was in her funny-girl mood.

I couldn't wait any longer to ask Peta about Paul. 'Your mate, what's-his-name, Rob, John, Jack, Sid? Anyway, he hasn't called.' I was trying to be as casual as possible.

'Paul,' she said.

'Paul, yes, I knew it was a one-syllable name.' Trying to act semi-uninterested.

'Who's Paul?' Liza and Dannie chorused.

'He's a friend of mine,' Peta told them, then looked back at me. 'Sorry, I forgot to tell you – his grandmother's dog died on Monday and he went back to Newcastle to stay with her for a few days. She was really upset about it. I think he mentioned something about buying her a new dog. You know, to keep her company at night. She's all alone up there. He told me to tell you he'd call when he got back, which is tomorrow I think.'

'Sounds promising, Alice! Just don't be pushy,' Dannie said.

Liza quickly followed her lead: 'And don't expect too much on the first meeting.'

Peta looked slyly at Dannie, then me. 'And before you ask, he's gorgeous.' I wasn't even listening to them. Of course Paul was with his grandmother, because that's the kind of gentle, caring and considerate guy he was. That was what made him so ... right. So *Mr Right*.

I smiled. I hadn't been rejected, and there were still two outcomes possible: that we lived happily ever after, or that *I* rejected *him*.

'Call for you, Alice!' Mickey had answered my mobile in the staff room as I made a cup of tea. My heart was pounding – it had to be Paul. Why now, why lunchtime, when everyone is here and will hear me sound like a teenager being asked to the school dance?

'Thanks, Mickey, who is it?' I said, as though I wasn't expecting a call.

Mickey covered the mouthpiece. 'Don't know, but he sure sounds cute.' Everyone suddenly stopped talking. There had been rumours for months that Mickey was gay, and most of the nuns and male teachers weren't at all happy about it. The principal had given a lecture about 'inappropriate, non-Christian behaviour' at an all-staff meeting recently, staring at Mickey and me the entire time. She had used the words 'promiscuous' and 'alternative lifestyles' a lot. So much for Christian tolerance.

I grabbed the phone, took a deep breath and said calmly, 'Alice Aigner.' Clear, non-warbled, confident. Nice work, I mentally congratulated myself.

'Hi, it's Peta's friend, Paul.'

'Oh, hi Paul. Peta told me about your grandmother losing her dog. I hope she's feeling brighter.' I was cruising through the conversation.

'Yes thanks, she's fine. I bought her a little black Scottish terrier and she's happy as Larry, as they say. Anyway, I was wondering if you'd like to have dinner with me this Friday, if you're not already busy. I understand it's close to Christmas and you've probably got a million invitations—'

'No I haven't,' I cut in, 'I mean, I have nothing on this Friday. I'd love to have dinner with you.'

'Great, I'll call you Friday to organise where to pick you up and I'll book a table for eight o'clock. By the way, do you like seafood?'

'I love seafood, Paul.'

I spent the rest of the day analysing word by word, sentence by sentence, everything Paul-the-Engineer had said in our two-minute phone call. He'd bought his grandmother a black dog. Black rather than white, that was a good sign, I thought.

He had invited me to dinner on a Friday night, too – it was a very positive sign. A lunch invitation is good, but a dinner invitation is much better. Dinner means a serious invite. A date on a Friday is a really serious date, much more serious than dinner on a Tuesday or Wednesday. He didn't say Thursday, because it's payday – not like Simple Simon. Yes, it was certainly looking good.

He'd thought I'd probably have lots of invitations. That meant he thought I was very popular. That everyone must want me at their parties. Of course they did, but how did *he* know that? I was grinning from ear to ear.

He was going to pick me up. He had a licence *and* a car. I loved him already. I wondered what sort of car it was. Didn't matter – as long as dinner didn't have to be on a train line, I didn't care.

Mental note to self: buy Peta something extra special for Christmas. She must've fed him a whole heap of info to make me sound deadly and desirable.

By half past twelve on Friday, most of the teachers and students had gone home, following the final assembly for the year, but I stayed back and pretended to clean out the fridge as a gesture of community service. The principal was suitably impressed but it was really an excuse to wait somewhere quiet for the phone to ring. I didn't want to be driving or shopping when Paul called me, so staying put until he had seemed the smartest option. My phone hadn't completed its first ring when I picked up.

'Hi Paul, you just caught me leaving school. How are you?' It sounded a bit false, but it was okay for an I'm-pretending-not-to-be-waiting-for-a-phone-call response.

'Great, looking forward to tonight. Hope we're still on. I've booked a table at the Harbourview for eight. That okay?'

'Sounds fab,' I said, trying not to sound eager. *Interested*, but not too eager.

I gave him my address and hung up before I wet my pants with excitement or said something too ridiculous. I was like a three-year-old whose parents had just told her the Wiggles were coming to dinner.

Paul said he'd pick me at seven-thirty, so I had approximately seven hours to get ready. I headed straight to the beautician to start the process of making myself look irresistible.

❤

'Okay, Kathy, do your magic. Brows, lip, chin, bikini, in any order. I want a deluxe facial, too.' Kathy was my trusted beautician who made an eyebrow wax feel like a surgical procedure. I loved it. Her attention to detail was matched by no other, and I always felt like I was on the operating table as she checked and double-checked that each brow was an exact replica of the other.

Eyebrows done, a quick line of hot wax across the upper lip, and any remnants of hair were completely gone. 'There's nothing on your chin, Alice,' Kathy said, 'Whaddya want me to do that for?'

'Because I can feel something there, a hard hair, just one. If I can feel it, he'll be able to feel it as well. Pluck it, wax it, nuke it if you have to, but get rid of the little sucker or it will ruin my night.' I was a woman on a mission.

'Who's the lucky guy then?'

'Oh, he's perfect, a friend of a friend, bought his grandmother a dog this week ...' I told Kathy every detail of the two two-minute conversations I'd had with Paul. She could tell I was excited. Kathy knew what a shortage of decent men there was in Sydney. She was single too.

I shut my eyes and imagined the night ahead of me – until she ripped the hair from my bikini line.

'Shit, Kathy, you trying to kill me or what?'

'Sorry, stubborn little buggers. You've got a couple of ingrowns – I'm going to have to dig them out.'

She soon declared the job done. 'Anything else? What about the legs?' She felt for any fur that might be growing.

'You know my theory, Kathy. If I shave my legs before I go on a date, it means I'm expecting to have someone else's hands running up them.' I *was* supposed to be sticking to the 'no sex until the third date' rule.

'Well don't you? I mean, what was the purpose of the bikini wax if you weren't thinking along those lines?'

She was right of course, but I always liked to act as if I were a bit saintly. I decided I should get my legs done just in case, for whatever opportunities might present themselves.

It hurt more than the lip, brows and bikini combined, but I felt completely touchable at the end of it. I might just have to ask him to touch my legs anyway, I thought, just to get my money's worth.

Waxing done, the lights were dimmed as I donned a terry-towelling strapless wrap and lay back for my deluxe-state-of-the-art-top-of-the-range-only-Kathy-can-do facial. I immediately relaxed as Kathy's hands massaged my décolletage, neck and face. Creams, exfoliants, oils, steam, hot towels and gentle fingers made their way over my face. I drifted away and imagined Paul-the-Engineer doing the same honours once we were a couple. Yes, that was another reason I wanted a husband: face, neck and head massages upon request. Mr I-Bought-My-Grandmother-a-Scottish-Terrier was sure to be the sort of guy who would see this sort of request as a privilege. I started to plan a lifelong program of massages and caressing.

Before she finished, Kathy massaged my hands and arms, and explained that she'd resisted squeezing the odd blackhead for fear of causing unnecessary holes in my face just before dinner. I looked and felt like a new woman, and could have gone straight home to bed and been happy. I had a better offer though – and it had been a while since I'd been able to say that.

At three-thirty I had less than two hours to buy something new to wear. Although my wardrobe was bulging, it was essential that I wore something specifically purchased to impress my date. Something to mark the beginning of my new life, a life that included Paul-the-Engineer, black dogs, lonely grandmothers and endless massages.

I held my breath and thanked Biami as the first shop I went into delivered the sexiest outfit I had worn in years. A slinky blue satin slip dress falling just below the knee. I was getting more and more excited.

'I have a date! With an engineer,' I proclaimed as I handed over the cash to the salesgirl.

'He won't be able to keep his hands off you.' The shop assistant was excited for me.

'That's the plan!'

Next I went three doors down Crown Street to my stylist Denis (who preferred to be called Den Den), pleading with him to do a quick wash and blow-dry, promising he could do the whole bridal party for the definitely-going-to-happen wedding. Den Den didn't even charge me – he believed, like me, that Paul-the-Engineer was the one. It seemed the whole world – the universe – was on my side.

Home by six, I eased myself into a tepid bath instead of a steamy shower, so as not to disturb my hair. I sat with a glass of red in hand and tried to calm down. With just over an hour to make myself gorgeous and prepare to begin the first night of the rest of my life, I set myself a new mantra: *I am beautiful, the world is beautiful, I am surrounded by love, I will be loved, I am loved.*

twenty

Mr Too-Right?

I looked at my watch impatiently, waiting for the buzzer on my door to go off. The shot of schnapps I'd had after the glass of red to calm my nerves had only made me feel ill. I loved how the Austrians drank schnapps for 'medicinal purposes' – to warm the legs in the cold, to settle the stomach after dinner, to cure almost anything. No wonder I never needed an excuse to drink – it was something I'd inherited from my father's family.

Finally, the door buzzer went. I took a deep breath, mumbled *I am beautiful, I will be loved*, turned the knob and gave a rehearsed smile. I needn't have. I was greeted by a warm, friendly face and a handsome – very handsome – man (even from a lookist's perspective). My nerves melted away.

'Hi.' Paul moved in and gave me a gentle peck on the cheek. No awkwardness at all. I breathed a sigh of relief. He was, it appeared at first glance, normal. 'Ready?'

'Yes, absolutely,' and before I knew it we were downstairs in his car, driving towards the city.

'Peta tells me you're an engineer.' I wanted to know all about him, while I discreetly checked out all the gadgets on the dash of his sporty silver Peugeot coupé. I loved his car. I loved that it had electronic windows and a CD player and if you pushed the dash, two drink holders popped out – they would be great for those drives in the country we'd be taking. I loved that we didn't have to take the train. I loved that I was a passenger for the first time in a long time. Was I that easily impressed?

'That's right, with the city council. First Blackfella they've ever had as an engineer. Actually, I'm the only Blackfella on indoor staff. You'd think a big city council like ours would have heaps of Kooris on staff. I mean, with so many living in Sydney.'

I was already falling in love, no doubt about it. From the moment I'd opened the door and seen his Colgate-ring-of-confidence smile beaming back at me, I knew it. Before I even got to the linen suit, and his oh-how-I-want-to-crawl-all-over-you aftershave hit my nostrils, I knew it. Now Mr Beyond-Right, Mr Perfect, had something intelligent to say about the lack of Blackfellas at the local council. He was my dream come true. Yes, I *would* be Mrs Paul-the-Engineer. *I would be Mrs Right!*

Soon we'd parked the car and I found myself seated across from him at the table, wine ordered, his jacket off – biceps pushing through his crisp white shirt – and I was completely hypnotised. I was in a dreamlike state. It was Friday night, I was looking the sexiest I'd ever looked, not a chin-hair in sight, and I was dining with Paul-the-Engineer, the only Blackfella working as indoor staff at Council, who drove his own car, could order a bottle of wine, *and* smelled like heaven.

'Oysters – I love oysters, don't you?' Paul smiled, raising one to his lips, the lips I was already dreaming about kissing.

'Oh yes, I love the way they slide down my throat.'

'You have the last one,' he offered.

'No, I'm right, it's all yours.' If I ate one more oyster I'd rip his clothes off right there at the table. I didn't need any more aphrodisiacs. It was better to be safe than sorry, or horny for that matter.

It was destiny: Paul and I ordered the same meal, salmon with olive tapenade. It came with garlic potatoes, which neither of us touched – clearly we were both expecting a kiss at some point during the night. I didn't even look at or really taste any of the food at all. I felt full of the sight, smell, touch of Paul.

The night was perfect. He laughed at all my jokes, told me stories about his youth and explained why he loved his grandmother so much. Both his parents had been killed in a car crash, and she had raised him. At the end of the meal he insisted on paying the bill.

'Only if you let *me* buy *you* dinner sometime soon.' I'd read in *Cleo* years before that one sure way to secure a second date was to let him pay for the first one and then offer to buy the next yourself. (Of course, if you didn't want to see him again, best to go Dutch.) Even men who aren't interested in a relationship will almost always say yes to a free feed.

'You don't have to, but I'd love to have dinner with you again,' he said. As *Cleo* had promised, it never failed.

We strolled around the Rocks, until Paul suggested we have a cocktail at the Park Hyatt, overlooking Circular Quay. My heart jumped. 'Park Hyatt sounds perfect, great idea.' The Park Hyatt was where I'd planned on spending my wedding night. How did he know? It wasn't just a coincidence. There were so many bars in the area, and he could have suggested any of them. It was a sign for sure. (Or maybe it was because it was the only *decent* bar close by.)

We sat and had a martini and just watched the world go by on foot, ferry and water taxi. Every time I looked at him, his smile made me weaker. I was either very drunk or falling in love. Or maybe he had slipped something in my drink? There'd been a lot of that going on around Sydney, but he was Peta's friend and I had no reason to mistrust him.

Paul couldn't be faulted. He was charming, sexy, good-looking; not only employed, but had a career. He knew who he was and didn't have to carry his Koori family tree round with him. He didn't have a tat or wear Koori beads to cement anything. It all seemed too perfect. I was suspicious.

'So you finished your degree in ninety-five – what were you doing before that?'

'Oh, just hanging around, as young lads do.'

He couldn't have been *that* young in ninety-five. Counting back quickly, I calculated he must have been around twenty-eight when he finished his degree.

'So, what is it that young lads do in their mid-twenties?' I couldn't help myself.

'Come on now, Aunty, what's with all the questions?' Paul mocked me, and I felt like a right twit. Why was I acting like some daggy old woman? He must've been out sowing his wild seeds or whatever boys do in their twenties, but, as Mum would say, 'That's what boys do.' He wasn't being mysterious; there just wasn't any need for me to ask so many questions on a first date – the best first date of my life.

I excused myself and went to the ladies room, surprised to find I was a little wobbly on my feet. I'd had a bit to drink, but not half as much as I would've if I'd been out with the girls. The martinis had gone straight to my head. Or perhaps I was just love-drunk.

I liked using toilets in flash hotels with marble vanities and fancy lights and mirrors; beats having to queue up in a nightclub where going to the loo is simply about necessity. The Park Hyatt toilets were the kind you'd like to spend time in. I fixed my make-up, checked my bra straps weren't showing, and made sure there wasn't any lint on my dress or paper stuck to the bottom of my shoe. I was looking so good I was turning myself on.

As I made my way back across the restaurant to our table, I wondered if Paul was going to kiss me or not. He'd only touched me lightly as we crossed the road and guided me out of the way of traffic. Maybe he wasn't interested at all. Maybe he was gay. Maybe he was just not that into me. Maybe I shouldn't have bothered leaving the garlic potatoes on the side of my plate.

'Paul, I thought maybe we could have a walk around the Opera House – what do you think?' I asked, before I even sat back down.

'I was just thinking the same thing. Ready now?'

He'd been thinking the same thing, oh my god, we were so connected, so in tune. It was scary. He got up and took my hand and my ridiculous theories were instantly washed away. He's *wasn't* gay, he *was* interested, and he *was* into me.

His strong engineer's hand squeezed mine, and my body went warm. Just hand-holding could have been enough to satisfy me.

Strolling along the quay, we saw a mime artist, a didj player, a clarinetist and a muso who sang just like Tracy Chapman. We were impressed.

We walked around Bennelong Point, wondering out loud what the corroborees were like there before invasion, when all the local clans would gather for their bush opera. The past and the present blended into one as we shared a moment that only Kooris could.

At the front of the Opera House we stopped. I leaned out over the rail that runs right around the edge of the pavement and looked out over the water. Paul stood behind me, arms around me. It was perfect. His mouth went to my neck and I closed my eyes so that my sense of touch was heightened. He gently caressed my collarbone and shoulders with his lips.

I slowly turned around. He was taller than me; I raised my eyes to meet his. They were smoky brown and I just lost myself in them. Our lips touched, slightly parted, and his tongue met mine. We kissed slowly, standing pressed hard against each other. When we eventually broke apart, I felt relaxed and comfortable, waiting for a sign from him, waiting to find out what would happen next.

He kissed my forehead, then the tip of my nose, and pecked my lips once more before motioning me back towards Circular Quay. We didn't speak, but walked arms linked, me holding on tightly to his arm. His bicep was massive! What do they say about men with big biceps? Or was that feet? I didn't care.

We stopped for a last drink at the Aqua Bar. I decided to have a lime and soda, so I could remember how good the sex was in the morning. I could definitely break the three-date rule: Paul was the one, Mr Right.

As I reached the bottom of my drink, he checked his watch. 'I should get you back to Coogee and me back to Rozelle soon, I've got a big day tomorrow. I'm building a deck and the boys are coming round at eight.'

'Sorry?'

'I'm building a new deck. I've been wanting to do it since I bought the house two years ago. Finally got the plans approved last month.' He beamed, but I just stood there, gobsmacked. I wanted to shout at him: *Build what deck? What about me? The night's over because you want to build some bloody deck you haven't mentioned all night?* I could hear Dillon chanting in my head: *He's just not that into you, he's just not that into you.* Why had Paul even started something back there if he had no intention of finishing it?

I realised I was thinking like a bloke. I'd always said how nice it would be to be able to have a passionate, sensual kiss, or kisses, that didn't necessarily always have to lead to sex. I should be grateful for the gentleman in front of me.

I smiled at him and said, 'I've had a lovely evening, Paul, the best in a long time. I hope you have good weather for your work tomorrow.' We headed home, to our separate beds.

❤

At eight am the door buzzer went. The weather was grey and overcast so I was still in bed. I knew who it was. It was Peta and Liza, wanting to get the goss on the Perfect Date. They both knew I wouldn't answer the door if I had a bloke with me, so I let them sweat it out, letting them at least *think* I was still in the throes of passion. Peta put her finger on the buzzer, though, and left it there for what seemed like ten minutes. I scrambled out of bed before the neighbours could lodge a complaint.

'I know what you were doing, Missy ... Can read you like a trashy novel.'

'How did you know he wasn't here?'

Liza handed me a smoothie and pulled some mangoes out of her bag. 'Thanks, love,' I said, and took a long suck on the straw.

'He's been talking about his deck-building for the last two months,' Peta said, 'and I'm going over there later. Anyway, he's not that kinda guy, too much of a gentleman.' It was true, and I grinned at her.

'So how was dinner?' Liza asked, mango dripping from her chin. I'd always believed the only place to eat a mango was in the bath: they were just so messy. Maybe Perfect Paul and I could eat mangoes in the bath in the happy future ahead.

'It was perfect. He was perfect. The food, the view, the whole thing. Perfect!'

'Wow, that's a big call, Alice. Haven't heard you rave about a date like that, ever!' Peta was proud that she'd set up the perfect date.

'Yes, well, my friend, I think you may have done good this time. Your friend Paul is simply perfect. I think he'd be a great husband.'

'Don't get carried away, all right? You need to have another date before you send out the invites and order the flowers.' Peta didn't want the whole perfect set-up to come crashing down just because I was being too … organised.

'She's right, Alice, just one step at a time, okay? Maybe that's something we should have put on your list of strategies for *not* meeting Mr Right. *Don't rush things.*' Liza went to the list on the fridge and pencilled it in.

I wasn't really listening to either of them, though. I was just content to go get dressed and head off Christmas shopping with my two friends, a spring in my step: I would be Mrs Paul-the-Engineer's-Wife by the time I was thirty.

twenty-one

He's the one, he's the one!

I woke on Christmas Eve to the sound of the garbage truck making its way up the hill. I'd missed them. I'd never missed them before – I couldn't believe it. I ran downstairs just in case I was wrong, but I was so tuned in to the sound of that truck I was sure I was right. The problem was, I'd been sleeping so soundly since meeting Perfect Paul that I was always dreaming, not wanting to wake.

There it was, though – not just my empty bin back in its designated spot, but a little present on top of it: a gorgeous cactus plant in a white porcelain pot with a red Christmas ribbon round it. Paul must have put it there after he'd dropped me off the night before. He was so thoughtful; he'd put my bin out too. Who had brought the bin in, though? And why hadn't the plant been stolen? Or ended up in the garbage truck? It didn't add up. Had Paul come back this morning to drop off the gift and brought the bin in then? Surely he wouldn't have had time to do that. No, he definitely wouldn't have had time. Was I over-analysing again? Probably. I was, as Dannie would say, one of those women who think too

215

much. I had to stop. I smiled at the cactus and walked back upstairs. *He's the one! He's the one!* I told myself.

I was happy but confused. I'd had the most romantic two weeks of my life with Paul-the-Engineer. We'd spent nearly every night together since we'd met. We'd eaten at Café Sydney following a day of Christmas shopping in the city; had fish and chips at Bondi (and the backpackers didn't even bother me); gone swimming at La Perouse at dusk and to a movie at Moonlight Cinema in Centennial Park. I couldn't even remember what the film had been, we'd been so absorbed in each other. He'd planned something special for Christmas Eve as well. I'd never met a guy who was so well organised, and I loved it.

Between all of that, we'd also managed to meet each other's friends over Christmas drinks. Everyone commented on how lovely we looked together. And we did. I knew it, he knew it, but neither of us actually said it to the other.

There was just one thing wrong: I couldn't help wondering when I might get the chance to grip on something other than his bicep. I called Dillon for his opinion.

'Look Alice, it sounds like he's into you.' Phew! 'Thing is, all men want the same outcome; it's just that some take a different route to get there. Some take the direct line and expect it straight away; nice guys will go round the long way; but essentially it's the same goal.'

'That makes sense to me. He's a really nice guy. He probably hasn't even been thinking about it that much. He's very respectful of women.'

'Okay Al, now you're just being naive. He's thinking about it all right. He's just respectful, as you say, though I reckon strategic might be a better word. Either way, he doesn't sound like he's gay, and he calls you and you have dates, right?'

'Yes, lots of calls and dates. And he gave me a cactus. Mum and Dad have met him, and they thought he was gorgeous. Mum's been calling me every day asking about him. She reckons we'd have beautiful kids.' Her calls hadn't even bothered me really. At least she was no longer trying to set me up with Cliff, and she'd stopped accusing me of lesbianism.

'You know she means *she'd* have beautiful grand-kids.' We both laughed.

'Yeah, I really wish she wouldn't confuse her desire for me to procreate with my desire at the immediate time to get laid.'

'Okay, too much information. I don't want to hear my sister speak like that, so I'm going. Good luck.' Dillon hung up, but I felt better for having spoken to him. I settled down to wait for Paul to pick me up for our Christmas Eve date.

❤

At twelve-thirty my buzzer rang and I grabbed my handbag and headed out the door, feeling comfortable in my white linen dress with navy flowers. I'd dropped two kilograms in the last couple of weeks, with excitement and increasing infatuation overtaking my appetite.

Paul looked gorgeous as ever, casual but sexy as hell. We drove towards the city and I tried to guess where he was taking me for lunch. He parked the car at the Park Hyatt and walked me to a room on the third floor overlooking the harbour. On the balcony was a feast of delights: fruits, cheeses and a cold seafood platter to die for.

'I hope you don't think this is too forward of me, but Merry Christmas, princess.' He kissed my hand and passed me a glass of champagne. It was the perfect moment. I pulled him close to me and we got lost in a passionate kiss. Always hopeful, I'd shaved my legs that morning just in case. I'm sure it didn't matter to him at all, but I felt glad I had as he ran his tongue up my legs and then kissed my knees. My knees! Who'd have thought they were an erogenous zone? It certainly wasn't something I'd ever talked about with the girls – but I would be. Toe-sucking yes, but knee kisses never. This was new for me.

Move higher, move higher, move higher, get to the thighs, get to the thighs. I was impatient with desire. Just one quick orgasm would be enough to satisfy me –

and then we could take the next four slowly. He was relishing every moment of making me wait, though. He'd get his – and he did, after I got mine.

❤

We finally got to the food on the balcony later in the afternoon and we were ravenous. Luckily everything was still almost edible. We left the oysters – too risky – but devoured just about everything else on offer, then I devoured Paul again, the most delicious of the lot.

The evening played out much the same. Paul made up for years of selfish lovers I'd suffered, and we both agreed that once you'd had Black you'd never look back.

'Life doesn't get much better than this,' Paul said. Suddenly I felt my Christmas gift of a CD and a tie weren't half as romantic as his offerings. Paul loved them nonetheless, and I'm sure he understood that a teacher's wage went nowhere near an engineer's income.

❤

I woke to the sun streaming through the balcony doors.

'Merry Christmas, princess.' Paul handed me a card. It was signed, 'To many more together, Paul.' Enclosed was another envelope and inside, two tickets to the Sydney Symphony Orchestra in January.

'Wow, I've always wanted to see them. How did you know?'

'Our friend Peta gave me a whole long list of things I could buy you. I thought I'd start at the bottom of it and work up. Thought it might have been a little too soon for the diamond brick.'

'I'll kill her, and thank her at the same time.' I went blood-red. I was already embarrassed at the expense Paul had gone to. I'd spent years paying for men who'd rather buy beer than food and rather place bets than book tickets or weekends away, though, so I figured it was karma – my turn to be spoilt.

Wanting to make the most of my Hyatt experience, I had one last lazy shower before we headed off to spend the rest of the day at my parents' house. Lunch was lovely, loads of food and laughs and presents. Dad played the perfect host, making sure the home-brew was flowing. We didn't have one family fight, and for the first time, we all had partners at the same time. Larissa and Arnie's girlfriend Cindy had both come along.

Arnie, Dillon and I carried out the family tradition and played hours of board games. Paul was a star at Trivial Pursuit, but wouldn't indulge in Twister. I was glad to opt out, not wanting to split already under-pressure-from-lunch seams. Arnie and Paul laughed hysterically at each other's childish jokes and I saw a side of my brother I'd never really appreciated before. He was a very funny guy, and easygoing to boot. I watched him all afternoon and saw why the girls liked him so much. While Dillon was wise, Arnie was fun. And tall, dark and handsome. He got the best of both Mum and Dad.

'Hey Paul, pull my bonbon,' Arnie said for the third time, 'Trust me.' And they both killed themselves laughing again, as Arnie acted like an old man and farted every time Paul pulled on the other end of the cracker. I blamed it on the after-meal schnapps we'd all had. Another Austrian tradition Dad carried out on special occasions: either everyone at the table had a nip or no-one did. There was terrible pressure on those who didn't want to drink, but then again, I'd never met a non-drinking Austrian. Funny thing was, contrary to media perceptions, I'd met quite a few non-drinking Kooris.

'Time for a spell, you two funny guys.' Larissa was holding her belly, sore from enjoying the laughs all afternoon. 'Let's perv on Michael Bublé for a while,' and she loaded a DVD into the machine. Everyone collapsed to spend the rest of the day in front of the telly.

Mum called me to the kitchen. 'Well?'

'Well what?' I was confused.

'Well, what's going on with you two? You look perfect together.'

'It's only been two weeks, Mum and, yes, he is a bit perfect.'

'You know if you're a bitch to this one, you *will* grow old all by yourself. You'll *have* to become one of those

221

lesbians, then. Is that what you want? I'm starting to think it might be.' I didn't even bite. It was clear where my irrational genes had come from.

I looked at Paul again, his eyes fixed on the movie, his profile just gorgeous. Dillon was sitting with Larissa and Arnie was with Cindy, whom he'd been with for several months – a record for Arnie. It looked like she was in for the long haul. Everyone seemed happy and content. There was something really right about the whole scene.

At seven we said goodbye to the family and went back to my place. Paul stayed for the first time, because he would be going away until New Year's Eve. This new sense of closeness made me happy. We took a stroll along Coogee Beach before sundown and bumped into Peta with her new man Michael, a colleague from the department. (She was big on the saying 'Don't dip your pen in the office ink', but it didn't seem to apply in this case.) We walked together for a while and it was really nice, like a double date. Surely I wasn't becoming one of those sad 'I'm no-one without my bloke attached to me' kind of girls?

Paul and I had an early night, and the sex was even better than the day before. I was almost glad he was going away for a week – I was already exhausted.

❤

I woke late, around ten. It'd been a long, busy night. Paul had left already, but not before going out and buying the paper and some pastries for me. I declared him a saint as I bit into a buttery croissant. A short note from him wished me a happy Boxing Day and said he'd call later. He hadn't wanted to wake me.

I spent the next four days at the sales and just hanging out at the beach, realising how much I really loved being around Paul. I missed his company – he was so easy to talk to and fuss over. I counted the days down until he'd be back, and started planning January, as we would both be on holidays.

I hadn't asked Paul to Bianca's wedding yet, but as luck would have it, Liza had met a bloke too, some guy named Luke she'd pub-pashed at the Palace on Christmas Eve. As she was taking him, we agreed that I should ask Paul as soon as he got back to Sydney – but I couldn't wait that long, so I called him.

'Would you like to come to my friend Bianca's wedding on January twenty-third?' I wanted to be organised, and to organise him if need be.

'Of course, princess, I'd love to. Just tell me where I have to be and when and I'll be there. Is it formal? I've got a tux.' He sounded as excited as the bride. Of course he'd have a tux – Mr Perfect would.

'I can't wait to see you, Paul.'

'Me too, princess, I'll see you tomorrow at yours, okay? Say four o'clock?'

I smiled as I put the receiver down and started to plan what I'd wear on the New Year's Eve Spectacular harbour cruise we'd be attending. The invite read 'Dress to the 9s,' so I thought long, black, backless, with a shawl. Paul hadn't seen that outfit and would love it. I didn't think I should have my knees showing, just in case.

At four sharp the buzzer went and I wondered for an instant if I should be offering Paul a key. Perhaps it was too early for that. I'd forgotten about it by the time I'd opened the door. He thrust a bunch of multi-coloured gerberas in my face.

'For you, my princess.' He smiled his Colgate smile and I went weak at the knees. The door had barely shut when we were on the floor making up for lost time.

We made our way to the dock at Rose Bay to meet Peta, Liza and Dannie, along with hundreds of other party-goers. There was a real New Year's buzz in the air, even if we were a little late starting the celebrations.

'Where the hell have you been, Missy? We were buzzing for twenty minutes.' Peta was a little miffed.

'Left without us, did you?' Liza asked. She wouldn't have believed that Paul had left me handcuffed to the bed while he went and showered, so I didn't even begin to tell her. I was just grateful that I hadn't peed myself with laughter while I waited for him to uncuff me. He'd threatened to shave me as well, while I lay there exposed, but I gave him a mouthful about itchy regrowth and told him I'd put him on rations if he came anywhere near me with a blade.

Within half an hour we were among a large flotilla of craft on the harbour, all seeking the ultimate position for the midnight fireworks. Both Paul and I had that post-coital glow. So did Dannie and George, I suspected, as the kids were with his parents for three days. We all settled ourselves in some chairs on the upper deck and sat on a couple of bottles of champagne as the harbour lights just passed us by. At that very moment I could've died an extremely happy women.

At midnight the fireworks went off over the bridge. They were beautiful, but I couldn't help thinking that they had cost $2 million, and yet there were people living in the streets of Sydney, Aboriginal communities without decent facilities, and soup kitchens that could use that kind of funding. I hesitated, but then voiced my concern to Paul. He agreed, adding, 'And what about what it does to the environment?' I hadn't spoiled the moment – he felt the same way! We kissed away the fireworks and toasted each other and the New Year. The year I would probably get engaged, and move another step closer to becoming Mrs Right. Mrs Alice Aigner-Right.

twenty-two

Someone else's wedding

'Rise and shine, princess, big day today.' Paul was more excited than Bianca probably was. He tickled my face with kisses to wake me.

'Can you kiss my knees instead?'

'It's seven-thirty, you better get up if we're going to be on the road by nine.' He kissed my breast lightly and pulled me out of bed.

One thing that both impressed and irritated me about Paul was his ability to organise. I soon understood how my own scheduling of everything pissed other people off. Paul was always on time and always thinking ahead.

'I've already got petrol, packed a little something to nibble on in the car, and left enough space in my bag for you to put most of your gear into. No point in taking two bags, is there? Oh, I've also got a spare suit bag for your dress.' I wasn't sure if I was annoyed or appreciative.

The phone rang and he answered it in five seconds flat.

'It's Liza – she wants to know what time we're picking her and Luke up. I said ten past nine. What do you think?' He'd already told her what time, so I didn't know why he was asking me. I really wished Liza would get a car, I was always chauffering her around. But because Paul was perfect, he'd never complain about something so insignificant as giving someone a lift somewhere. I had to stop being so negative.

'Nine-ten is fine, sweetheart.'

Dannie and George had left the eastern suburbs before us, having to drop the kids off at his parents' on the way. It was the kind of extra organisation that Paul would be great at. No doubt about it, he'd be an excellent father. Liza, Luke, Paul and I made our own fun driving out west, laughing like adolescents at the name 'Rooty Hill' and singing along to some old hits by Racey, Amii Stewart and Blondie along the way. 'The Tide is High' brought back memories of a trip to Fiji for Liza and me, and we threw each other a glance, thinking of fun times in our younger days, back when we really were happy to be single. I liked Liza's man Luke, though: he was really laid-back. A little rough around the edges, but a down-to-earth kinda guy – a good match for Liza, who didn't handle bourgeouis bullshit well. I could fake handling it when I had to. It was a requirement of working in a private school.

'We should all take a trip somewhere together!' Liza shouted. I saw an immediate flash of doubt cross her face, as she realised that we'd only been seeing these fellas for a short while. Luke and I were both quick to agree with her, even if we didn't quite mean it, and I gave him brownie points for being smart enough to take what Liza said seriously and act interested. Paul, on the other hand, remained silent. Was he thinking it was too early to make plans together?

'What about you, babe? Not interested in a trip to the tropics?' I needed to know. After all, I was in this relationship for the long haul.

'Oh, yes, of course – it's just that I'm not that big on flying.' He wasn't at all convincing.

'Have a few drinks!' Liza and I chorused, sounding like the complete lushes that we were. Paul laughed, but didn't say anything else. I was still curious, but didn't push it.

We had a pit stop so Liza and I could talk about the boys.

'So, Luke's nice, Liza,' I called to her from my cubicle as we both peed.

'So's Paul. He's really generous and friendly. Dannie thinks so too.' So the girls had been gossiping, fair enough. Would've been more worried if they'd had nothing to say about him.

'Did you notice he hesitated about your idea of a trip? He didn't seem keen to me.' I was worried, and it would play on my mind until we'd cleared it up.

'Al, don't go over-analysing again. He was probably just concentrating on the traffic.' I thought that a strange response from a non-driver, but she was probably right.

We arrived at Rooty Hill around ten-thirty and went straight to our hotel, not far from where the ceremony would be held.

Paul and I spent the afternoon getting ready: him resting and me doing my nails, hair and make-up. I wore a slinky red dress with the highest heels I'd ever owned. Peta had loaned me a diamond necklet and earrings and I felt like a million dollars.

As I held my hair up, Paul did up the clasp on the necklet.

'Do you really not like flying?' I was going to get to the bottom of this. I had to know whether we'd ever be able to take a trip together or not.

'You look beautiful.' He smiled as he took me in with his eyes.

'*Flying?*'

'Short flights are okay, like in Australia, but I wouldn't be keen to go much further.'

'What about Broome?' I asked. I'd always wanted to stay at Cable Beach Club and ride a camel along the sand at sunset.

'Yeah, Broome, I'd love to go there and ride a camel.' Everything automatically seemed all right again.

'You know it's quicker to fly to Noumea than to Broome,' I said, 'so we could still do the Pacific with Liza and Luke.' Actually, I thought, we could do both over the next couple of years.

Paul looked doubtful again. 'It's the flying over masses of water that frightens me. What if we crash?'

'We've got more chance of survival crashing into the water than into the desert between here and Broome.' He and I both knew I was right, but we didn't have time to argue – we had to leave for the wedding.

The ceremony took place at Watt's Cottage. Paul told us that it had been built at the turn of the century by Frank Watt, a descendant of the original white settlers in the Rooty Hill area. I smiled back at Liza and Dannie, proud that my man was a walking fount of trivia. I think Liza felt a little put out, as I usually relied on her for such details. She couldn't keep her hands off Luke, though, so she was over it pretty quickly. Dannie and George seemed to be soaking up their time away from the kids, enjoying just being a couple for a while. Dannie actually looked our age again, and not really grown-up, as married women with kids often do. Bianca had started looking that way from the moment she got engaged.

As we stood around waiting for the bride, Liza and I tried to dodge the hateful stares of the women from the hens' night who'd been offended by Liza's outbursts and our drunken antics. The cake-cooker sure as hell hated Liza, and only managed to throw me a barely-there smile. I was hoping that no-one would say anything to Paul about my community-service-to-youth at the Retro Club that night.

The bride arrived in a black Cadillac that oozed class and style and I wondered what had happened to the daggy hen I'd seen walking through the city with a veil and sixteen henners a few weeks before. Her father helped her out of the car and the entire group took a deep breath in awe.

Bianca wore a long, sleeveless silk dress with a sweetheart neckline and a fitted bodice with little pearls that matched the ones in her ears. Her long white satin gloves and long chiffon shawl draped across her décolletage and flowing down the length of her dress were impressively elegant. Bianca looked angelic as she carried her bouquet of white lilies and beamed at Ben, her groom, waiting anxiously for his wife-to-be. Just before she reached him, though, he pulled up both trouser legs to reveal one blue and one gold sock. Most of the men cheered. Dannie laughed, but I didn't get the joke.

'What's it mean? I don't get it,' I whispered in Liza's ear. She just shrugged – she didn't get it either.

The ceremony was romantic and sincere; tissues dabbed eyes all round me. Paul had his arm around my waist and leaned over to whisper in my ear, 'You'll make a beautiful bride.' I tilted my head to meet his peck on my cheek, happy, but thought to myself, 'Will it be by the time I'm thirty?'

As the bride and groom left to have their photos taken, the six of us went straight to the reception centre. The venue was the local club, and pre-dinner drinks consisted of schooners and Barcardi Breezers in one of the many bars – we could take our pick. The guys went hunting for the best bar for us eastern-suburbs types in full wedding regalia. We settled for the unbelievably named 'Rooters Bar' – the only one that didn't have footy TAB and card machines ringing in the background.

Before long, most of the other wedding guests had made their way to Rooters Bar, too, but we kept to ourselves, making small talk, reliving the ceremony and discussing the bride's outfit. I was conscious, though, of the single women guests looking awkward and out of place. I'd never understood why wedding invites weren't automatically extended to partners – at least for those who wouldn't know anyone else attending. One or two women were obviously by themselves; I smiled at one, who stopped to talk.

'Hi, I'm Tara. I'm actually here by myself, do you mind if I hang with you guys? I'm feeling a bit awkward.' God, I felt for her. I'd been there before.

'Sure, no worries. I think there's a couple of other women in the same boat. We're on table seven if you want to change your place card around too.'

She appeared to be glad about that, and brought one or two other girls into our circle. I patted myself on the back for not becoming one of those 'I've got a man now, so the rest of the single world can drop off' kind of women. I'd lost count of the times I'd been at weddings by myself and had to make small talk until the bridal waltz was done and I could leave.

After a few drinks, Liza and I were soon giggling like schoolgirls. Dannie was getting a bit of a glow up as well, but it had taken her several days to recover from the hens' night and she'd vowed to take it slower at the wedding. Luke seemed like a bit of a boozer and downed at least five schooners while we waited (I was counting). My Paul just smiled and organised everyone, and George sipped a couple of bourbons.

When we were finally ushered into the reception room, Liza and I burst into laughter, turned to each other, and said, 'You've got to be kidding.' Ben, Bianca's now-husband, was a minor league player for the Parramatta Eels, and the colours of the decorations were blue and gold. Blue and gold serviettes on every table, blue and gold candle centrepieces, blue and gold balloons forming an arch along the wall behind the bridal table. It looked like Grand Final night. We both looked at each other and said, 'The socks.'

'Don't be bitches. It's Bianca's day, she can have it any way she likes,' Dannie said.

She was right, of course, but Liza and I were both gobsmacked that the classy bride had not only endorsed the decorations, but helped to put them up. It got worse: as we headed to our table, right up the back, we passed a champagne-glass pyramid.

Before sitting down, Liza moved a few name tags around and made sure the few people there who liked us were on our table. We didn't want too many single pretty ones, though: we were both new to our relationships and didn't need any outside competition this early on.

Seated, we waited for something decent to drink, as music started to play in the background. Regurgitator followed Powderfinger followed Silverchair and Something for Kate. Even Paul commented on the unusual repertoire for a wedding dinner.

Liza, Dannie and I got stuck into the carafes of wine on the table, until Paul offered to save us from the dreadful hangover the cheap wine would bring on. We put down our glasses of moselle in shame as he walked off into the fluorescent light towards the bar. 'He *is* gorgeous', I said, as much to myself as to the girls, who agreed with me.

I couldn't take my eyes off him, admiring his rounded butt in his tuxedo. Thankfully George and Luke had worn tuxes, too, or we'd all have had to leave. They were the only men attired so formally, and the girls and I were all dressed to the hilt. Collectively we stuck out like sore thumbs.

Liza and I carried on bitching about the appalling decorations, the cheapness of things and the lack of class we saw as inherent in the western suburbs. Dannie was disgusted. She was always telling us about the snobbery in her Paddington street, and now she became a vocal advocate for the 'down-to-earth suburbanites', Bianca and Ben.

'For someone who works in community law, Liza, you can be incredibly bourgeois and pretentious when you want to be.'

'Yeah, Liza,' I added in support.

'You too, Alice!' Dannie said. Thank god, Paul came back at that exact moment with a bottle of Yellowglen – 'the best they had,' he said.

'Oh, this is going to be a looonngggg night,' Liza said to no-one in particular.

Half an hour later, Bianca and Ben finally arrived to a rowdy fanfare. We all stood clapping as they walked through the archway of chicken wire covered in blue and yellow paper flowers to ABBA's 'I do, I do, I do, I do, I do'. It was the best music played so far.

After dinner, the best man took his place at the microphone. He was a bald-headed, goateed, stocky bloke with a tooth missing in the front and a shirt too tight around the collar. 'Mr and Mrs Willis, ladies and gentlemen, Eels-supporters,' he started, and the room went up in a chorus of 'Oi, oi, oi!'

'I am Christopher, otherwise known as the Crusher, and I'll be your MC for tonight. I 'ope you've enjoyed your meal, dessert is in the form of wedding cake, and we'll be carvin' that up straight after the speeches.' Liza slumped back in her chair, both hands wrapped around her glass, and rolled her eyes. Crusher rattled on for half an hour about how Ben loved Bianca almost as much as football, and their plans for her to give birth to an entire Parramatta side in the next few years. I couldn't understand how Bianca could find any of the speech funny, but she appeared to be laughing constantly. Maybe I had been at St Christina's too long, maybe Dannie was right. I was a bourgeois Black, and so was Peta. (It wasn't hard to be in the Aboriginal community – you just had to have a job and own your own car and you were regarded as middle class.)

We toasted the bride and groom as newlyweds and Crusher wished them the best for their honeymoon to Noumea. The thought of the honeymoon set me off again. I nudged Paul.

'I've always wanted to go to Noumea. What about it? You and me? We don't have to go with the others, if that's what you're worried about.' He didn't answer.

Why he was reluctant to travel with me? Perhaps with his mortgage and new deck, money might be tight – that was understandable. The man wasn't a bottomless pit of cash. I should've thought of that earlier.

'There's often good specials on, you know, second person goes half-price. We could wait for the best deal, doesn't have to be straight away or anything.' All I wanted was a glimmer of interest at this point and I'd be happy.

But Paul just grabbed my hand, pecked my cheek and told me I shouldn't talk through the speeches.

'I might have bad table manners, but at least I'm not afraid to fly,' I sulked.

Up on stage, Ben said that Bianca looked so beautiful he was glad he'd married her, and we all ooohed and aaaahed. When he commented that the bridesmaids looked stunning, though, I couldn't help myself.

'Oh puuulleease. They look like sticks of fairy floss in those dresses.' Liza agreed, but I looked at Paul to make sure that he did too. To my sheer horror, I saw that he had started in on the carafe wine. I'd clearly upset him.

Every speech was more appalling than the one before, and the telegrams didn't bring a change of pace. One after another made reference to Ben's own 'performing eel', with puns on scoring, tries and the sin-bin. Crusher seemed to have found his calling in life. We were all grateful when the wedding waltz was finally called and Bianca and Ben took to the floor to Shania Twain's 'From This Moment'.

The DJ took the microphone from Crusher: 'Okay girls, if your man doesn't ask you to dance now, he doesn't really love you.' Very subtle. Liza and I stared straight ahead, not knowing where to look. Paul took a firm grip of my hand, not saying a word, but led me onto the dance floor, and Luke followed suit with Liza. George and Dannie had beaten us there.

Paul was a brilliant dancer, but he was uncharacteristically quiet. I tried to make eye contact, but his eyes evaded mine. He just pulled me closer and said we'd talk about it later.

'I wish they'd cut the cake so we can leave. I want to get Luke out of that tux.' Liza was really into Luke, and fair enough, I thought. I also wanted to get Paul back to the hotel to talk – or at least make up – but I really thought we should stay until Ben and Bianca had headed off.

I couldn't wait to see the cake. I imagined it in the shape of a football, or perhaps it was one of those huge ones that a cheerleader might pop out of. Liza and I were both pleased to see it wasn't blue and yellow, but a standard white-iced fruitcake – although we would have been happier with a mud cake. The cake was cut and everyone took to the dance floor again for what seemed like hours. Paul and I only danced to a select few: things weren't right between us. I was angry with myself for being pushy.

Then the floor was cleared by Crusher, who was rounding up all the single women for the tossing of the bouquet. 'Come on all you girlies, shake your twats over this way!' He'd had way too much to drink, but no-one seemed to be saying anything about it.

Luke and Paul encouraged both Liza and I to be in the running, but we knew there was nothing more pathetic than women our age fighting over a bouquet of flowers to see who was supposed to get married next. 'Up you go, girls,' Dannie scoffed. She saw the humiliation as our payback for being mean. She was spared the embarrassment because she was married.

Liza and Dannie both knew I planned to be the next, but no bouquet was going to make it happen any faster, especially in light of the mess I seemed to have gotten myself into with Paul. Glaring at Dannie, I stayed put. Paul asked 'Don't you want to get married?' It wasn't a proposal, of course, but I wasn't sure if he meant *ever*, or if he meant *next*, or *to him*, or what. I was more confused than I'd been an hour before, and that was something.

Then it was time to throw the garter. Crusher was a little over-enthusiastic: he struggled to hold the mike and have a chance at catching at the same time. George attempted to take the floor, but Dannie swiftly pulled him back into his seat as we laughed. Both Luke and Paul joined in the rumble to catch the garter, but neither was lucky; Liza and I were relieved.

We formed a guard of honour as Bianca and Ben left for their honeymoon, but I could only think about getting back to our hotel so I could talk to Paul. I wasn't quite sure why, but I felt the need to apologise.

We were all well over the limit, so we got a cab. Paul and I didn't speak or touch at all, sitting in the back seat. I don't know if Liza and Luke could tell – they were both comatose.

Back in our room, Perfect Paul hung his suit up properly and then had a shower. By the time he came to bed, I was two-thirds asleep. He gave me a peck on the forehead.

'Good night, princess.'

♥

Morning brought seediness and sunshine.

'Do we need to talk?' I said hopefully.

Paul just held me, gave me his Colgate smile, and said 'Later', as he went to kiss my knees. Who was I to argue? At ten-thirty our phone rang. Luke and Liza were waiting in the foyer. Dannie and George had already left to pick up the kids.

All was as it should be in the world of Perfect Paul and Princess Alice as we cruised along the motorway back to the eastern suburbs and civilisation. None of us could wait to get to the coast, as the overcast day was proving anything but cool. Liza and I talked again about the prospect of the four of us taking a holiday to the Pacific at some stage. We'd both been to Fiji and had worn the islands out over there, so we tossed up between the Cook Islands or Samoa.

Paul finally joined in the discussion. 'I don't have a passport.'

'That's a cinch, only takes a couple of weeks to organise. You should do it anyway, in case we want to go somewhere on the spur of the moment.' Paul still looked concerned, but things seemed to be okay again. I'd just have to workshop his fear of flying.

We dropped Liza and Luke at Bondi and headed back to my place, then on to Coogee Beach, where we spent the afternoon, the sun streaming down and the alcohol gradually seeping out of our pores. Just before dark, Paul suggested a drink at the Coogee Bay. I was surprised; he knew it wasn't one of my favourite hangs. There were too many backpackers, and the number of brawls there had been growing in recent months too, but I wanted to please my man any way I could, so I just said, 'Sure.' Getting to my feet, I started to brush the sand from my legs.

''Ullo love, wanna drink?' The half-pissed Pommy backpacker's accent got my back up straight away.

'No thanks. My boyfriend's getting me one.' Where the hell was Paul? In fifteen minutes I'd been approached four times. It was never that way when I was single, I thought, and I set off through the beer garden looking for him.

'Here she is.' Paul put his arm around my waist and handed me a lukewarm drink.

'I thought you must be queuing to get served.' Why had he left me standing like an idiot for fifteen minutes?

'Oh no, I just bumped into an old mate of mine. This is Cropper.' His tattooed and bearded mate didn't look like a mate at all, more like a crony. Given a choice, I'd have preferred the backpacker who'd just pinched my arse to Cropper, but I was polite.

'Hi. So how do you know each other?' I always liked to know someone's context; where they fit into other people's worlds. Especially now that Paul's world was mine as well.

'Just around,' Cropper mumbled evasively, and took another sip of his schooner, looking away.

'Where around?' He didn't look at all like the type of character Paul would normally hang out with.

'Your woman asks a lot of questions, Pumper.'

'Pumper? What the hell kind of name is that, Pauly?' Paul pinched my waist slightly, laughing nervously.

Cropper stood up. 'I'll get us another beer, Paauully. Would the little woman like something?'

'No thanks, I'm off.' I was pissed off, but I was trying hard to be the understanding girlfriend, conscious of the fact that I hadn't actually *been* a girlfriend for some time. I kissed Paul quickly. 'Why don't you stay and have a drink with your mate, and come up when you're ready?'

❤

At ten, Paul stumbled in my door absolutely rotten. I let him sleep where he fell on the lounge, a bit disturbed

243

that my Perfect Paul had changed so much in the last twenty-four hours. Then I reminded myself that he looked after me when I'd had too much to drink. I gently put a blanket over him and kissed his forehead before going back to bed.

twenty-three

I've got a Valentine!

I'd been looking forward to Valentine's Day for weeks, ignoring all the cynics who say it's nothing more than a commercial scam to sell flowers, chocolates and tasteless red underwear. I've always admitted that I'm an ad exec's dream audience when scouting the lingerie outlets in Double Bay arming myself with the sexiest underwear I could buy. This year I made a special trip. I bought a black chemise and dusky-pink bra with matching French knickers (red is so tacky and obvious for Valentine's Day). I didn't concern myself with comfort, as they weren't meant to stay on too long anyway.

At home I did a fashion parade for myself. I lit some candles, pulled the shades and struck a few practice poses to see which were the most flattering. There were only three out of about fifteen that did any real justice to my curves. These would be the ones I'd use with Paul.

This year would be perfect. Not like last year, when I'd had no-one to buy lingerie or pose for. Last year had been awful. I'd been feeling depressed and unloved, and took a rare sickie from work, not wanting to see all the obscenely huge bunches of roses I'd imagined being delivered to the staff room. ('Yeah, right,' Mickey had snorted. 'For this lot?') Mum was having dinner at the RSL with Dad, and asked me along, but I'd decided to stay in with Norah Jones, a block of chocolate and a bottle of Moët. By eight pm I'd been convinced the whole Valentine's Day thing was a plot by happily married marketing executives to make usually happy single women feel bad, so that they'd go and spend lots of money to make themselves feel better.

This year I had decided to treat myself. On February 13, I took myself to the Korean Bathhouse in Kings Cross for some pampering. It was my first time there. I spent three hours bathing, steaming in the sauna and being scrubbed, massaged and shiatsu-ed. It took me some time to get used to it, but once I had, I never wanted this indulgence to end. I lay naked on a vinyl massage table as a Korean lady scrubbed every inch of my body with her tiny hands. From the tips of my toes right to the backs of my ears, she didn't miss an inch, or a millimetre for that matter. I had to strain not to pull a face as she scissored my legs apart and scrubbed between my thighs, lifted my breasts and scoured my butt. My mother would definitely have regarded it as a lesbian act, so I vowed never to tell her about it.

Later I sat in the ginseng bath and scanned the room, hoping that no-one would notice I was checking them out. I was relieved to find that I wasn't that different to other women. I realised how hairless I was, though, and also noted that many of the other women there had incredibly small breasts. I actually began to feel quite good about being a DD myself. I compared stretch marks and cellulite and realised I was doing all right for a woman my age. My self-esteem didn't rise, but it didn't plummet either, so all in all I thought it was a valuable pre-Valentine's gift to myself.

I woke on Valentine's Day to the sound of the surf and started the day by pounding the pavement up Arden Street towards South Coogee. The morning sun kissed my cheeks and shoulders as I walked east to the headland, down along the beachfront and up to the Ladies' Baths. The air was full of the chatter of old women excited about their early morning dip. I breathed in the sea tang and filled my lungs with the peace I only ever found when I was at home in Coogee. My mantra was: *I am surrounded by love, and I am loved.*

I turned back, walked past Barzura to see if there was anyone in there I knew, then headed home, wondering if there might be flowers from Paul waiting for me. There weren't, but I wasn't worried – there was plenty of time yet.

Sweat dripped down my spine as I took the steps to my front door two at a time, stripping off the minute it closed behind me. As I lathered myself in the shower, aware of how clean my skin felt after the scrub the night before, I heard the familiar beep of my mobile and knew that a text message was coming through. It was only seven-thirty, a little early for messages. I hadn't dried myself completely when it went off again. My heart jumped in anticipation, but they were only messages from Dannie, hoping I'd text her back, because she didn't think George would get her anything. George was a bloke's bloke, but he sometimes showed up with roses from fashionable Oxford Street florists. Dannie was proud that her man, although he rarely bought flowers, made sure they never came from a bucket at the mixed-business shop down the corner. Another message arrived, this time from Mickey, just to tease me.

I replied to both and then sent a couple messages to those I thought would appreciate the beep of their own phones, including Paul. He sent one back:

Happy Valentine's Day, Princess

Then I heard the sound of the postie's bike, surprisingly early, and squashed my face against the window. I should have just opened it and saved myself the job of cleaning the smudge afterwards. Peering desperately down on Arden Street, I saw him flying down the other side of the road, delivering post to the shops. I figured by the time I got downstairs, he'd likely have already done my block of flats.

He was still there when I arrived at my letterbox. He'd brought me only my phone bill, my rates bill and a real estate agent's flyer saying 'We have buyers in your area.' Nothing from Paul. I looked at the bills and commented to the postie, 'Bill, the only reliable man in my life!' He laughed and said, 'Well he must be gay, *and* he's two-timing you, 'cos he's in my life as well.'

My feet were heavier going upstairs than they had been coming down; it was time to go to school.

Driving to work it was obvious what day it was: bouquets of flowers were travelling through crowds, workmen covered in dust carried long-stemmed roses for their wives, and schoolboys and girls hugged stuffed toys. It made me smile. Jewellery shops seemed to be busier than usual, with couples shopping for engagement rings. I looked at my own fingers. Soon *I'd* have an engagement ring. I was sure of it.

I blamed Mum for my obsession with Valentine's Day. Ever since I could remember, she had always given Dad something: a card, chocolates, a cake. I used to buy gifts for Dad to give to my mother when I was in school. I'd meet him at the gate, arm him with his romantic weaponry and send him inside to his valentine. When I left school, he suddenly started buying the roses himself, stuffed toys, a plant. Even cards. He never wrote on them, though, just left them in the paper bag from the newsagent. It was about the effort he'd made to buy it. Mum knew that. In more recent years, he'd started taking her to the RSL for dinner as well. That was the joy of growing old with someone.

Mum always gave Arnie, Dillon and I a Valentine's Day surprise as well. We all knew they came from her, but there'd be a parcel on the table from a secret admirer for each of us. It was really cute – until I was twenty-one and she was still doing it. Then one year it just stopped, but the damage was already done. I was an addict.

This year I had Paul, so I didn't need to worry. Mum and Dad didn't need to invite me to the RSL for dinner. I didn't need to take a day off work or buy my own flowers or champagne. It was all taken care of and I was anxiety free.

❤

At school many of the senior girls had boyfriends, so there were red hearts, teddy bears and a few flowers in the room. I thought I'd lighten the history lesson up and see how much the girls actually knew about Valentine's Day.

'I see some of you are into the international day of love, and a few of you are even lucky enough to have received gifts. Does anyone know how or where the first Valentine's Day happened?' I turned to write 'Valentine's Day' on the board.

'Someone told me it's named after a woman named Val and a guy nicknamed Tiny and they were so in love, their village – probably in France somewhere, because the French are the most romantic – declared a Val and Tiny Day, which became Valentine's Day!' one student sung out, only to be mocked and jeered by the other girls. 'It's just a theory,' she responded.

'Well, you're not completely off base – there is some French involved.' I looked around the room at the class. They were interested, but no light bulbs were going on above heads. I could see they'd need some help. 'Anyone want to have another guess?' One hand slowly crept up.

'Yes, Clair?'

'I know there's a Saint Valentine – has it got something to do with him?'

'Actually, yes. Valentine was a priest in Roman times. He died on 14 February 269 AD, after being jailed by the Emperor Claudius. The priest apparently left a note to his jailer's daughter and signed it "from your Valentine". Some say that Pope Gelasius set aside the day Saint Valentine died, Februrary 14, as a day to honour him, and called it Saint Valentine's day.' I was writing the main points on the board.

'But where did the love and romance come into it, Miss?'

'Good question, and yes, this is where the French are involved. Charles, a Duke of Orleans, was taken

251

prisoner by the English, and from his cell in the Tower of London he sent a love poem to his wife on 14 February 1416. And so it became known as the day for sending romantic verse to the one you loved. Saint Valentine then became the patron saint of lovers.' There was a warm sigh throughout the classroom.

'There are other theories and stories behind where the day came from and how it has evolved over the centuries.' Some of the girls were looking out the window; following their glance, I saw a massive bouquet of roses travelling across the playground to the school's administration office.

'Now, for the rest of this class, I want you to go to the library and do some research, and for Friday's class I want you to bring five hundred words on the history of Valentine's Day. Be conscious of your sources and don't rely too heavily on internet research. You can use the media as well – I'm sure there'll be articles in today's papers.'

The girls all got up quickly, grateful for a light-hearted assignment. It was a change from the Cold War or the rise of Nazism.

When the girls had gone to the library I headed straight for the canteen, oddly hungry for midmorning. I grabbed an apple and mineral water and went to my office, where the huge bunch of roses we'd all seen in the playground was waiting on my desk. They looked a little out of place with the NAIDOC posters on the wall and the Aboriginal flag draped on the door as a claim of place. The pretty and the political didn't seem to blend well, but there was no reason why they shouldn't. Paul had gone to the trouble of organising roses. He thought – *knew* – I was worth the effort. I read the card out loud:

> *Roses are red*
> *Violets are blue*
> *No rubbish*
> *I fancy you!*

I wasn't quite sure about the verse, but I was thrilled by the flowers. Paul clearly wasn't afraid to show his affection or to spend money on me. How lucky was I? It was the most beautiful bouquet of roses I'd ever seen – and my twenty-ninth birthday was only six months away, a great time to get engaged, I thought.

At eight o'clock that evening, Paul showed up with an even bigger and more beautiful bunch of roses. It was slightly over the top, given he'd already spent a fortune.

'Wow, I'm spoiled, aren't I?' I was truly surprised.

'I wanted to send you something to school, but I wasn't sure if you'd be there or not. Peta said you took a sickie last year.'

'Very funny. I got the flowers and I loved the verse, but stick to engineering rather than poetry.' I took the roses from him and went into the kitchen to get a vase.

'What flowers?' He followed me into the kitchen.

'The flowers you sent me at school. I left them in my office as a reminder to all that I'm hooked up.' Paul laughed strangely as I filled two vases with water to accommodate the masses of roses he'd just given me. Why would he pretend he hadn't sent the flowers to school? Trying not to over-analyse the situation, I just played along with the game. Who was I to complain, with dozens of roses around me? Paul *must* have sent them. Unless it had been Simple Simon – but it couldn't have been, he was too cheap. And if Mickey had done it as a joke, he sure as hell would have let me know before the end of the day, because he'd want the glory and glamour for the gift. No, Mickey wouldn't have been able to keep it a secret the entire day.

It had to be Paul: there was no-one else it could have been.

He took me to a fine little Italian restaurant in Paddington, where we had good food and gazed into each other's eyes. I was happy. He seemed happy. We had moved to the next level, that place where the *L* word just needed to be said. So I did: 'I'm in love with you, Paul.'

Then silence.

'I don't know what to say.'

What kind of response was that?

'You don't have to say anything. I just needed you to know.' I was being very grown-up. I knew he loved me. No man did the things Paul did for me without being in love. He just couldn't say it. That was cool. I could wait. I thought it was odd, but I could wait. We finished dinner, went home, made love and all was good.

twenty-four

Men suck and I am just too deadly

A week later Paul dumped me. It was exactly two months, one week, three days and twelve hours since we'd met. I was checking my emails at work and read:

> I really enjoy being with you, Alice, but I need time to think! Perhaps we could be friends.

What the fuck! Time? Think? Friends?

Luckily I had no more classes that day and I left school straight away. I called him on the way home, but he didn't pick up. I waited for the beep and left a message: 'Is this how you treat your friends, Paul? Do you fuck your friends, Paul? Do you take them to the Hyatt, Paul?'

Why, when everything was going so well? When we had just had the best Valentine's Day ever? And Mr Perfect-Colgate-Smile-Peugeot-Driving-Smell-So-Good-Build-His-Own-Deck didn't have the balls to tell me face to face – or even over the phone! He'd used the most impersonal means of communication currently known to humanity.

What could've happened? Why did he need time to think? And how much time did he need? What did he need to think about? Did he need me to help him think? What the hell was going on?

He wouldn't take my calls and he didn't return them. He didn't return my text messages or my emails either. He was completely incommunicado. I was helpless. Distraught and helpless. Sad, lonely, confused and PISSED OFF!

There were so many questions I needed answered – preferably by Paul, but anyone would do.

I didn't want to go to Peta just yet – I thought he might go to her first. I'd wait to see if she called me. Instead I went to Dannie, the only one of us in a truly long-term relationship. I knew she'd give me logical and rational advice. At least I hoped so.

Dannie just said, 'Give him the time to think.'

'How much time?' Could I set a limit?

'I don't know. As much as it takes?'

'What? Don't be ridiculous.' Why had I come to Dannie for advice? In all honesty, she'd tolerated more as a wife than I ever would. George adored Dannie, and would never cheat on or criticise her. But George ran his own race, did his own thing. She did most of the running around with the kids, picking them up and dropping them off at sports and activities so he could play golf most weekends. The only real 'Dannie time' she got was when she was with us girls, and that wasn't even monthly. On top of going to the golf club every Tuesday night for a drink with the boys, George never lifted a finger around the house. I was sorry I'd asked Dannie for her opinion: clearly she needed to sort her own relationship out before she could help anyone else with theirs.

Next I called Liza, still not wanting to drag Peta in. With a Cosmopolitan in hand at the Cushion Bar, Liza said, 'Forget him. He was too effortlessly nice anyway. That Colgate smile always worried me. How many other women do you think he wooed with that dental work?'

I'd thought the same thing a couple of times as well, but I couldn't just forget him. I could still smell him all over my sheets, and I didn't want to wash them until the problem was solved and I had him back.

'I need another drink.' I slid off my stool and walked purposefully over to the bar.

'Hi there!' It was Shirt Guy — so he *was* a Cushion local. Once I'd have been thrilled by his efforts to strike up a conversation, but I was so totally over men right now that I didn't even care that this stranger was the only straight male in my life, family excepted, speaking to me.

'Whatever,' I said rudely. It was all I could manage. I took our drinks back to the table.

Liza was curious. 'What did you say to that guy? Do you know him? He looks shattered.'

'Shattered, schmattered. He's Cushion Bar furniture, like us. I call him Shirt Guy. But tonight's about me, how *I* feel and what *I* need. I really don't care what anyone else, least of all a *man* might feel.'

'I'll drink to that.' Liza raised her glass. We drank Cosmopolitan after Cosmopolitan. If I were lucky, I'd be able to puke Paul right out of my life at the end of the night.

❤

Five days passed before I called Peta to ask her advice. I'd hoped that I'd hear from Paul before then. That he'd have done his thinking and realised his future was with me. My phone never rang. Clearly he was still thinking.

So I called her. It was *her* fault anyway: she had introduced us.

'Peta, it's Alice, I need to talk to you. Paul dumped me by email, and I haven't got a clue why.'

'He *what*? I'll be right over.'

Within fifteen minutes she was on my couch and I was telling her everything.

'I don't get it. It doesn't make sense. He went from perfection to rejection overnight,' I sobbed.

'What do you think sparked the change in his behaviour towards you, Al?' Peta was being kind, rubbing my shoulder, passing me tissues. I just sobbed harder, trying to talk, sniff up tears and sip wine at the same time. I had manage to down almost a whole bottle of verdelho in half an hour. Paul wasn't just responsible for my broken heart, I was also becoming an alcoholic.

'He's a lowlife, scumbag, dirtbag, grandmother's boy, yellow-bellied liar,' I ranted. 'Prick, arsehole, fuckwit … What else?'

'Jerk,' Peta added.

'Jerk? *Jerk*? You think so? Just *slightly*. I hope the loser rots in hell.'

'No you don't, not really. I know you love him. That's why it hurts so much.'

'Yeah, maybe I should just give him time to think.' I was confused. I was emotionally all over the place. I drained my glass.

'The messed up dirtbag managed to mess me up as well.' I blew hard into a soggy tissue.

'That's what men do, Missy, they mess up their women so they can have something in common – fuckedness!'

I found the biggest glass I could – in fact, it may have been a vase – and walked through my flat with the longest G&T known to humankind, shaking my head in disbelief, leaving a trail of snotty tissues behind, in front and to the side of me. I couldn't believe I had that many tears inside me; I'd never cried like that before. And where the hell was all the snot coming from?

There was knock on the door; Peta answered it. It was Liza, with a box of chocolates in her hand.

'Peta sent me a text,' she said as she handed me the box, which I tore open immediately. I shoved several pieces in my mouth and almost gagged – it was all I'd eaten all day and not much more than I'd eaten since the beginning of the week.

'Everything seemed all right. He never said anything,' I started again.

'How was the sex?' Peta was straight to the point.

'There was plenty, and it was fantastic, obviously.'

'Obviously.' Both friends confirmed what I knew was true. That's what good friends did. They didn't need to ask any more.

'Then why did he send me a fucken email?' Somehow I found myself sucking on a joint that Peta had rolled. I didn't even smoke tobacco, but it filled my lungs easily, without coughs or dramas. Great! I thought. I was a closet yarndi-head as well.

'I reckon it was his mate, the one you said you saw at the Coogee Bay Hotel that day,' Liza said. I passed her the joint, but she handed it straight on to Peta. Liza was always uncomfortable on the rare occasions when we smoked in her presence, but she had learned to deal with it. 'I remember thinking there was something odd about that, when you told me.'

'His mate, that's it. He didn't look like the kind of fella Paul would hang out with. Something must've happened at the pub, but what?'

'Oh Missy, he hasn't told you, has he? About his past?' Peta sat with a bowl of corn chips resting in her lap, looking suddenly guilty.

'Told me about *what* past? What the hell are you talking about?' I was crying and laughing at the same time, ripped and confused, but still desperate for answers. I had the munchies, too, so I motioned to Liza to go to the pantry.

'Grab the Tim Tams, water crackers and salsa. Oh, and the Jaffas. Thanks'

'Our sweet Paul spent some time in prison not long ago,' Peta said, beginning to laugh, and as Liza walked back into the room, she fell completely off the lounge. I wasn't quite sure I had heard her correctly.

'Did you say Paul had been in prison?' Liza was suddenly more interested.

'That's right.' Peta climbed up off the floor, wiping the tears from her eyes. She was totally smashed.

'You've got to be kidding. That's not even slightly funny, Peta.'

Liza had said exactly what I was thinking. I was suddenly nervous.

'I'm sorry, but it's true, sweetie. Back in the nineties he was in Bathurst for a break and enter.' She was still gasping for breath, tears running down her face from laughing so hard.

'What break and enter, and what's so fucken funny?' I wanted the end of the story. I was angry, and sick to the stomach from eating an entire box of chocolates, washed down with a vaseful of G&T.

'I'm sorry, Missy. It's funny because the idiot was trying to break into this place, and when he went to smash the security camera with a cricket bat he ended up knocking himself out. Police found him spread-eagled at the scene of the crime.' She doubled over again. Liza had started laughing now too – she was dribbling ice-cream, she was laughing so hard.

'What? What?' I was in total disbelief. 'So you're telling me that not only is he a criminal, but he's a lousy crim at that? Can't even manage to do a job without knocking himself out? Fucken idiot!'

'It all makes sense, Alice,' said Liza. 'My bet is that he knew he could never tell you that, and with you talking about going overseas all the time, and him having trouble getting a passport, not wanting any searches done on him, my guess is he was really embarrassed about it.' Lawerly Liza had solved the case.

'So he fucken should be! But why did he need to steal? He makes heaps of money, why would he even do it?'

'Yeah I know,' said Peta. 'He's a smart guy, always has been, but a few years back he was heavy into the oky-doke and needed more money than he had. He's clean now, of course, or I'd never have set you up. He's completely on the straight and narrow. I reckon that fella he met at the Coogee Bay Hotel was probably from the old crowd and it reminded him of what he was capable of and probably spun him out a bit. Just leave it, Missy, give him some time. He'll figure it out or he won't, and if he doesn't, well his loss big-time, eh?'

It was good advice, but it didn't make the heartache any easier. I sobbed myself to sleep that night and every night for what seemed like months. I even had to replace my pillows because they were ruined by the waterfalls of sadness I had cried. My mantra had become: *I will never love again*. It was only in a few brief moments of breakthrough that I acknowledged that at least I'd known the amazing feeling of being in love for a little while, which was better than never feeling it at all.

I took the break-up with Paul hard. Who wouldn't? I'd thought he was perfect. I'd thought *we* were perfect. I sat and listened to every sad love song CD in my collection. I had plenty. I played them over and over and over, drinking enough gin to pickle myself. Before I'd go to sleep every night I'd have one last blast of U2's 'I Still Haven't Found What I'm Looking For' as I cried into my gin.

I resisted telling Mum for nearly two months, concerned I'd get a lecture about how I'd ruined another relationship and I'd *have* to become a lesbian. I was worried for nothing. Mum was just loving and supportive – and by the time I told her she'd worked it out for herself anyway.

'Just focus on the nice memories, Al,' she advised. Although she was probably right, her words of wisdom didn't really help the immediate heartache. I had so many questions – about myself, about men, about how someone could just shut off like that. I needed reassurance that I wasn't to blame. I needed to speak to Dillon.

♥

I sat on my couch under the doona with a cup of peppermint tea. I'm sure Dillon thought I hadn't left my flat for weeks. I had, but just to go to work.

'What's wrong with me?' I sobbed into my tea.

'I don't know.' He was sincere, but it wasn't the answer I was looking for, obviously. He had brought a pizza with him – a first. My baby brother was growing up and looking after his big sister. While there was something loving and precious in that thought, it also depressed me that I needed taking care of.

'What do you mean, you don't know?' He knew I was fishing.

'There's *nothing* wrong with you. You just need to find someone who's comfortable with the way you are.'

'No, I need to find someone who's comfortable in *himself*, so he can be comfortable with me.' Dillon tilted his head, as if to say, 'Fair call.'

'Why didn't he just tell me the truth, Dillon?'

'Men aren't good with the truth, Al.'

'What? So it's a whole gender of liars we're talking about then, is it? I've got no chance. What chance have women got?' There was desperation in my voice.

'It's just that we don't want confrontation. We don't want to hurt women, not on purpose, anyway.'

'So he thought dumping me via email wasn't going to hurt me? It wouldn't have hurt me if he'd just told me the truth. It's not like he broke into *my* place. I would've been disgusted, but not hurt.'

'Geez, Al, how embarrassed do you reckon he was. Spread-eagled at the scene of his own crime. The bloke's a complete fuckwit. He knew it, and he wasn't going to be the one to point that fact out to you. You don't deal with fuckwits very well.'

'Well, I think he's a bigger fuckwit just letting me go.'

'I agree.'

❤

My debrief with Mickey was much gentler. We met in Giuseppe's pizza place in Darlinghurst. Mickey's traditional country, he joked. He always made me acknowledge 'the gay community whose land we gathered on' each time we met in 'his' space.

'It sux, Al, and I am sick of it. We are both such great, fantastic, unbelievable catches, and yet nobody seems to be able to handle us. It could be that we're so far developed and know exactly and intuitively what is right in a relationship, people subconsciously realise

they don't come up to scratch and run for their lives.'
Mickey was very philosophical and theoretical about it
all, but I found his words comforting.

'They all suck, Al, no exceptions.' That was more like
the Mickey I knew, and he was as passionate about his
speech as he was about biting into his second piece of
Giuseppe's pizza.

'Maybe you're right. Truth and communication are
essential in a relationship, and most straight men are
liars, I've been told.'

'It sux, Al!' Mickey's favourite phrase was 'It sux'
and it near killed him at school not to use it. He let it
fly while we were out, though, and it always made me
laugh. It was such an eighties thing to say.

'Look Al, you need to remember that I, like most
normal people, think highly of you, and know you are
worth so much more than a bloke like Prisoner Paul
– or any of the other cocksuckers out there. You are a
beautiful, intelligent woman with a giving heart. What
more could the prick ask for? You are way too deadly
for this shit.' Tears welled in my eyes, but I was laughing
inside: when whitefellas use the word 'deadly' it just
sounds ridiculous. But I felt better. Men did suck, and I
was worthy of great things. My new mantra would be:
Men suck and I am way too deadly for their shit.

'Now let's talk about me, Al. I've got men problems
too.'

'Of course, Mickey. What's happening on the man
front for you then?' It was good for me to change seats

and play counsellor for a while. Mickey burst into tears, like a child who'd been told he couldn't have his favourite dessert.

'What's wrong, Mickey? Tell me, what sux?'

'I'm sorry. I'm a bit depressed 'cos Tom told me this morning that I was his life goal. I suddenly realised that's what I've been for so many men in the past.' Tom was Mickey's latest squeeze. They'd met at the Empire Hotel in Erskineville and had been seeing each other for about three weeks. He was much younger than Mickey, but Mickey was hooked on the sex, and happy, or at least he had been until now.

'Go on, I want to hear about this life goal business.' And I did.

'I was something they wanted and strived hard to obtain.' He took a sip of cheap chianti. 'You see, I'm known to be unobtainable in my community, Al.' Anyone as promiscuous as Mickey didn't seem that unobtainable to me, but I didn't say anything.

'Anyway, once they've experienced me – maybe they'd say *conquered* me – they always just move to the next one – don't fucken mind me. No, forget Big Mickey.' Mickey was always making reference to his penis size. I had grown used to it and stopped asking him not to.

'That sux, Mickey.' It was the answer I knew he was looking for.

'I am so over it, Al. I'm never going through it again. I'm tired of the cling-ons, the users.'

'Why do you put up with that shit, Mickey? You're nearly forty.' I was a little upset that he was in such a state. 'You are gorgeous, sexy, smart, witty, loving, generous, honest and kind. You're the kind of guy every girl dreams of. You're just on the wrong fucken team!'

'Sweetheart,' and he turned all camp, '*you've* just got the wrong plumbing for me is all. It sux!' He took a longer sip of his wine. 'All I know is that life is full of little challenges like Tommy Tzaziki and Paul the Prick, and if there is a god, I can't wait to slap her face for all this shit.' I spat my drink all over him as I laughed.

'Al, I think it's time to change our focus. I think our mistake is that we're stuck on the idea of romantic love. All I have to offer men is mystery and challenge, and once that's gone, I hold no more interest or promise. Maybe I should just do as the black widow spider does ...'

'Sorry love, but you'd have to be a white widow spider.' And we raised our glasses to cheers.

twenty-five

I should be loved, cherished and worshipped

August arrived, and with it my twenty-ninth birthday – and the realisation that my deadline for meeting and marrying Mr Right was only twelve months away. I needed to get back to the strategy. Peta often said the quickest way to get over a man was in the arms of another. It had always worked for her.

There were no banquets organised for me at the Park Hyatt, but Dannie, Liza and Peta threw me a surprise birthday dinner at a local Italian restaurant. Dannie and George, Liza and Luke (who'd been around since Bianca's wedding but still wouldn't commit to anything more than two weeks ahead), Arnie and Cindy (she'd broken the one year record with Arnie), Dillon and Larissa, Mickey and Tom (who was obviously getting another chance), and Peta with a guy she'd met at a conference that week. And me. Just me. No-partner me!

'What? You couldn't ask *anyone* so that I had a date as well? You couldn't hire me a bloody escort?' I asked Peta, but loud enough for the whole table to hear. I couldn't

271

believe that after everything I'd been through, they had managed to organise my birthday dinner so that I was the only one without a partner at the table. Were they being heartless? Stupid even? Were they too scared to set me up with someone for fear of failing, *again*? Or was I just being ungrateful? Perhaps they believed I was capable of being a happy single among a roomful of happy couples. God knows, I'd once been okay with it.

'Open your pressies, Alice.' Larissa was trying to break the tension and handed me her gift. I could tell it was a book. It wouldn't want to be a self-help-dial-a-man-how-not-to-be-single-forever kind of book, or I'd throw it at her. Luckily, it wasn't.

'Wow, just what I wanted – Aria's *Leo Star Guide*. This will see me through till the end of the year. I love it, Larissa, thanks so much.' I could see her and Dillon breathe a sigh of relief that she'd made a good choice. I started reading out the forecast for the rest of the year: *'Health: You will take more interest in your wellbeing this year, Ms Leo. More exercise, less of the finer things. It's okay to indulge sometimes, but everything in moderation. You may even think about losing something from your diet all together.*

'If Aria thinks I'm giving up the gin and tonic she's wrong. I think it's the vegetable juices I'll do in moderation.' Everyone laughed.

'*Work: Your work situation might also provide you with some social opportunities in the next twelve months, Ms Leo, so be open to playing a little with your work colleagues. All work and no play makes Ms Leo another star sign, and you don't want that.'*

Maybe that meant I would have to find a different place to work. There was nothing happening on the social front at St Christina's. I hadn't thought of a change of career as part of my strategy before, but maybe it was something I should consider.

'Relationships: The next twelve months promise to bring you better responses to your attempts in the relationship sector of your life, Ms Leo. You will be sexier and more attractive to men. You need to be aware when someone is interested in you, though, and don't be closed off to potential partners who mightn't normally make their way into your heart.'

❤

With Aria's words still in my thoughts, I had my annual birthday dinner with Mum and Dad the next night. Takeaway Chinese and a homemade birthday cake. It was a ritual. No-one mentioned Paul. I'm fairly certain that Dillon had been doing some counselling before I arrived.

'*How to Be a Sex Goddess.* Interesting choice, Mum. What made you pick this for me?' She'd given me a guide on how to be a sex goddess 'with or without a man'.

'The young guy in the shop suggested it when I told him you needed help finding a man. Unfortunately, he was gay, so he wasn't interested in taking you out. I invited Cliff tonight, too, but he wasn't very interested either. Said he had something on in Erskineville.'

I rolled my eyes and started flipping through the book. It did have some good tips. 'Listen to this one!' I said, and read it out loud: 'Treat yourself to expensive jewellery. A goddess deserves a Gucci watch!'

'A teacher's wage would never go that far, Mum, but I'm looking forward to reading the tips for working-class girls.'

♥

I woke to the sound of the garbage truck picking up and dumping down bins below in Arden Street. 'Damn, shit, I forgot!' I had a rare day off, and had planned to sleep in. I raced out of bed and downstairs in less than five seconds and heaved the bin down the path, looking like something the cat dragged in. I was in my ratty old pyjamas and had thrown on dark sunglasses to hide the panda eyes I had from not taking off my make-up before I went to bed.

'Morning,' one of the garbos smiled at me, offering a surprisingly gentle hand with getting my bin down the three steps from the property to the footpath.

'Oh, I'm sorry, I forget every week.'

'I know, that's okay. Shouldn't your husband do this?' I tilted my head pathetically, as if to say, 'Yes, he should!' This guy was familiar; I tried to place his face.

I watched my bin being emptied into the orange truck and was surprised when the garbo took the bin back up the steps for me.

'Wow, chivalry's alive and well at the local council these days, then?'

'It's part of our professional development.' He grinned, showing a dangerously beautiful set of white teeth. I had a fleeting flashback to Paul.

'What? To help damsels in distress?' Was I flirting with him?

'No, to help damsels in pyjamas in public.' Shit, I was in my pjs and hadn't even brushed my hair. God knows what he must have thought.

'Thanks, mate!' I sounded blokey all of a sudden.

'It's Gary.'

'Gary,' I repeated. Then the penny dropped. 'You're Shirt Guy!' I pointed my finger at him like an idiot.

'Sorry?' He looked down at his fluoro-yellow, council-issued shirt, puzzled.

'Oh, I've seen you in a really nice shirt, at Cushion.' I remembered how rude I'd been to him last time. 'God, I'm so sorry for being rude that night, I was a bit—'

'Drunk?' and he laughed.

I was embarrassed. 'Yes, it was one of those days.' I extended my hand, 'I'm Alice.'

'Gotta run, there's an old lady in a housecoat and rollers I have to help at the top of the hill. She might get jealous if she knows she's got competition.'

As the truck pulled out from the curb, Gary-the-Garbo threw me a wave. Was he flirting with me? Or did he think I had a useless husband who couldn't even put the bins out? Did he actually feel sorry for me?

Back in the warmth of my flat I thought about what I'd do with the rest of the day, and decided to lie in bed and read my latest self-help book, *How to Avoid Mummy's Boys* – a gift from Larissa, of course. I really should've been going for a walk, but the exercise-guilt passed before I'd read the first three pages. Soon I dozed off again. It was a gentle reminder of the joys of singledom. Sleep and reading! It made me think of Dannie, going without both, and I felt lucky.

In the evening I ran a long, hot bath and added a few dozen droplets of lavender oil. I slid into the tub, placed a face cloth over my eyes and lay back, relaxed, plugging the tap with one big toe to stop the hot beads of water that fell every so often. All I could hear then was the toilet running. I needed a plumber in to look at it; one more reason why it would be handy to have a bloke around, of course. Most men can just fix stuff like that.

Until I found Mr Right, I'd just have to get Dad over to look at the loo for me.

twenty-six

I will be kind and compassionate to all the white people I meet today

Gary-the-Garbo's sympathy spurred me on: it was time to get back to my strategy for meeting Mr Right. I consulted the list on my fridge. Phase II was attending professional gatherings. Time to call in Peta, my expert on the conference circuit. She'd only just returned from her last trip. We met at Cushion as usual for cocktails and a catch-up. When I arrived she was sitting outside, facing the beach, but with her head in a magazine, already halfway through a Manhattan.

'So where have you been this time?' I asked. 'I hope you're not working too hard?'

'I've been at a conference in Canberra on improving Indigenous literacy, facilitated some workshops, was great stuff, really inspiring. Met some interesting men, too. Seriously, Alice, if you *really* want to meet someone, you'll have to get on the conference circuit – it's like a dating agency on the road. You're guaranteed a shag if you want one, you just need to be discreet.'

'I'm not looking for a simple shag, Peta, I'm looking for a commitment to a lifetime of shags!'

'Whatever! I just think you need to start with one night of lust and romance before planning an eternity of them.' She headed inside to the bar for another cocktail. It looked like it was going to be a big night. I peered in through the glass doors to see who or what was on offer. A few local rugby players drank beers, a gaggle of women celebrated someone's birthday, a couple sat huddled on a couch looking out the large windows towards the sea. One guy stood alone at the bar, and we caught each other's eye. He raised an eyebrow and smiled, lifting his beer to suggest 'Cheers,' and then I saw it: a wedding ring. Most men in bars were jerks, just looking for that one-night shag, even if they had someone to go home to anyway. In my books, that was just being greedy.

Peta had started me thinking: I really did need to get out of bars. I needed to be among professionals who shared an interest in the things I did. I was always receiving invitations to events run by history associations, but I never went. I'd heard they were full of old whitefellas. Then again, my dad was an old whitefella, and he was the 'deadliest man on the planet' as Mum always said. I decided that as part of Phase II of the strategy I would attend some professional gatherings and see what they offered a single girl.

A week later an invite arrived for a function celebrating a local historian's forty years of service in the eastern suburbs. I was excited about the prospect of meeting new people, even new white people. I should probably have more of them in my life anyway, I thought, do a bit more for reconciliation. I laughed out loud at that thought. My mantra became: *I will be kind and compassionate to all the white people I meet today.*

❤

Walking down the narrow hallway of the heritage-listed building, I tried to seem confident, even though I didn't know a soul. I signed the visitors' book, got my name tag and looked around. The room was already full of whitefellas huddled in little groups chatting and being very civilised. There were no brown faces in sight. I found the self-serve bar, poured a generous glass of wine and strolled around the edges of the room, looking at old framed black and white images of Bondi Beach from times gone by. No wonder history was boring to Aussie kids if this was the best a local history association could do to present it. I kept walking slowly, hoping that someone might recognise me, but who would? I'd never attended any of these gigs before – what was the likelihood of anyone knowing me? I would have to make conversation with a stranger, there was no other way. At least everyone here had something in common – a passion for history.

I looked around the room and saw one young, groovy, academic-looking guy come in alone. Not much taller than myself, in jeans, white shirt and dark blazer, he looked interesting, even shaggable. That's the only thing you can really tell about someone from first glance. How we look communicates a lot about how we feel about ourselves and this fella was well dressed and groomed: he had good self-esteem and took care of himself. I didn't want to seem too obvious by approaching him straight away, so I thought I'd slowly make my way around the room and bump into him accidentally a little later. That would give him a chance to approach me if he was having reciprocal thoughts.

I attempted a sexy saunter, feigning interest in the black and white photos, and soon found myself next to two greying men in suits laughing that deep belly laugh that old men do. I quietly mumbled my mantra: *I am daunting and desirable and determined. I will be kind and compassionate to white people. I am daunting...* Before I knew it I was being introduced to Suit #1, who described himself as 'a descendant of the first people of the area'. I was fairly sure he didn't mean he was Gadigal – he would've just said so if that were the case – but I asked him anyway, giving him the benefit of the doubt: 'So you're Gadigal, then?'

'No, don't know *that* family. I'm a descendant of the Colllinses – you know the Colllins family, that's Colllins with three *el*s. There's a park named after us.'

I refrained from commenting about the family with the misspelt name and got straight to the important details.

'So you're a descendant of the first family who were *given* a land grant after the local Aboriginal clan, the Gadigal, were *dispossessed* of their land, then?'

Both men laughed that belly laugh again, as though I were a child who had said something cute but meaningless. They were starting to piss me off. I tried not to raise my voice, but continued, 'Seriously, this *is* a history association – surely you recognise *all* history and not just that which serves the coloniser?'

'Of course, you are right, Miss …?'

'Aigner – Alice Aigner. I head up the history department at St Christina's.' They both seemed a little surprised, but impressed. They still hadn't guessed I was Koori, though. Probably never even met one before, not knowingly anyway.

Suit #1 continued, 'We here at the Eastern Suburbs Local History Association recognise Australian history, Aboriginal history and prehistory as well.'

My blood started to boil. I could feel the colour move right up my neck. Was there steam coming out of my ears? The mantra about being nice to white people was gone.

'What Aboriginal history? Everything that happened post-invasion is *Australian* history. Aboriginal people didn't dispossess themselves, they didn't poison their own watering holes or place themselves on government-run reserves and church-run missions. The colonisers and settlers – the so-called *Australians* – did that. That's

Australian history. And as for prehistory, what the hell does that mean?' I knew what he meant, but wanted to hear him say it.

'History before the British settled Sydney Cove, of course!' He was unashamedly adamant.

'You mean history before the British *invaded* Sydney Cove, don't you? Or is it regarded as prehistory because in your eyes nothing *apparently* happened here for the tens of thousands of years before that?'

'Why do you keep saying *invasion*? It was *colonisation.* Someone would have colonised Australia eventually. Better the Brits than the frogs, don't you think?' This was Suit #2's intelligent contribution.

'*Invasion* was what happened in 1788 when the boats arrived, *mate,* and *colonisation* is the process that followed. You should really get up to date with the terminology. And for the record, at least if the French had colonised us, we'd have better food and fashion!'

I threw back the last of my wine, mentally blaming white people for making Blackfellas *have* to drink. They drive us to it. They make us need to escape their narrow-minded, in-denial, racist, imperialistic bullshit.

As I made my way out the door, I spotted a lecturer I'd had at university, a staunch lefty unionist. Ruby Timberton seemed to remember me too. We made eye contact, both shrugging our shoulders, as if to say neither of us belonged. I was happy for her to stay, but I was already tired of being the thorn in everyone's side. I couldn't have managed another exchange like the one I'd just had with the Suits, and didn't even want to chance it with the good-looking fella I'd seen earlier. Ruby's stomach might've been stronger and her skin must've been thicker than mine, or maybe the discussions would never be as personal for her – she was white.

I drove home along Campbell Parade, wondering if I would ever meet a man I could respect as an equal. He would *definitely* have to have a good mind, share my passion for history, have a sense of humanity and appreciate the everyday wonders of life. I hadn't realised how important it was to me until now. Even at the most 'civilised' of events, I had somehow managed to get into an argument – but only because these issues were basic, everyday concerns for me, and completely non-negotiable.

♥

'Integrity is so much more important than romance, isn't it?' I asked Mickey twenty minutes later, as we sat on stools at the Cushion Bar. I needed a drink after my latest attempt at meeting Mr Right, and Tom had just dumped Mickey *again*, this time apparently forever.

'I just want a nice bloke, Al.'

'And you're different to everyone else *how*?'

'I keep sending telepathic messages out to the one who is supposed to love me. Problem is he never messages me back.'

'Perhaps you should try text messages, then.' I was trying to be funny, but Mickey just frowned and continued.

'Sometimes I feel like I have to be a different person before anyone will find me attractive. It sux, Al. I don't want to be a different person. I want someone to love me just the way I am.'

'I'll drink to that.' I raised my glass to Mickey's and we sat silently for a minute or so. Then I spotted Gary-the-Garbo at the bar, and suddenly felt thirsty again. 'Be right back, Mickey!'

I made my way towards Gary. 'Hello!'

He turned and smiled but I wasn't sure he knew who I was. I extended my hand. 'I'm Alice, you probably don't recognise me with clothes and make-up on. Oh, that sounds bad, doesn't it? What I mean is I live in Arden Street and you helped me with my bin. I was in my pyjamas.' I sounded like an idiot. No wonder he laughed.

'Yes, I know who you are, Alice. How are you?'

'Just unwinding after a tough day is all.'

'Another one? Perhaps I should steer clear, then?' He was funny. I liked his humour.

'No, you're safe at the moment. So what about you? Quiet drink with the boys?' There were few men actually in the bar.

'Sister's birthday.' He motioned to a woman near the far doors. 'That's Liesl, we're just having a drink before

dinner. She didn't have a bloke to take her out, so I am.'
Thank god! I wasn't the only one then.

'Better go, or knowing my sister she'll have us
married off in no time,' Gary said with a wink.

I suddenly felt better, and walked back to a depressed
Mickey thinking how much I loved the Cushion Bar.
They had great happy hour cocktails to loosen the
inhibitions, lots of young fellas to perv on, hardly any
backpackers to cringe at, and staff who flirted when
required and, judging by the full jar on the bar, were
tipped well, too. Best of all, it was an easy crawl home
afterwards.

twenty-seven

Trawling the classifieds

With my recent experience with the old historical farts fresh in my mind, I couldn't even bring myself to register for the national education conference that Peta was going to. I couldn't bear a similar exchange lasting three or four days. I moved straight onto Phase III: checking out the classifieds.

I sat on my balcony with a cup of tea and the personal pages and searched, highlighter poised to mark the first advert that looked remotely like it had some potential. After thirty minutes I found one that looked promising:

> VO4936: Schoolteacher, n/s, loves reading, cooking, movies, the beach, intelligent conversation. Seeking similar in sassy single.

Seeing as he was a teacher and I was, after all, sassy, I decided to give it a go. First I prepared my reply and rehearsed it in my sexiest bourgeois-Black voice.

'Hi. I'm a sassy, non-smoking schoolteacher, and I live at the beach all year round. I love literary fiction and having meaningful conversation over a home-cooked meal. And I really appreciate being cooked for. I'm a Leo, so I can be a bit fiery. If you'd like to meet for a drink or coffee, give me a call.'

Once I was ready, I dialled the number warily and listened to his message. He sounded as sincere as a stranger on a phone message could, articulate *and* enthusiastic, but I was put off responding when he finished: 'Okay, speak soon, lots of love, Max.'

Lots of love? *Lots of love?* What the hell was that? Generally speaking it's hard enough to get to the *L* word after six months of sex, dinners, shared baths and family events. Paul had *never* managed to say it *at all* and had freaked out when I did. Now there was someone saying it to the universe – in a voicemail message – for *anyone* to receive. Nup, Max was definite clingy stalker material and didn't know the true value of the *L* word. I hung up without leaving a message.

I didn't throw in the towel, though, but kept trawling column after column, searching until I found one that just might be a goer: VO2869. I liked the number – twenty-eight was my birth date; sixty-nine, well obviously got to love that one. The ad read:

> 38, financially secure, GSOH, n/s, no children, animals or baggage.

Well, the last bit was a lie – we've all got baggage – but he got a brownie point for recognising that it existed! It went on:

Love the sunrise and the sound of rain falling on a tin roof.

Okay, so he'd ripped that off from Norah Jones's 'Come Away With Me' but that was fine, because I loved her music and I gave him a brownie point for that too. I dialled the number and listened to his chirpy message: 'Hi, this is Rod, thanks for calling. Leave a message, and we'll talk.'

He sounded like a cool dude, so I left a few choice words of my own and waited for a response. Within an hour my mobile rang. He was either checking his messages constantly – meaning he was *really* desperate – or it was a fluke that he'd checked just then. Hoping it was the latter, I answered my phone with the sultriest voice possible.

During our short conversation, Rod sounded pleasant enough. He was on the Gold Coast for a few days, back in Sydney on the weekend. Sales rep for a pool company and lived in Lane Cove. Was keen to catch up when he got back. We agreed to meet in the city somewhere, depending on time and weather.

'Why don't I call you when I get back and we can meet on Saturday?'

'Sounds like a plan.' I wasn't even nervous or embarrassed about the process of organising the date. Let's face it, we were both in the same boat.

'Can you email me a photo of yourself in the meantime, so I know who to look out for on Saturday?' he asked. A fair request. I asked for the same back.

289

'Great, Alice. Well, I guess we'll speak soon.' Signed, sealed and delivered – or at least it would be on Saturday.

'Okay.' I felt a bit weird, but this new way of lining up dates was proving to be manageable, and a lot easier than going through friends.

That night his emailed photo arrived. He was gorgeous: green eyes, sandy hair, warm smile. It was taken on the water, but I couldn't work out where. I sent back a photo of myself almost immediately. It had been taken at Message Sticks, the Indigenous arts festival held down at the Opera House, when we took students on an excursion to see *Ten Canoes*. I looked fabulous. Big smile. Luscious red lips. I was standing next to the Message Sticks banner holding a small Aboriginal flag Clair had stuck in my hand at the last minute. I didn't intentionally want to send anything *Indigenised*, but it was a great photo of me.

He didn't call the next day, or the next day, or the next day. On Friday I sent him an email, just so I could make other plans if he couldn't do Saturday now.

> Hi Rod, hope you're well. Just wondering if you're still on
> for coffee tomorrow? Or is there a problem? Alice

He responded a couple of hours later.

> Hi Alice. Sorry, been really busy. Just wondering about your
> photo. You look gorgeous, but what's with the flag? Rod

I knew it. He couldn't cope with the Black stuff. Should I have sent a different photo? Would it really have made a difference? Flag or not? I would still be the same woman. I was furious and fired an email back.

> Rod, if you're trying to ask whether I'm Aboriginal or not, the answer is yes. Is that a problem? Alice

But already I knew it was, if not for him, then definitely for me. I knew I wouldn't hear from him again and I didn't.

❤

I called Dillon and told him I'd made his favourite chicken and olive dish, if he was in the area and wanted to drop by. We both knew what that meant: I needed to talk. We enjoyed our meal, then, as I washed the dishes and he dried, I said, 'Dillon, I'm thinking of trying internet dating.'

'Al, I think that's dangerous *and* it's a bit … desperate, isn't it? I know you want to get married and have kids, but you know you can always get artificially inseminated.'

'What? I'm not a cow, Dillon! I can get laid!'

My little brother went through my pantry for something sweet and then left. So began Phase IV.

twenty-eight

Getadate.com.au

It was already late September and I was panicking. So much for spring being in the air or spring romances for that matter: it was pouring with rain outside, and chilly, and I was sitting with a glass of gluhwein, staring at Google on my laptop, looking for love in cyberspace. Internet dating was all the rage, I told myself; Mickey was on the net constantly, and in chat rooms. He might've been looking for something slightly different to me though, as he seemed to be dating someone new every other day. I'd never done either: chatted online or checked out any websites designed for singles. I couldn't believe I was even contemplating it, but Mr VO2869 had really taken the wind out of my sails. I didn't want to believe all men were racist jerks, so, if for no other reason but to give me back my faith in humanity, I got back on the job and logged on to find Mr Right.

There was no turning back once I'd registered with Getadate.com.au, Australia's latest singles site. I promised myself that once I hit that return button I would remain seriously committed to finding myself some internet lurv. So I pressed return, then spent literally hours poring over the pages and pages of profiles and pics of men from all walks of life, all over Sydney, with different looks, different kinds of faces and smiles, various political persuasions and wide-ranging but definite tastes in women.

It disturbed me that many of the men indicated in their profiles that they didn't have strong political views and they didn't mind the political views of their women. I wondered if the Palestinian guy with 'no firm beliefs' would mind if a Jewish woman sent him an email. I knew it was unlikely to happen, but something similar could: what if the guy in the National Front got a message from someone who *wasn't* 'full-blood Anglo-Australian'. I'd say most had pretty firm expectations about race and political views, even if they weren't aware of it, especially given my experience with Mr Pool-Cleaner from Lane Cove.

While some men listed very little on their profile and seemed to have only limited expectations in meeting women, others were quite definite about what they wanted their perfect woman to look like. 'Must be petite, Caucasian, big-breasted, long-legged, naturally blonde' and so on. I couldn't believe how shallow some of the men were, many of whom wouldn't rank as pretty boys themselves, even though it was obvious many of the photos posted had been 'assisted' by technology.

I found a picture of a guy who looked pleasant enough, but not too pretty. (Rule Number 1: Don't date a guy who's prettier than me and then I won't have to worry about every woman and half the men in the room wanting him too.) I was no longer a lookist anyway, after Charlie. I'd learnt my lesson.

My chosen internet guy said he liked reading and the beach, was politically left of centre, didn't have kids but wanted them eventually, and had no criteria specifying what his ideal woman looked like or what her nationality or political persuasion should be. Yep, he'd do. I sent him a non-committal email just to say hello, giving him a bit of basic information about myself:

> I like reading historical novels, I literally live at the beach, have done a wine appreciation course and am tertiary educated. I am a champagne socialist with a sense of social justice.

I invited him to email me back with some questions if he was interested, then signed off with a carefully chosen internet name: Koori Rose. I wanted to be up-front about my identity right from the start. (He called himself the White Knight – so was definitely not a Blackfella.)

A few weeks later, after numerous emails, we planned to meet at Bronte Beach for breakfast on Saturday morning.

I checked with Aria before leaving home and she said I'd need to be very organised to get through the day ahead, so I gave myself thirty minutes to make the ten-minute trek from Coogee to Bronte. Finding a park was a struggle – it was all revenue-generating one-hour metered spots. Who the hell would want to be at the beach for under an hour? Finally I found a park a short distance away and hiked back down to the beach-front cafes.

I grabbed a table at Swell, as agreed in our last email, and took in the sights, surrounded by pretentious latte drinkers, remembering how the area looked when I was a kid at school: there had been a milk bar, and you could only buy fish and chips and ice-cream cones.

I was early, but I wanted to be well seated and relaxed when the White Knight finally arrived. I ordered a juice and some water, then just sat and soaked up the view and the atmosphere. Bronte was bordering on chaotic, with the cars and kids and people walking dogs.

Time passed quickly; glancing at my left wrist, I realised Mr White Knight was twenty-five minutes late. More pissed off than disappointed, I called for the bill, paid it and left.

I hated people wasting my time. It wasn't as though I didn't have better things – or at least *other* things – to do. The hassle with the parking was another frustration, and I was pretty damned furious by the time I'd trudged back up the hill to my car. Why had he stood me up? The jerk had probably been watching from across the road and hadn't liked what he'd seen. Fine, he didn't know what he was missing out on.

'Prick, bastard, wanker, LOSER!' I got in my car and drove to Bondi to meet Liza at her place. We'd planned on conducting a post-mortem of the breakfast date anyway, but she wasn't expecting me so early.

❤

Liza was mid-sentence, trying again to persuade me to meet her cousin Marco – 'Did I tell you he works in international trade and is quite politically astute, impressive eh?' – when my mobile rang. Saved! I looked to the sky and mouthed 'Thank you, Biami.'

'Alice Aigner,' I said.

'Where were *you* this morning?' It was the White Knight, sounding angry.

'Where was *I*? Where the hell were *you*?' I was angrier than he was ever going to be.

'I was fifteen minutes late.'

'No you weren't. I was there till nearly half-past-eight and there was no sign of you. If you were just running late, why didn't you call me and let me know?'

'I didn't have your number on me. Anyway, I asked one of the staff if anyone had been waiting and she said no.' He was insinuating that I was lying!

'Well, I was there at seven-fifty-five, reading a book and enjoying the view. Perhaps I didn't look like a desperate woman with nothing better to do than wait for a loser to have breakfast with me.'

'Well do you want to organise to meet next week, then – have another try?'

'I don't think so. I made enough effort this time round. If you *really* wanted to meet me, you would've been there. See ya!' I hung up.

'You are unbelievable!' Liza was disgusted. 'He was just running late. He didn't stand you up.'

'Liza, Liza, Liza. Don't make excuses. I may not have met my Mr Right, but I'm sure as hell not going to tolerate someone being half an hour late for the *first* date. No way. I'm not waiting for anyone who can't be bothered, or who isn't smart enough to ring me when he's running late. Shit, Liza, he should've been there half an hour early.' I was ruthless.

'Maybe my cousin Marco's not the fella for you then, either. I mean, he's a great bloke, but works his arse off and has been known to be late on occasion. In fact maybe there is *no* fella for you at all, Alice.' Things were a bit cool between us, and I soon left, determined to prove Liza wrong.

An old mantra came to mind: *Try anything twice!* I went online and started scrolling through pics and bios again. I scrolled right past the really good-looking guys and stopped at a fella who wasn't Brad Pitt, but wasn't offensive either. He liked boating, good food and wine, 'ladies who are ladies' (whatever that meant), and had studied Swedish massage. I sent him an email and we arranged to meet up the following weekend.

♥

He had asked me to meet him in the car park of a swanky Sydney yacht club. 'An RSL on the water' I'd joked to him on the phone, but he hadn't laughed.

From the minute I saw him I had that sinking feeling. Think *Titanic* × 1000. There was no chemistry between us and the venue seemed to have had an atmosphere bypass. All would have been forgiven, though, if the restaurant attached to the club had actually been open. I opted not to eat rather than order something fried from the bistro. I was already feeling ill, and then he started talking about how much money he had, his weekends out on his yacht and how he could imagine me as a yachtie's wife, G&T in hand, wind in the hair, ocean in the background.

'Well, I like gin and tonic,' I said, making an effort to be polite.

'Tick!' he responded.

'But I get seasick,' I lied, so I'd never have to go on his boat.

'Cross!' What the hell?

I decided on a new tack: 'I watched *Amélie* on DVD last night and loved it. Have you seen it?'

'Yes, tick!' Weirdo. I threw one more hook at him.

'I can't wait till winter comes round. It's my favourite season.' I was lying: his profile had said he preferred the warmer climate, and I wanted to see how he'd react.

'Cross!' That did it.

'What the fuck are you doing with your ticks and crosses?'

'I'm giving you a tick for the things I like about you, and a cross for the things I don't. I'd give you a cross for saying "fuck". I like ladies who behave like ladies.'

'What?'

I thought you'd like the feedback.'

'Well, that's a cross from me, then.'

'Why?'

'I'm a teacher, I don't want ticks and crosses. Actually, no-one really does on a date.'

'Isn't it a good way to work out if we want to see each other again?'

'I'll help you out. I'm giving you one big cross!' With that I got up and walked out.

On the way home, I received a text message:

> I'm giving you a big tick anyway! Look forward to seeing you again.

I didn't even waste the cost of an SMS to tell him what I thought of him. A week later he texted me again:

> Did I tell you I give really good full-body massages?

I couldn't ever consume enough G&Ts to make *that* happen. I blocked his number on my phone and swore off men with boats.

My two internet dates so far had been disasters. I decided not to try for three times lucky, so that was the end of Phase IV.

twenty-nine

Uprising

I gave the blind dating a miss for a while and instead pinned my hopes on an email invitation to the up-coming 'Singles Uprising at Bondi Beach' that I found in my inbox. It read:

> You're invited to Sydney's Annual Singles Uprising at Bondi Beach, but you will only be admitted if:
>
> - You are single
> - You bring another single person of the opposite sex
> - You are smart, attractive and funny

Liza had clearly put me on the mailing list. It was good to know she hadn't given up on me finding Mr Right after our recent spat, but my immediate reaction was to avoid the event at all costs. I considered the loads of backpackers likely to be hanging around Bondi Beach, lobster-red and full of booze. I could hang out at Coogee any day and witness the same painful behaviour from my balcony. Still, I was supposed to be open to *all* opportunities to meet heterosexual, single members of the opposite sex, and that included attending events I hadn't yet or wouldn't necessarily otherwise attend. I met the criteria outlined in the invitation, so why not? I decided to go to the uprising and drag Mickey with me for moral support. Peta and Liza were still with their fellas, and Mickey was really the only one buying into my strategy 120 per cent at this stage. He was looking for a new 'friend' anyway, after Tom. At least taking each other along wouldn't cramp either of our styles, just in case there was someone with potential there.

It was the hottest day Sydney had seen in fifty-six years, and the humidity didn't help my attempt at looking good when foundation just kept sliding off my face. I struggled to see how I looked from behind, and was thankful I had, because I was so hot and sweaty I had a wet g-string mark on my white pants. I changed into a lilac slip dress, wore no knickers at all, and grabbed a hat as I ran out the door to meet Mickey waiting downstairs.

'Doesn't get more desperate than this!' we said simultaneously as we spied the two-metre-tall glittering red *U* pegged into the ground near a blue shed at South Bondi. The skateboard ramp looked more inviting to me at that very moment than Sydney's Singles Uprising. Mickey and I were both wary, so rather than lunging right into the experience, we circled the designated space three times, searching desperately for someone within the singles precinct who didn't look totally desperate. Someone who looked more like us, with a take-it-or-leave-it attitude.

'They should have a fucken big *L* for loser there, that'd be more apt,' Mickey said cynically, and I agreed wholeheartedly. I wondered *why* the event was 'invitation only' when it would *never* attract gatecrashers anyway!

We were confident that we met all the criteria for attending, but we were also just as confident that no-one else did. Our collective self-esteem was soaring at this point.

As we slowed down to do a final circle of the space, I felt Mickey's hand reach into my bag, searching frantically for the bottle of bubbly and glasses we'd packed in case we needed to make other people more attractive and interesting. I let him dig it out, as I looked around despairingly for the bright, adaptable folk, the unattached thirties, forties and fifties who were outgoing and socially capable, good for a laugh, keen to meet others – keen to meet *us*! I looked for the singles the invitation had promised we'd meet.

Mickey and I had no doubts at all that we looked as interesting as the people we'd like to meet and, perhaps slightly arrogant, we assumed that if we stood still, people would just find themselves gathering around us. Arrogant or not, we parked ourselves about five metres from the main crowd of only twenty, cracked open our bottle and toasted each other, proud of ourselves for giving it a go. At least I'd able to tick off 'Singles Uprising' from the strategy list on my fridge.

'God, there's some unattractive people around, Alice,' Mickey complained. We *were* looking pretty gorgeous compared to the rest, but then we hadn't had much to drink. A couple of glasses of bubbly always managed to make the least appealing person look like a fox.

By the time the bottle was drained of its last drop we had met at least half-a-dozen of Sydney's singles, all tired of being around couples apparently, and all sure they had something to offer the opposite sex.

There was one guy who caught my eye, but he was South African, and Peta and I had always agreed that the Afrikaner accent made us think of the devil. I gave him the benefit of the doubt until he made a comment about Blacks being 'primitive', and how they should be grateful for 'us civilising whites'. It was painfully clear it was time to go. It was not the sun or the wine or the other desperadoes I'd had enough of, but this jerk, who'd made me realise that the only uprising happening was his racist one, something I didn't want to be a part of.

Mickey and I went to the Clovelly Hotel and ate and drank the rest of the day and night away.

thirty

Holiday romance

As a last-ditch effort I decided to try for a holiday romance, an expensive strategic move, but strategic nonetheless. It was late October and Christmas was fast approaching; memories of Paul were soon going to choke me from within. I needed to meet someone who'd at least get me through the festive season, if not all the way to my thirtieth birthday and the altar.

I dug into my savings to take a trip to Aotearoa, and the windy city, Wellington. While I was looking forward to going to the Downstage Theatre to see the latest offering from young playwright Briar Grace-Smith, and visiting the national museum Te Papa, I was more excited about the prospects of a holiday romance. Mr Right needn't be right in my pocket in Sydney. He could well be across the Tasman. Yes, a trans-Tasman romance might be the thing for me.

I aimed to use the trip to brush up on my flirting techniques. I re-read *How to Be a Sex Goddess* and *How to Talk to Cute Guys*, finishing the last page of the latter just before leaving for the airport. I flirted with the assistant in the duty-free shop where I bought an iPod.

I batted my eyelashes more than once at the customs officer, which just seemed to make him suspicious. I was super-friendly to the guy at the service-desk in the Qantas Club, because I knew there were definite bonuses to dating an airline employee – all those discounted trips I'd heard about. Smiling broadly, I felt good as I made my way to Gate 23.

The flight wasn't full and I was grateful. I took my window seat and sank into a relaxed mental space, preparing for four days of rest and relaxation. As I looked out the window at the rain falling lightly on the wing, a handsome male sat down in the aisle seat. He was wearing running shoes with jeans and a black roll-neck jumper, Jerry Seinfeld style. An empty seat separated us; my black winter coat and sky-blue scarf rested on it. We exchanged smiles and 'hellos' and he ever-so-politely asked the flight attendant to hang 'the lady's coat'. I was impressed. He had a sexy, cultured voice and was obviously older than me, pushing late forties probably, and I made a note of his old-fashioned manners and style, something lacking in many of the younger men in Sydney these days. Many of them would sooner sit on a woman's coat than ask someone to hang it.

We made small talk for the first hour of the flight. He'd just spent forty-five days touring Australia. He worked for himself, something to do with the music industry, but he didn't give too much away – he was very mysterious on that front. Although he told me he was 'proudly Pakeha', he seemed to think he knew all there was to know about being Maori.

'The haka is too commercialised these days. It's lost its meaning and they should stop doing it at the rugby,' he said, with the authority and arrogance only a whiteman would dare assume when discussing the culture of 'the other'.

'Hell, that's the only part of the rugby I even watch.' *His* views on the haka meant as much to me as a man's opinion of women's business, but I thought I might as well talk to him as practice for the weekend ahead.

We ate our meal and continued to chat and I asked him what the highlight of his journey to Oz was. I had already clued him in on my 'ethnic extraction' and with that in mind he began: 'Well, this is probably going to upset you ...'

It always fascinated me when someone opened their dialogue with a comment like that and then proceeded, as they had predicted, to upset me! If they already knew what the consequences of their actions would be, why did they carry on?

He continued, 'The highlight of my trip was climbing Ayers Rock.' Of course it was. It would have been impossible for this man who knew *all* about Maoris not to know *all* about Aboriginal people too.

'Well, I guess that's the end of our conversation then, isn't it? I don't want to begin my relaxing trip away with conflict.'

He didn't take the hint, clearly feeling the need to justify himself, to make sure I understood why he had done it. 'I respect the religious views of others, I just don't think they should be rammed down my throat. I respect the wishes of the Aboriginal people, but they should respect mine too.' He had wished to climb 'the rock'. It had been a 'spiritual experience' for him. What he got personally from the climb was worth denying those who cherished Uluru the respect they deserved.

'Do you think you could climb St Mary's Cathedral in Sydney? Do you think you'd get anywhere near the top of the Vatican? They're a couple of "spiritual experiences" worth climbing for, don't you think? Or do you *really* respect the Catholic faith?'

I was over it. I couldn't be bothered re-educating this man at 20,000 feet in the air. I put the headphones on and pretended to watch the movie, an action film with Will Smith I had no interest in whatsoever.

As we made our descent, the flight attendant came to collect the headphones. I tried not to make eye contact with Mr Pakeha, aiming to get off the plane without any further communication at all.

'How was the film?' he asked.

'I wasn't watching it.' He finally understood that I didn't want to speak to him.

❤

At the end of day one I sat in the restaurant of my hotel, waiting patiently and quietly to be noticed.

'Sit in the woods and wait for the timid deer to come eat from your hands, Alice. Be patient and quiet.' These were the final words my father had spoken as he dropped me at the airport that morning. Mum had obviously had a word with him. But 'patient' and 'quiet' had never been adjectives used to describe me.

It had already been fifteen minutes, how long would it take anyway? While sitting and waiting I became increasingly conscious of my posture, of the way I was drinking my wine, of whether or not my arse was hanging out the back of the chair. It *felt* as though it was practically touching the ground. I checked discreetly: of course it wasn't. I'd drunk too much.

With my man-antennae up, it was only seconds before I registered a guy enter the bar attached to the restaurant. I'd seen him earlier at the pool, wearing budgie-smugglers, while I was people-watching from the spa. I liked the elegant dive he did into the pool and the fact he effortlessly swam lap after lap. He was still going long after I'd gone all pruney and decided to head back to my room.

I was under pressure to order as the waiter approached me for the third time. I was starving, but couldn't make up my mind: should I order a delicate, ladylike salad or the side of beef I really felt like? What if Mr Budgie-Smuggler came into the restaurant and saw me eating half a cow? 'How ridiculous, Alice,' I chastised myself. 'Women should eat whatever they want, not be concerned about what men think of their eating habits.' I'd told my girls at school the same thing in the past, and I'd meant it. Now I settled for a caesar salad with Cajun chicken, knowing I could always order some room service later on and scoff myself stupid in privacy.

Mr Budgie-Smuggler did in fact head into the restaurant and straight for my table. 'Hi, would you mind if I joined you? The restaurant is full and I don't really want to travel far from the hotel – a bit tired from swimming today. Didn't I see you near the pool in a red swimsuit?' I didn't answer immediately. I was dry in the mouth, but my palms were sweaty. Was he interested in me? I didn't want to get carried away. The restaurant was full, and he had to sit somewhere. But he'd said he remembered seeing me at the pool, was that a clue?

'Sure, happy for you to join me.' What seemed like ages had passed, but he finally sat.

His name was Jack. He was a philanthropist from Sydney, living in Bronte (a pleasant coastal walk from my place in Coogee), and was in NZ to help set up a philanthropic foundation of some sort. He had a full head of grey hair and hazel eyes. I gave him my brief biography and he seemed to hang on every word I said.

Jack was older than me, possibly mid-fifties, ex-wife, three grown-up kids, and travelled the world doing philanthropic deeds like Bruce Wayne. By the end of dinner and two bottles of wine, I didn't know who was putty in whose hands. Jack offered to pay for dinner, and I accepted graciously (and thankfully, as he had ordered the most expensive wine on the menu, the sort of stuff teachers rarely if ever got to drink). As we headed to the lift, I had already gone through my criteria in my head and Mr Budgie-Smuggler had a pretty good strike rate. Lots of ticks, as Mr Yachtie would have said.

In the lift Jack yawned and stretched. 'I might head to the spa, always helps me sleep better,' he said casually. Was I supposed to take this as a hint and meet him there? I had no idea, until he added, 'What about you? Do you need something to help you sleep better?'

'Sometimes. I might join you,' I said nonchalantly as I stepped out of the lift. I waited for the doors to close, then ran to my room, desperate to get to the spa before he did so I could position myself to my best advantage. I slipped into my still damp and cold cozzie, checked that everything was tucked in where it should be and I had enough cleavage. I threw a dress over the top, pulled my hair up, grabbed a towel and did a fast walk to the lift in as ladylike a fashion as possible.

He wasn't there when I arrived and I rushed to get into the water and start the bubbles. The water was hot, and so was I, because of all the alcohol. I sat with my back to a jet and shut my eyes, remembering Peta's old saying: 'Low speed is good, medium speed is better, high speed ... who needs a man?'

'Looks like you're having a great time already.'

Jack had arrived.

'You were smiling.'

'Oh yes, just remembering a story a friend told me.'

'Want to share it?'

'Ah, no. It's not really for public consumption.' He eased into the water at a comfortable distance from me. He looked even better in his tight swimmers at close range, and I wondered why a man with so much 'plumbing' didn't wear something more concealing. I'd answered my own question almost before I'd finished asking it.

We sat in the spa silent for some minutes before I felt his foot on mine, and at first I shied away. St Christina's had clearly had an influence on me. Within seconds, though, I slid my foot on top of his, and then suddenly felt his hands all over me. I was straddling him, the straps coming off my shoulders, his tongue in my mouth, on my neck, on my breasts. I could feel him hard against me and wondered where the hell I was going to put that plumbing. I'd forgotten about my 'No one-night stands or sex on the first date' rules. Sex on holidays didn't really count. Not when no-one else would ever know about it – unless we ended up getting married, which was always possible, wasn't it?

Putting on a condom in the spa seemed a bit tricky, so we headed upstairs before we reached the point of no return.

We were barely dry, and laughing like two kids about to shag in their parents' car, when we stepped out of the lift on his floor, the penthouse suite. I felt like Julia Roberts in *Pretty Woman*, but I refused to think of myself as cheap. I simply hadn't had sex since Perfect Paul almost eight months ago, and I wanted to feel desirable again. Jack seemed like a decent guy, apparently not concerned about the obvious age difference, lived in the next suburb back home. In fact, he appeared to be quite perfect for a holiday romance – one that even had the potential to grow into something more permanent once on home turf again. I was trying to give myself 'permission' to do the deed. I needed to have that one night, as Peta had said, before planning a million of them. I was still thinking this as he led me to the shower, big enough to hold twelve people. We got each other into a lather, which helped dilute the un-sexy reek of chlorine.

We spent plenty of time in the shower, an added bonus (Sydney had had water restrictions in place for the past few years, and I was always conscious of how much water I used when showering back home). We were both wrinkly when we stumbled dripping wet into the bed.

Jack flipped me around like some soft porn star – and to my surprise, I enjoyed it. I had no idea people his age had sex like that. I drifted off to sleep only to be woken at irregular intervals during the night for encore performances.

'So, what a night!' Jack put my thoughts into words as we sat eating breakfast in his suite. I just nodded and smiled. I was too physically exhausted to speak. I couldn't remember ever feeling that way.

'I fly to Auckland this afternoon and then to Sydney at the end of the week. Do you want to catch up on the weekend?' Was I hearing things? Was Jack really that charming, organised and capable, a star in bed *and* asking me out for another date?

'That'd be great.' Sitting there looking like crap with nothing but a sheet around me, I suddenly realised that in the rush of getting from the spa to his room, I'd left my dress in the pool area. It was only seven am: I could still make it back to my room without attracting attention. Jack offered to fetch my dress and was back in less than five minutes.

The day passed slowly and I savoured every minute, walking around the micro-city of Wellington, browsing in clothes shops, spending money in second-hand bookstores, stopping for a coffee or something to nibble when the urge took me. I was content and glowing. I went back to the hotel at three pm to say goodbye to

Jack, but he'd already left. There was a message waiting under my door:

You're an exciting woman, I'm glad we met!
Wish we were flying back together. Jack

He wished we were travelling home together! He was definitely better than Mr I-Know-Everything-About-Maoris. I'd given him my card, he'd call for sure. He was a philanthropist – of course he'd call. He had integrity, and ethics, and morals *and* a huge dick. He'd *have* to call. Too tired to analyse anything further right then, I lay down to have a nap, and didn't wake until the next morning.

Two days later, having done the Te Papa museum and library and all the other sights the Windy City had to offer, I headed to the airport. On board the plane I was excited about heading home and seeing Jack again. That one night had been like having just a single Tim Tam out of the packet. I just couldn't stop at one.

'You are now free to move about the cabin ...'

I was ready for a stretch. There wasn't anyone sitting next to me, so I made an easy escape to the toilet. The flight attendants were preparing a snack behind the curtain as I went to enter the vacant cubicle.

'Did you hear about that man flying from Auckland to Sydney yesterday? Spent the whole flight chatting up Robyn Tyson – you know her, don't you?' I had to stop and listen; a girl couldn't pass up the opportunity for a good bit of gossip.

'Yeah, I heard the story this morning, about some old fart – philanthropist, he said.'

'Isn't that someone who collects stamps?' another attendant butted in. No wonder they called them trolley dollies!

'No it's someone who works in charity, has lots of money and donates it all over the place. Anyway, that's not the story – thing is, he asked Robyn about the Mile High Club.'

'What?'

'Yeah, asked if she was interested in joining it with him. He had to be in his late fifties.'

'Robyn's only twenty-five!'

'Yeah, I know, that's what she said. He didn't care. Just kept hassling her. Must have been one horny old bloke. Wanting to spread his money and *seed* all over the place.'

'You're sick.'

But I was the one feeling sick. It had to be Jack, but I needed to know for sure. It wasn't as though I could ask them, so I just waited, busting for the toilet now, but hoping some more information was forthcoming.

The dippy one finally asked, 'So, did we get his name so we know who to look out for?'

'We just called him Jack-the-lad, but Robyn gave him such a serve I don't think he'll bother anyone again.

She was only worried she might spot him at the beach – said he lives in Bronte and she's only at Bondi.' My stomach nearly gave way and I violently pushed my way into the toilet. I'd never thrown up on a plane before but I had that watery-mouthed feeling happening and sure enough, *pfffwooaarrr*. I'd have to say leaning over an airline toilet, breathing in that antiseptic smell, was one of the most unpleasant experiences I'd ever had. Then I sat, peed, and got myself together. I splashed my face with cold water before stumbling out and dribbling my way back up the aisle. I'd been gone a while: afternoon tea had already been served and cleared.

Staring out the window, I wondered how I could be such a poor judge of character. I soon stopped beating myself up, though, and started to smile. The sex had been GREAT; vomiting on a plane had been worth it. I just wished I hadn't heard the story, so I'd never have known. The old fart had probably done 'it' up there a dozen times. Hell, I probably would've done it with him myself if it were on offer.

I grabbed some duty-free gin on my way towards customs, figuring I was going to need it to get through the next few weeks of self-deprecation and the number of times I was going to have to tell the story to the girls. I didn't even bother to check which customs desk had the cutest guy, I was over meeting Mr Right. My only concern at this point was not getting caught for the gorgeous new bag I'd picked up from a local Maori weaver. I planned to say that I didn't know it was natural fibres, I thought it was plastic. I hoped that would work. I pulled the front of my top down slightly just in case the dumb-brunette act didn't work, and I had to use cleavage to get through. Desperate times called for desperate measures.

I got my passport checked and was directed to the baggage carousel without question, but I panicked at the sight of a sniffer dog. I was convinced he was going to smell out the bag – that's what they're trained for. I saw my suitcase on the carousel but I didn't pick it up – I'd wait until the dog and his master had passed me. Then the master, the customs officer, threw me a huge smile. Shit! He knew. I was a goner and there'd be a huge fine. I started talking to myself. Act dumb, act sexy, and be sure and act cool. Calm down and don't panic!

The dog and the customs officer were heading right for me and my suitcase was going round again. There was nothing in my hand luggage, but the dog stopped and sniffed and sniffed and sniffed. Shit! Could he smell my desperation to meet Mr Right? Or, just maybe, the customs officer was looking for a woman. He was in the perfect job: plenty of opportunities to frisk women, pat them down, get them in compromising positions. Just maybe, this poor cute beagle was being used to help its master meet *his* Ms Right.

Well bugger that. I wasn't going to be part of someone else's sleazy ploy or underhanded attempt at meeting a woman. Just let him threaten to take me in for a strip search. I'd expose him in front of everyone here at the carousel!

I stopped myself suddenly: I was totally irrational, tired and stupid. The dog and his master had moved well and truly on. They were now two carousels along and neither of them were looking back in my direction. I grabbed my case as it swung by, and headed out.

Back at school, Mickey was weirdly interested in all that Mr Budgie-Smuggler and I had got up too. I would've thought that images of hetero sex would have made him ill, but apparently not. Mickey was convinced Mr Dick-Sticker ('dick-stickers' was Mickey's name for Speedos) would call, if for no other reason than another shag.

'Great, thanks! That's what a girl wants to hear!'

'Well, if he comes back for more, it means he enjoyed it,' was Mickey's rationale.

'Oh he enjoyed it all right, but it didn't stop him looking for more of it on his flight home. He won't call – he's an arsehole. They all are.'

Mickey gave me a hug. It was the first time I'd been held with any real affection by a man in months. It meant a lot to me.

'Alice, it's Jack – Jack the philanthropist—'

I cut in immediately. 'Don't you mean *philanderer*, Jack-the-lad? Visited the Mile High Club lately?'

He laughed, thinking I was just kidding around.

'I hear you're barred from trans-Tasman Qantas flights, something about being a pedophile ...' That was below the belt, I knew, but seriously, twenty-five was just a little too young for him.

'She was old enough,' he said defensively, openly admitting he had tried something.

'Not old enough for you, you old geezer!'

'So I guess dinner and a spa is out of the question, then?'

'Have you got thick skin, or are you just thick?' I was quicker than usual, and gave myself the big thumbs up for that response, but it elicited nothing from Jack.

'Right, well, I'm putting the phone down now mate, and it's the *only* thing that'll be *going down* between me and you!' I hung up – and so ended my final attempt at meeting Mr Right.

I'd reached the end of my list of strategies and failed in every effort I'd made to find a man. I didn't feel deadly or desirable, loved or lovable – just over it. It was time to go back to the SWOT analysis and remind myself of Peta's arguments against married life. If I was going to be single forever, I might as well enjoy it.

thirty-one

Love yourself and you will be loved

On Melbourne Cup Day, the sun rose over Wedding Cake Island, the waves crashed on the shore of Coogee Beach, joggers made their way up and down Arden Street, and life continued as it had for the past months, years, decades. Nothing had changed. I was still single, even though I'd spent the past year dragging myself through disastrous dates.

I was all dated, researched and strategied out. Men were now merely objects to be observed, researched and reviewed; specimens to be dissected and studied, analysed and taken apart bit by bit in an effort to understand them. All I wanted to know was why they made it so damned hard to like them, love them, be with them or marry them – why it was so hard to find one worthy to be called Mr Right.

Liza had invited Peta and I to a Melbourne Cup luncheon at the Park Hyatt. She had finally let go of Luke – not organised enough for her – and she'd been dating a sales rep for Moët & Chandon, who smuggled us in. Peta had rung in sick, and my history students were all away on retreat, so I wouldn't be missed at school. Even Liza was playing hooky, a rare thing for our legal eagle to do.

Sitting with Peta, looking around at the crowd, I thought I'd try to summarise my findings for her. 'You know what I reckon?' I said as I adjusted my fascinator.

'What d'ya reckon, Missy?' Peta fidgeted with her hands. I could see she was desperate for a cigarette.

'I reckon that the really nice men are dingo ugly, the hot men are not that nice, and the hot and nice men 99.9 per cent of the time are gay. The hot, nice and straight men are mostly married; the men who aren't that hot, but are nice, have no financial security; while the men who aren't so hot, but are nice, with financial security, think I am only after *their* security—' I took a breath and Peta jumped in.

'And the hot men without security are after *your* security, right?'

'That's right, but I wasn't finished … The hot men who are not so nice and are straight don't think I'm beautiful enough, and the men who think I'm beautiful, who are straight, and nice enough, usually have financial security but are cowards.'

'Missy, you're fucken depressing me.' Peta didn't want to hear any more.

I kept going anyway. 'Aaaaand the men who are the slightest bit hot, generally nice and have adequate financial security *and* happen to be straight are usually too fucken shy to make the first move! Farkkkkkk!!!!! To make it harder, the men who never make the first move automatically lose interest if I take the initiative. And that's about all I understand about men.' Glad that I'd got it all off my chest, I poured us both another glass.

'I'll drink to that.' Peta tipped her glass to mine.

Scanning the room I noticed an inordinate number of couples. 'Paul and I came here on our first date.' I said, and felt tears well.

'Oh god, don't start on about Paul, Missy, he's history.'

'I know, but I always wanted to have my wedding reception here. *Your company is requested at the wedding of Mr and Mrs Right at the Park Hyatt ...* It should have been splashed across hundreds of invitations and mailed out to all corners of the globe by now.'

'Let it go, Alice, for both our sakes.' Peta looked straight at me and her tone said *I'm over it.*

'A string quartet would be playing as guests made small talk and sipped fine wines. Mr Right and I would be swanning around and having our photos taken while passers-by ooohed and aaaahed at the sight of us.'

'Alice, this really isn't healthy.' Peta was getting annoyed.

'Just humour me, please. Let me finish. I promise it'll be the end of it.

'I'd be wearing my Tiffany ring and a tiara and Mr Right would be the happiest man in the world. Life would be complete. We'd take the honeymoon to Venice and Paris, have a couple of kids, I'd end up principal at St Christina's, and we'd live where Wedding Cake Island couldn't be seen and would never need to be mentioned ever, ever again. We *would* live happily ever after.' I wiped a single tear from my cheek with as much dignity as I could.

'And that's the end of it, Alice. No more.' Peta stood up and walked away.

No more, Alice. No more.

By half-past-five the ballroom was a flurry of gorgeous women and men, TV cameras and Sydney socialites, bubbles being poured to the left, right and centre of me. I'd already had way too much champagne, but it didn't stop me holding out my glass every time a waiter went past. I hadn't had a win and I couldn't even remember what horse I'd backed ten minutes after the race had been run, but the eye candy was incredible – even the waiters looked promising. It was a reminder that being single meant you could do all the guilt-free perving you wanted.

Liza had spent hours schmoozing with the mob from Moët, and why not? It was a big change from her clients at the ALS. It was funny to see her so posh. Her new man seemed like a dream, and unlike Luke, could show her affection without putting her in a headlock. I took a photo of Liza and me together on my mobile phone and sent it to Dannie, who'd watched the race at the school with the kids.

I spied Peta across the room, talking endlessly with a group of women who all looked suitably impressed. She had always been an engaging storyteller, or should I say bullshit artist. Rather than go into the whole Indigenous education issue on Melbourne Cup Day, my guess was she was spinning some yarn about being the interior designer of the ballroom we were in, or perhaps she was someone's agent, or had just patented some great invention.

I tried to saunter as goddess-like as possible out to the balcony for some space to myself and fresh air. I put my shades on to shield the glare off the harbour, and smiled at the warmth of the afternoon sun on my face. Leaning over the railing, I closed my eyes and just enjoyed being there, trying hard not to drift off to the wedding that never was. *No more, Alice. No more.* I didn't know how long I'd been there when Peta arrived.

'What're you doing out here?' she asked as she handed me another glass of bubbles.

'Just thinking.' I took a careful sip – I *was* trying to sober up. 'Not about weddings, so don't worry.' I didn't want her walking away again. She smiled her broad white smile.

'Life's not bad, eh?' Peta was cheerful, not drunk cheerful, just happy-with-her-lot cheerful. As I looked at how content Peta was, and where we were, and how gorgeous we both looked, it happened. I had an epiphany.

'You know what Peta? You're right. Life isn't bad at all, is it?'

'Not at all,' she agreed.

'Being single isn't the end of the world.'

'Not even close to it.' Peta was looking through her glass at the Opera House.

'I could go back in there and flirt, or score, if I wanted to – right now.'

'You could.' Peta shifted her champagne eye-glass to the Quay.

'Or I could just go home, crawl into my pyjamas and eat toast for dinner, without worrying about a man or kids.'

'Or you, Liza and I could just drink bubbly for the rest of the night.' She touched her glass to mine.

'I mean, when you think about the men who've been on offer over the past year in Sydney, I'm *clearly* better off single anyway.'

'God, I wish Dannie could hear this.' I could see the glimmer of victory in Peta's eye as she recalled their SWOT analysis.

'Leave Dannie out of this, Peta, it's about me.' I leapt to my feet and proclaimed, ' I love my life!'

'Thank god you're back! I missed you!' Peta stood up, too, excited. 'I'll go grab some more bubbles, and Liza, and we'll drink to your reclaimed singledom.' She spun around and her mass of hair followed as she headed back into the ballroom. I sat down on the stool and closed my eyes, smiling with a sense of resolution.

Beside me, I heard someone say, 'It's a beautiful spot, don't you think?' I wasn't sure if the comment was meant for me, so I didn't open my eyes, but waited. Nothing further was said. Peering over the top of my sunnies, I saw the most luxurious hair, a rounded olive face, hypnotising green eyes. Oh yes, I really, really loved my life.

Could I possibly speak? Could I say something without making a complete gig of myself? The vision spoke again. 'Sorry, I didn't mean to bother you. I've been standing here for a while, but since you came out the view is twice as beautiful.' I guessed he was pretty pissed too.

I love my life, I love my life, I love my life.

'So did you back a winner?' I had to say something; it was all I could think of.

'Actually, I missed the race, was caught up at work. Dead loss in the office sweep too.' He had the sexiest voice. I was sure he was younger than me, but I was giving it a go, and every minute he hung around the more points he got. Of course he was staying; the view was *twice* as beautiful since I'd arrived.

What he said next surprised me.

'I was meant to be at a wedding here this month, but it was called off. The guy was a cad – lucky she found out sooner rather than later, eh?'

That sobered me up pretty quickly.

'I was meant to come to a wedding here once, too. It's not happening now either.' I sounded positive, not whiny or moany at all. 'There's probably enough Moët functions to keep this place busy, though, I'm sure. Do you work for Moët?' I was trying to see where he fit in, and whether or not he was a mate of Liza's new man.

'No, I run an importing agency. I'm a ring-in here today. I'm Mark.' He extended his hand and smiled broadly.

'I'm Alice, and I'm a gatecrasher too – probably best we hide ourselves out here, don't you think?' He laughed and so did I.

The party seemed to be breaking up inside. Mark asked for my number. I gave it to him, but without expectations, just as Peta and Liza came looking for me on the balcony. It was eight pm and Liza was hungry. 'So, Alice, I see you've finally met my cousin Marco. Didn't take you long to find the most gorgeous woman in the room, did it, Marco?'

I was dumbfounded, and so was he.

'You're *Marco*?'

'You're *that* Alice?'

Liza's new man walked out with a bottle of Moët and topped up our glasses. I made a toast, 'To *not* meeting Mr Right—'

'Until the time is right!' Liza added.

Marco turned to me. 'So, Liza said you weren't interested in dating any of her family.'

'*Other* members of her family, Marco. I didn't mean the good-looking ones.'

'Would you like to have dinner, then?'

'Sure. When?'

'Tonight?'

Liza grabbed my arm and pulled me aside.

'I told you so.'

'You did, and I will *never* not listen to you again! Thank you!'

Epilogue

Spending time with Marco gave me faith in men again. He proved to me that there *were* men out there who were charming and honest and kind, and with no specific agendas or baggage (well, noticeable baggage that is).

The only problem was, without alcohol, we had no real chemistry. We partied and got on well as mates, but soon realised we were never going to be anything more than that. We both agreed that chemistry isn't something that will develop over time, like companionship or conversation, and that sex is actually a very important part of a relationship, especially a young one.

Liza was pleased that we'd at least given it a try, and I enjoyed hanging out with a straight, single male for a while, but Marco and I didn't last long. I was on my own again.

❤

The week before Christmas I was still looking for gifts, even though St Christina's broke up weeks before the state schools. I just didn't seem to have the energy to spend days on end shopping among the growing crowds of Bondi Junction after a long year as full-time department head and husband seeker. I needed to relax a bit and take it slowly, which is why I hadn't finished any Christmas shopping. The upside was that I was loving my single life. Marco had helped me find a comfortable space between serial dater, husband hunter, female friend and satisfied single. I was truly content for the first time in ages.

I roamed a busy bookstore in Bondi Junction until I'd found the right book for Larissa. It had become a joke between us, giving self-help books. I'd moved on, and was standing in the history section when I saw him: Gary-the-Garbo, only a metre from me in the same aisle. He caught me staring.

'Alice, fancy meeting you here!' Gary-the-Garbo sounded surprised, but looked pleased to see me.

'Why do you seem so surprised? You think I can't read?'

'Its just that I've only ever seen you on the street in your pyjamas and at Cushion. I thought you only slept and drank.' Gary-the-Garbo had a sense of humour. I liked that.

'Reaaaallly? I could say the same for you, *mate*.' The banter was flowing easily.

'I only go to Cushion to see you, surely you know that.' He turned to put a book back on the shelf, so I couldn't see his eyes. I couldn't tell if he was serious or not. I hoped he was, but I kept it light.

'And *I* thought it was for the happy hour prices!' My mouth was dry and my palms sweaty. The silence that followed was awkward. We both turned to the shelves.

'So, looking for something specific?' I asked, not wanting the conversation to end.

'Yeah, I'm supposed to be getting something for my father, but I always end up here buying something for myself. I'm a bit of a history buff.'

'What a coincidence. I'm a history teacher at St Christina's.' We had more than bins and booze in common.

'Maybe you could recommend a book, then. I'm looking for something on the first Gulf War – I'm trying to understand the link between the US involvement in the Middle East then and today.' Wow, he was a reader of history with an interest in world politics as well. Gary-the-Garbo was *interesting*. Mental note to self: stop referring to him as Gary-the-Garbo. World wars weren't my area of expertise, so I couldn't really suggest anything, but I did help him scan the shelves briefly. Neither of us was really concentrating on books anyway.

'What about you?' Gary took Larissa's Christmas present out of my hand and read the title out loud: *Women Who Think Too Much.* He looked back at me with a smile. 'Interesting. For you?'

I half-heartedly snatched it back. 'It's not for me.' I didn't want him to think that I was the over-analysing, paranoid type, even if I had been known to be. 'It's for my brother's girlfriend — kind of a joke.' He didn't need to know that I had planned on reading it as well, later.

Then it was awkward again. The kind of awkwardness two people feel when they like each other but are both too nervous to do anything about it. Fear of rejection is often more powerful than desire for happiness. It had been ten months since I was with Paul and even though I'd had other dates, the scars had not completely healed. I wasn't going to be making the first move with a man for a while, not after a year of disastrous dates and failed relationships. I'd see him around again, I always did, so there was no need to push it.

I dug into my bag for my purse. 'I best be off, got Christmas lights to struggle with. It's a tradition of mine. The annual light-hanging nightmare, I like to call it.'

His face lit up. 'Do you need a hand with them? I'm actually an electrician by trade. Christmas lights are my specialty.'

'Are you being funny, Gary? I'll have to call you Funny Guy.'

'I thought I was Shirt Guy.' He'd remembered. He was good with details too. I liked that. How could I refuse the assistance of the only man to ever offer to hang my lights who could *also* read *and* was funny *and* remembered details *and* wasn't related to me?

'I'd really love your help with the lights, if you have some spare time.'

'I'm free this afternoon, after I have a swim. How about three?'

'Perfect. I'll give you the address... oh, right.' He didn't need it. I was still nervous.

Gary came round and hung my Christmas lights, changed a globe in the hallway, fixed a dripping tap with his bare hands, and even helped me trim my tree. All the while we talked easily. He told me stories about the weird things people left out with their garbage and summarised the Vietnam War for me too. I told him about school and cleverly raised as many potentially problematic topics as I could – from the stolen generations to Aboriginal arts and culture. I wasn't looking at him as a possible partner, but I didn't want a racist hanging my lights either. I'd sooner sit in the dark. But I needn't have worried. He was surprisingly clued in, for a garbo.

'Just because I pick up your garbage, doesn't mean I don't read the broadsheets or watch current affairs programs, Ms Alice.' I liked that he stood up to my snobbishness and narrow thinking too!

That Saturday turned out to be the best I'd had in a year, not only because I got so many 'man-jobs' done, but because my new straight, male, single friend was just that – a friend. He was obviously keen, but was taking it slowly in getting to know me and vice versa.

It was comfortable: he didn't come on too strong. I was tempted to think of a mantra, but decided to leave those behind with the failed strategy.

The following week Gary took me to a nursery. We went shopping for some herbs to sit on my kitchen windowsill. He didn't try to woo me with promises of yachts or expensive dinners.

I didn't spoil our friendship by thinking about weddings, or taking him home on Christmas Day. I didn't need the pressure from my family, and neither did he. His sister Liesl would be on his case anyway, he said. She was his equivalent to Dillon, but a little like Mum too, wanting to marry him off. That's what proud sisters do, so I was with her on that one.

Our shared passion for history made conversation easy. I learned so much from him talking about the Cold War, Vietnam and the rise and fall of Hitler. He taught me about world history, and I taught him about Australian history. Between us we had the globe covered.

At first glance, many women wouldn't consider a garbo or someone they only ever saw at a bar as an impressive option. It worked for me, though. I liked drinking a lot, and I hated putting my bin out. Gary was the complete package. His life would fit perfectly with mine. And there was plenty of chemistry.

♥

Six months later it wasn't the ringing of wedding bells that woke me, but life was certainly heading in that direction as the council garbage truck ground its way down Arden Street. I sprang out of bed, then raced to splash some water on my face and took a swig of Listerine. I even managed to find the time to run some lipstick across my lips before running downstairs. I didn't rush to drag the bin out, though.

It was just on winter, but I didn't even feel the cool coastal air – the fullness in my heart kept me warm as Gary drove the truck towards me. Who'd have thought, eh, that all those mornings he'd laughed at me as I ran out on the street in my pyjamas, sleep-encrusted eyes and hair like a witch, that he was perving on me, desperately wanting to take me out?

Who'd have thought that the cactus plant left on top of my garbage bin so long ago had been his way of dropping the hint? Why hadn't I realised back then that Shirt Guy was Gary? I must have been completely blind not to see him right under my nose. My very own Mr I-Can-Put-Out-and-Pick-Up-the-Trash-*and*-Say-'I-Love-You', too.

Dating Gary I was happier than I had been in years. My parents, too. Mum was relieved I wasn't a lesbian. Dad didn't have to come and fix anything. Even Dillon was glad he didn't have to hear all the personal details of his sister's sex- and love-life anymore. Bianca started calling again when she came back from her honeymoon and things settled down for her. Sometimes we all met at Dannie's for dinner. Peta was with a new guy, still happily 'serial dating'. Liza was with Mr Moët ... and we were *all* happy about nurturing *that* relationship.

Life with Gary around was good. No expectations, no disappointments, no dick-fiddling, no break and enters, no uprisings – emotional or otherwise – no moonwalking, no victim mentality, no more blind dates or mixed messages or excuses, and no more dripping taps or dragging bags of shopping up too many flights of stairs. Most importantly I had no concerns about being married by my thirtieth. All that mattered now when I looked out at Wedding Cake Island were the endless laughs, love and don't-have-to-go-looking-for-it-passionate sex, which neither of us was ever too busy or tired for. And, as it happens, the bin is always out the night before.

Acknowledgements

I would like to thank:

Josef and Mark Heiss, Phillipa McDermott, Linda Mirabilio, Darrell Sibosado and Bernadine Knorr for inspiration. The bits you love are all *you*. The bits you don't like are not you, they are fictional!

Terri Janke, Kerry Reed-Gilbert, Rosie Scott, Josie and Bella Vendramini for reading and commenting on early drafts.

Nicola O'Shea for her expert structural edit and for 'getting it'.

Tara Wynne from Curtis Brown for working in my best interests with professionalism and humour.

Meredith Curnow and Larissa Edwards from Random House for having a vision for Australian publishing that includes me in it. I'd also like to thank my editor Elizabeth Cowell, who unnecessarily stroked my ego, laughed at all my jokes, and taught me the difference between 'uninterested' and 'disinterested'. She is possibly one of the most patient people I know.

The Arthur Boyd Estate and the Australia Council – for the time and space to write the first 20,000 words.

Warawara Department of Indigenous Studies at Macquarie University – for the time and space, as Writer in Residence, to write the next 50,000.

The National Centre for Indigenous Studies, the Faculty of Arts and the School of Humanities at the ANU – for the time and space, as visiting fellow, to do the final edits.

Geraldine Star, for being my life coach and personal guru.

All the Heiss family – for watering my plants when I'm away writing, feeding me when I'm too tired to cook, picking me up from airports late at night, and simply for loving and supporting me unconditionally. I am, undeniably, the luckiest daughter and sister in the world.

Finally, all the men who have ever lied to or cheated on me, told me they loved me then not returned my call, led me on and then run off, stood me up or put me down – you're all bastards!

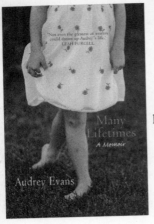

'My father died thinking that none of us would ever amount to anything worthwhile . . . He had told each of us from a young age that Aboriginal people had bad blood . . . that we were incapable of learning beyond elementary level because Aboriginal people were not as bright as white people.'

Growing up in the 1930s and 40s, Audrey Evans felt like an outsider living between two worlds. Perceived as neither white nor black, at school she was made to sit in the front of the class so that the teachers could look over her, and the only real education she received was in violence, alcoholism and poverty. In an era when many subjects were taboo, Audrey found herself pregnant at 17 before she was even aware she had lost her virginity. She was barely an adult when she was forced to work as a prostitute and was battling loneliness, depression and the brandy bottle.

In the years that followed, Audrey faced more than most women could bear in many lifetimes, but she stubbornly refused to believe that it was too late to turn her life around. At the same age that most people are thinking of retiring, Audrey applied for a place at university, changing her life – and the lives of those around her – forever.

Many Lifetimes is an extraordinary and ultimately uplifting tale of one woman's triumph over adversity and a powerful reminder that anything is possible.

'This is an inspiring memoir, and a real eye-opener as to what Aboriginal people – particularly women – had to go through to survive.'
Good Reading

'Many Lifetimes has been published posthumously ... At Evans' funeral, her children made a promise that they would publish her work no matter what it took. A little more than five years later, here is a beautiful promise fulfilled.'
The Sunday Telegraph

A BANTAM BOOK
ISBN 978 1 86325 479 3